A Fiery Secret

Diane Craver

Cover Art Design by
The Killion Group
http://thekilliongroupinc.com

Visit the author at www.dianecraver.com

Published in the United States of America

A Fiery Secret is a work of fiction. Though some actual towns, cities, and locations may be mentioned, they are used in a fictitious manner and the events and occurrences were invented in the mind and imagination of the author. Any similarities of characters or names used within to any person past, present, or future is coincidental.

Praise for Diane Craver's A Fiery Secret

"Catherine, as a character, is interesting. She is both worldly and innocent. She is a modern, independent woman who has a career and is capable of looking after herself. But then she has some 'old fashioned' values that make her not want to settle for second best. However, Catherine and the book do not come across as moralistic or preachy. It's just that Catherine has standards and makes choices based on them. So, to me, it's not the classic chick-lit book. It has more depth than that. ...I like the flirtatious start to *A Fiery Secret*. The whole relationship between Catherine and Jake is slow and sweet. ...I liked that the character of Catherine had more in her life than just investigating. That made her more realistic in my eyes as everyone has more than one thing going on in their lives. ...I believe there are a lot of different types of secrets in *A Fiery Secret*. Some are evil, some are wrong and some are through choice. It is a sweet, modern romance where the normal everyday complications of life meet a mystery head on. But above all, this book has a nice feel good ending that makes you smile."

~Janet Davies, Once Upon A Romance

"Author Diane Craver has a way with mystery. This enchanting Chick Lit voiced novel will have you suspecting just about everyone when it comes down to just who killed the janitor? And why? She keeps investigative reporter, Catherine Steel on the chase, not just for her story, but her hot co-worker, Jake Michaels as well...Without thinking about her own safety, Catherine ferrets out the truth behind the news."

~JoEllen Conger, Gotta Write Network

"Diane Craver sure knows how to write mystery yet add a tinge of romance to it. From the start the author grips you into the mystery of Max. Here is a janitor who always worked in the boiler room and one day is dead. I loved the fact that each chapter contained more information about Max's life and the woman he loved. Diane Craver did a beautiful job with this book and I hope to read more of her books."

~Lena C., Fallen Angel Reviews

Dedication

For my loving and fabulous daughter, Christina

Chapter One

Jake Michaels made me throw up on prom night ten years ago. I never really got over it. And now he was back in my life. Obviously, we weren't the same people. Both of us graduated from college and had real careers. I was an investigative reporter for the local newspaper, *The Messenger*.

When the paper's editor-in-chief and owner, Jane Gibbons, recently decided to have a larger sports section to increase circulation, she hired Jake as the new sports editor. We both worked now at *The Messenger* in Park City, Ohio, where we were born and raised.

My name is Catherine Steel, and I'm five-eight with pale blue eyes. Unfortunately, being outdoors a lot last summer had made a few freckles pop out on my face. But the sun had done something good by giving my light brown hair some natural blondish highlights. Gone were the days when I pulled my hair back into a ponytail and my work uniform consisted of dress pants with a boring pastel shirt. When Jake Michaels moved back and started working at the newspaper, I knew my wardrobe had to include tight, short skirts and stiletto heels so that picking up dropped pens by his desk would be sure to drive him wild with passion. He broke my heart in high school. What he did to me was deplorable and he ruined my sophomore year. Even so, I didn't want to ruin him. Seeing him squirm like the snake he was seemed to restore my self-respect and take some of the pain out of our past history.

But at the moment, I wasn't the one making Jake squirm. He was doing that to me. He stood next to me as I slurped water from the fountain in the hallway. He smelled so good I knew I had to take the longest drink in *Messenger* history. If I lifted my head and made eye contact, I'd be a goner. What was he wearing? Every man should use that aftershave.

"Well, water kid," Jake said to me, "maybe I've been wrong about you all this time."

I stopped drinking and licked the excess moisture below my lip. "What do you mean?"

"I thought you've been getting all these drinks so you could constantly walk in front of my office and show me what I've been missing out on."

I shook my head, noticing how he still had a summer tan. He wore a white shirt with the sleeves rolled up. Jake had an athletic look but he pulled off appearing preppy at the same time. I saw the challenge in his brown eyes, daring me to deny his observation. "I try to drink lots of water every day. It's good for you, flushes all the toxins out of your body."

"I've tried to ignore you walking by my office for the past four weeks, but I can't take it any more." He pushed me against the wall, but I didn't object. A tingling raced through me as his hands lingered on my shoulders. "And each time you've made your drink run, I've seen how you look at me, like you're all hot and bothered. I have a suggestion. You say you'll go out with me and then stand me up. We'll be even.

Then we can move on and get together. Like this." He tilted my chin and lowered his face to mine. He covered my lips with a breathtaking kiss, then his mouth lingered sweetly against mine.

I gave him a shove. No way was he getting off that easy. His solution grated on my nerves. I retorted with cold sarcasm, "Oh yeah, even. You're really something. You never showed up to take me to the prom. I waited for hours in my dress, which, by the way, I spent a fortune on, and I shelled out money to get my hair done." I decided not to mention the further humiliation when I faced my friends at school. I'd told them I was going to the prom with popular Jake, so they'd wanted to know what happened.

"Catherine, I apologized years ago. And when I asked you to the prom, I told you I'd be late."

"Being a bit late and never showing up is a little different."

"The track meet took longer than I thought. And my parents wanted me to wait for my medals. I told you to go ahead if you didn't want to wait on me."

"You could've called."

"I did. I thought you were at the prom. Your brother said you left."

Jake didn't show, and I got so upset that by the time he called, I was throwing up in the toilet. No way had I wanted him to know that. My brother was supposed to say I'd left with a hot guy, but instead he'd said I wasn't home.

I glared at Jake. "What about the dinner date we had and then you canceled? You said out-of-town relatives were visiting. Then I heard you went out with a cute girl."

His brown eyes glinted with anger. "She was my cousin."

I thought about saying, “And your cousin didn’t wear braces and glasses,” but I kept my mouth shut for once. No need to remind Jake that in my sophomore year I didn’t have my contacts or straight teeth yet. I shrugged. “Whatever. I need to get to work.”

“Go out with me this Friday. I’ll make it up to you.”

“I can’t.”

“Catherine, give me a break.” He ran his fingers through his black hair. “We’ll have fun.”

I took a step away from Jake, thinking up a quick excuse for Friday night. “I have a date.”

He raised his eyebrows. “Do I know him?”

“I doubt it. You don’t travel in the same social circles.” How could Jake know him? I don’t know him. I shouldn’t lie, but Friday was a few days away. I could get a date by then. Anything was possible.

“Hey, I forgot to invite you to my parents’ Halloween party. It’s a week from this Friday. Bring your boyfriend.”

“I’ll let you know if we can make it. I have to get back to work.”

Walking back to my desk, I was proud of how I’d handled Jake’s kiss. He’d excited me, but I hadn’t given in. I broke it off quickly. He probably wondered how I could be so cool around him. I smiled, thinking how awesome I was with giving a little and pulling back. Even though Jake was a louse to me in high school, I did intend to go out with him sometime. With a definite chemistry between us, I couldn’t help myself. But I wasn’t going to rush it. The chase was too entertaining.

It might be fun to go to his parents’ Halloween party and wear an unbelievably sexy costume. I could kill the boyfriend off or say he had a death in the family. No. That wouldn't work. Jake might think I was heartless not going with my boyfriend to the funeral. My mother was right. You should never lie.

I had just sat down at my desk in the middle of the newsroom when Jake appeared by my right side.

He held a paperback in his hand. "I believe this romance novel is yours. You left it in the meeting room." He glanced at it before handing it to me. "So you like romances. I think I might be more interesting than you reading about a character kissing her man in a book."

I grabbed my paperback, noticing several sets of eyes watching us. Sometimes I like being surrounded by other reporters and other times I'd like to have my own private office. "I'm researching romance novelists. We have several successful Ohio romance writers in our area, and I'm going to ask them how their novels are different now from several years ago."

He grinned. "You're just full of surprises. I never would've guessed you like investigating romances. If you need any help doing research, you know my number."

I clenched my jaw as he walked away whistling. Although I made that up about interviewing romance writers, maybe I would. Jake didn't need to know my reading habits. Truthfully, I loved contemporary and historical romances, especially ones by British authors. I did vary my reading and enjoyed mysteries a lot, but I always had a supply of romances to read. When I was a teenager, Grandma Nelson got me started on reading her favorite British author, Georgette Heyer, and I got her interested in regencies by American author, Candice Hern. I smiled, remembering Jane loved romances. I would suggest having a section on romance novelists.

When I wasn't writing investigative articles, I wrote fluff pieces—just when I needed extra money. On my investigative reporter's income, I could pay the bills, but when I wrote articles for the singles crowd in magazines and newspapers, I had money for cool clothes, books, movies, and toys for my godchild, Connor.

"What to Wear to Get Noticed" was a favorite article I wrote. In it I explained how you wanted to stand out from everyone else when you go out at night. I definitely had an awesome outfit that I'd worn a few times to bars. It was a skirt my best friend Angie created as a fashion design student at the University of Cincinnati. It consisted of belts and it was pretty short since she ran out of them. I think she did it on purpose because when I modeled the skirt, she said, "Catherine, you have great legs." Whenever I wore it, I got smiles and glances. Or maybe dancing on the bar counters helped too. I tell you, I was a different woman in this skirt—I became a nightlife star after a few drinks.

With the skirt, I wore this incredibly soft shirt which looked like different shades of lavender in various lights. Guys loved to touch to see what the shirt felt like. I only allowed pawing at the shoulders—no place else. And, of course, I wore my long hair down.

Although the clothing was important, a pickup line was vital in bars. I happened to have a sure-fire one that landed me dates.

My mom said I had to stop trying to help every single female out there catch a man. I wrote a column recently for a woman's magazine and gave a lot of tips on how to grab a guy's attention. She was livid and said, "You just limited your own chances of getting married before you're thirty."

I shrugged. "Hey, I just turned twenty-five. I have plenty of time."

Secretly, I knew she was also correct in saying there are too few available men for all of us women looking for Mr. Right. But what the heck, even though I've never written my great pickup line into an article, here it is—I look the guy directly in the eye and say, "You're hot."

Short, but definitely got the guy's attention. And they were shocked because it was unexpected for a girl to go to a guy and say that. A lot of times, he'd give a big grin and start talking to me.

After I met a new guy and started dating him, I wondered what he'd think of my secret fantasy. No one knew it. I hadn't even told Angie. I could see her telling everyone, and I didn't want to have every guy ask me if they could participate in part of my fantasy. And I knew some might laugh at me and think it was out of this world. But the adventuresome ones would go for it. It was my sexual fantasy and I didn't want to share it with anyone—well, obviously I wanted to share it with the right guy someday. But then, I pulled the daydream out when I felt down and visualized it happening. Fortunately, I have an active imagination. Although it seemed unrealistic, I believed it could actually happen to me. I mean you have to believe in your dreams, even the big fantasies. Right?

My daydreaming came to a stop when the phone rang. It was Adam, my brother. He didn't waste any time and said, "I need to talk to you about Tracy. She's upset and she doesn't want to talk to her dad about it."

Tracy is the daughter of Mayor Pat Connelly and presently Adam's girlfriend. Adam is an architect and works for a company in Park City. Adam knew my dislike for Mayor Connelly didn't include Tracy. When the mayor tried to put an unnecessary higher city tax on the citizens of Park City, I wrote a scathing article in the paper. Mayor Connelly said my facts were misleading. He demanded an apology, which I refused to give.

I leaned forward in my chair. "What's she upset about?"

"She found a hidden box in her mom's closet with pictures of Max Hartman when he was younger."

Before Max died in a freak accident, he'd been a janitor in Park City High School. "That's strange. Why would Karen Connelly have pictures of Max?"

"It appears Max was her boyfriend. There are several pictures of them together. Max apparently went to the same high school as Karen. Tracy thinks it's strange her mom never mentioned it, but there's more."

Tracy must have found something big. "What is it?"

"Tracy wants to show you a note. The note reads, 'I know your secret. It's going to cost you.' "

"Maybe she should ask her mom."

"Her mom's out of town. Tracy doesn't want to talk to her on the phone, and she's afraid her mom won't tell her the truth." Adam sighed. "Tracy said after Max died, her mom was preoccupied all the time and looked like she'd lost her best friend. She asked her mom what was wrong. And get this, Karen said, 'Tracy, never rush into anything. Always think about the consequences.' "

I bit my lip and thought for a moment. "I remember Max saying he grew up in Columbus, so if Karen went to high school with him, then I wonder if she's the reason he moved here. I doubt he moved here for the custodian job."

"Tracy mentioned that, since Max never talked about having any family here. Except Dana, but that was a lot later."

"That's right. She moved here a year before he died. Max said he divorced Dana's mom before he moved to Park City."

"And Dana told Tracy how she loved Max like a father."

Jake stopped a few feet away from my desk, and I watched him pretending to drink from a cup and pointing to the direction of the break room. I shook my head at his pantomime of asking me if I wanted coffee. He winked and grinned at me before he walked away. Of course, he had a sexy grin. And hey, I knew he did that on purpose to torment me like I tried to do to him with my hundreds of drinks a day.

"Catherine, you still there?" Adam asked.

"I'm thinking about the note Tracy found." I moved a lock of hair off my forehead. "I bet someone was or is blackmailing Mrs. Connelly and maybe she couldn't go to her husband about it. But she decided to confide in Max since he loved her enough to move back to Park City."

"If she did, I wonder if Max took care of it before he died."

Max's death. Maybe it wasn't an accident. He'd been efficient in the maintenance of the school building. Nothing got past him. When he wasn't keeping everything clean and running smoothly, Max was there for the students. Five years ago when he died, I thought how strange it was that the fire department and police blamed Max for the explosion. Mom knew him from teaching at Park City High School and had said, "I never thought Max would make a fatal human error in the place he loved."

I tapped a finger against my mouse pad. “Oh, Adam, you don’t think Max was murdered, do you?”

“It was definitely weird the fire marshal claimed Max’s carelessness caused the boiler room explosion.”

“Maybe Max was being blackmailed and he showed the note to Mrs. Connelly because the secret involved her.”

“That occurred to me too.”

I poised my fingers over my keyboard and typed in my favorite word, *investigation*. “We need to investigate Max’s death.”

“I was hoping you’d say that.”

I peered at my cup of coffee and saw a nasty film on the top. I should’ve nodded to Jake when he wanted to get me a fresh cup of coffee. I heard Adam say he’d check with Tracy to see when we could get together to brainstorm about Max, the note and Mrs. Connelly. I felt like a terrific cup of Mom’s coffee. “Hey, if it’s okay with Tracy, we can meet at the coffeehouse this evening.”

I was proud of Mom. She quit teaching after Adam graduated from high school. Actually it was the same year Max died. After teaching ten years, she wanted to own a coffeehouse with a bookstore included. She worked at Starbucks for a year to learn as much as possible before opening her own shop. I remembered her researching the coffee and tea industry by reading trade manuals, visiting different shops and interviewing the owners and workers. She even went back to college to take finance courses.

I’d talk to Jane about writing the story after I listened to what Tracy told me. From that little bit of information Adam had given me, my mind churned all kinds of possible scenarios and my fingers flew over the keys. I couldn’t wait to get the go-ahead from Jane. I loved being an investigative reporter.

Adam and I were fortunate in getting certain genes from both parents' academic strengths. From my math professor dad, Harrison Steel, I received the deductive and analytic skills I used in solving problems. My love of words and interest in news work had to come from my mom, Leslie Steel. She majored in English and Speech. I always went to her when I got stuck in unraveling a case since she had a creative, imaginative mind.

I stared at my monitor for a moment before I started typing again. I listed several questions.

Why had Karen Connelly been upset after Max died?

Had she still been in love with him?

Or was she distressed because she knew someone murdered him?

Was the note Tracy found from a blackmailer?

Who would want to blackmail Karen Connelly?

Was Max murdered?

If so, what was the motive?

Because everyone loved Max, our class had dedicated our yearbook to him. The decision had been unanimous among the seniors. As yearbook editor, I still remembered one person's opposition to our selection. The school secretary, Miss Evelyn Kent, flung open the door to the yearbook room, shouting, "The yearbook shouldn't be dedicated to a janitor. Mercy, students, think. Teachers, administration, coaches... All have had positive influence on your lives. How could you choose Max for this honor?"

But Miss Kent was wrong. Max deserved the honor.

When a student had a low test score, a fight with a best friend or just seemed lonely, Max had been there to help with a warm smile, reassuring words or advice. With his big heart and compassion, there was nothing to dislike about Max. I hoped he hadn't been murdered. It would be sad. But if he had been, I planned on finding the killer.

I sighed. Thinking of Max brought up many memories of being in school again. And in love. I needed a fix. People were addicted to different things when they feel low, and ice cream made me feel much better. Well, I ate ice cream when I was happy too.

In fact, enjoying spoonfuls of chocolate chip cookie dough ice cream was up there with my sexual fantasy. Hey, don't even think it. My fantasy was not having a guy lick ice cream off my body.

I'm classier than that.

Okay, I'll spill what my fantasy was. I wanted to lose my virginity with Mr. Right on our honeymoon in a famous London landmark. Maybe even Buckingham Palace. I suppose my love of British romance authors influenced me in wanting this particular honeymoon. And I saw so much footage of the wedding of Prince William, Duke of Cambridge, and Catherine Middleton that I decided London would be the perfect setting for consummating my marriage. I deserved a super-romantic honeymoon after waiting to lose my virginity to the man of my dreams.

Angie thought my mom hypnotized me when I was a wee girl to remain a virgin until my wedding night.

If good old Mom did, then it might just rub off with Jake back in my life.

Chapter Two

Perched on the seat of a flowered chair with my heels off, I felt comfortable. I laughed each time my godson's butt went straight into the air as he put his blond-haired head against the blue carpeted floor. "I guess Connor gets a thrill out of feeling he's upside down."

Angie grinned. She had a small gap between her front teeth, but she could care less and says it makes it easier to floss. "Or he's a butt person."

"You're lucky having Connor."

Angie nodded. "Brian and I think he's the greatest little kid."

"I'd love to have what you have. I'm never going to find a guy like Brian."

"Sometimes you have to settle."

I raised my eyebrows. "What do you mean, settle?"

"Now don't get mad at me, but you've dated some great guys and..."

"And what?" I stared at Angie, who wore a gray T-shirt and faded jeans. Since she had Connor, many days she grabbed one of Brian's shirts to wear and on her petite body it looked gigantic.

"This is just my opinion, but you seem to find fault with

the nicest and cutest guys. And you know I love Brian, but he's not perfect and he can drive me crazy sometimes." Angie's blonde curls fell forward as she picked up Connor. She sat on her tan leather sofa and watched Connor chewing on his finger. "Poor baby, he's teething."

"It's not always me. After a few dates, they want to jump my bones. And when I don't give in, they dump me." I reached for my glass of Coke and took a sip.

"I think you blew it with Sean. He had looks and personality."

"I was really into him until I realized he was self-centered and not very ambitious." While I dated Sean, he worked at King's Island theme park and during the winter he had little to do.

Connor wriggled on Angie's lap. Leaning down, she put him on a baby quilt. "You complain if you're smarter than the guy is, and you complain if he's not smart enough."

I shrugged, thinking Angie was partially right. I seemed to find something wrong and it was over before the relationship had a chance to make it. But I was young yet and I could afford to be choosy. "I'm not settling. I know what I want in a man and I don't think I'm being too picky."

"How's it going with Jake?"

Angie must have liked hearing my reports about Jake romancing me at the office because she frequently asked about him. "He shoved me against the wall and kissed me at work today."

"Now he's my kind of a guy. Not the shoving, but the kissing part. He doesn't mess around and goes after what he wants. I think you should go out with him. He definitely has the hots for you and you do for him too."

I shook my head. "I don't have the hots for him."

Angie sighed. "I know it was terrible you missed going to the prom with him, but he did have a good reason. It was important that he didn't miss his track meet since he ended up getting a full track scholarship to Ball State."

I shrugged. "It wasn't just being stood up twice. When Jake went away to college, I went to see him in a track meet and he ignored me."

"He's definitely not ignoring you now."

"Jake invited me to his parents' house for a Halloween party. I'm thinking of playing it safe so I don't get stood up again and going to it." I rolled my eyes. "Might as well see what happens."

"You better go to it. Jake invited us too. In fact, he joined us last Friday night when we went out and mentioned the party then."

My jaw tightened and I was afraid to ask but had to know. "Please say he didn't invite Hilary."

"Afraid so."

Hilary was a handful and the drama queen in our group of friends. I hated missing out on Friday since Angie and Brian don't go out as much since having Connor. It would've been like old times—Angie and Brian, Tim and Susanne, Hilary and Keith, Ben, Will, and me. We all went to University of Cincinnati together except for Tim and Ben. They both went to Xavier, which was a rival of University of Cincinnati, especially during basketball season.

Angie had hired a babysitter for Connor, and the whole group apparently went out without me. When Angie had called to tell me to meet them, I was tied up with an expert source about car repair fraud and wanted to get my story in before other reporters got wind of the car scams.

"Great," I said, irritated. "She'll ruin the night."

"She'll be fine if she doesn't drink too much."

Angie and I didn't always agree about Hilary. We were both bridesmaids for Angie's wedding. At the reception Hilary said a guest attacked her. She found the wife and told her how she had to fight the husband off her. Now, Hilary was gorgeous with long auburn hair and a perfect body, so it was possible.

"He even tore my spaghetti straps on my dress," Hilary had said in the loudest voice she could muster.

The husband said he never touched her and insisted Hilary was a liar. I think she hated not being the center of attention at the wedding and she decided to cause a ruckus. Or she was jealous that Angie got married before she did. Hilary's boyfriend, Keith, punched the husband in the face so hard that his glasses flew off and blood spurted out of his nose. Angie was upset with Hilary, but she forgave her.

"I have to look better than Hilary. Could you help me with my costume?"

Angie gave me a worried look. "There's not much time and I don't have costumes for us. And I have to get a dress done for a customer yet this week."

"It only has to be the greatest costume at the party." I shook my head. "I'm kidding. It just has to be sexy so Jake can't take his eyes off me. Sexy won't be hard for you. You're the woman who designed that great belt skirt for me."

"You know, Catherine, Jake might be the one. And you can give up your bar-hopping nights."

Sometimes I wished I had an unmarried close friend. Angie wanted me to get married and be just like her. And have a baby so we could raise them together. When I saw how happy she was with Brian and Connor, I wanted a hubby and a family. But other times, I loved being single and doing what I wanted. Besides, I waited this long for the right guy, I could be patient and wait longer. There was one for me. I just hadn't found him yet. But in the meantime, there was a party to attend and I loved parties. Especially costume parties.

"Nope." I carried my glass to the kitchen, saying over my shoulder, "I'm sure he's not."

"But you both obviously love to write."

I rolled my eyes. "I can't see me getting serious about a sports writer. But now, an editor at a big publishing house or an agent would be perfect when I write my book about unsolved mysteries. Or maybe about some unusual solved cases."

"I know whatever you write will be great."

I plopped down on the sofa, giving her an appreciative look. "Thanks."

That's what I liked about Angie. She was supportive of my ideas. Of course, she had a motive. She wanted me to dedicate my first book to her. That would be difficult since I had a feeling my mom would be hurt if it wasn't dedicated to her. I'd figure it out when the book was written and I had a contract for it.

Angie folded Connor's clean laundry and asked, "Are Adam and Tracy still together?"

I nodded, grabbing a baby blanket out of the basket to fold. "I might have a case about Max Hartman to put in my book."

She stopped folding, looking intrigued. "What does Max's death have to do with me asking you about Adam and

Tracy?"

"It might be nothing, but Tracy learned that her mom went to school with Max, and she found a threatening note in her mother's box of mementos. She wants to talk to me about it. Max's death might not have been accidental."

"I guess Mrs. Connelly never told Tracy about the note."

"She probably hasn't told anyone. Tracy found it hidden and her mom's away. It might not even be Mrs. Connelly's note."

"What does it say?"

"Something about knowing your secret and it's going to cost you."

We watched Connor squeak the duck on his quilt for a few moments. With a thoughtful expression, Angie said, "I do remember Mrs. Connelly helping a lot with school activities. Maybe she volunteered to be around Max."

I nodded. "He was good-looking. I had a crush on him when I was in school."

The phone rang and while Angie answered it, I wondered about Max. He had never talked about any family except he'd mentioned Dana a few times. I guess the school children had been his family. Did Mrs. Connelly and Max have an affair? Had Mayor Connelly noticed his wife spent too much time at school and learned that Max was her lover?

Angie replaced the phone. "It was Brian. He's going to bring Chinese home for dinner. You're welcome to stay."

I wrinkled my nose because I hated Chinese food. "Thanks, but I'll pass."

"You can pick out what you don't like and just eat the rice, and he's getting egg rolls too."

I did like egg rolls and rice, but glanced at my watch. "I

need to leave soon anyhow. I'm meeting Adam and Tracy this evening. She's going to show me the note."

"I can't imagine anyone killing kind Max." While Angie removed Connor's soiled diaper and pulled a wipe out of the dispenser, she said, "I wish babies came out of the womb potty-trained."

"Or it'd be great to be rich and hire a nanny to do diaper duty."

"That might be nice to have a nanny." After Connor's butt was clean, Angie said, "I heard on the news that the candidate polls show Mayor Connelly is ahead. You better be careful. He won't like any scandal about his wife being involved somehow with the janitor."

Mayor Connelly was running for a seat in the United States House of Representatives to replace his father. Representative Connelly was retiring. "I heard and I hope he loses."

"I love what you're wearing. The back lacing reminds me of the old corset styles."

"Thanks. The sweater's new from Victoria's Secret." I wore a slim black skirt with a back pleat and a white lace-up sweater.

Angie grinned. "Since Jake kissed you right in the office, your change of clothing must be working."

"Since Jake seems to want to be included in our circle of friends—"

Angie interrupted, "Remember, Brian and Jake were friends in high school and they stayed in touch while Jake was away at college."

I slipped on my heels. "I'm afraid I lied to Jake. I told him I have a boyfriend."

"Why'd you tell him that?"

"He asked me to go out with him this Friday. I didn't want him to think there's no one in my life and he can just step right back into it."

Angie frowned. "Tell me you didn't say your boyfriend's going to the Halloween party."

I gave her a small smile. "Jake did tell me to bring my boyfriend to the party. You have to help me think of a name for this guy."

She put her hands on her hips. "How about Elmer?"

I made a face, knowing she was teasing me. "That won't do. The name has to sound like it belongs to a hot guy."

"Ernie."

"Very funny." I rubbed my lower lip. "I got it. We'll say his name is Richard."

"I'm getting a teething toy for Connor." On her way to the kitchen, she said, "Let's make him British."

Angie kept a couple of teething toys in the refrigerator because the coldness helped Connor cope with his erupting teeth. I gave Connor a kiss while watching her open the refrigerator.

"I did love the British actor, Henry Cavill, in *Man of Steel*, but..." Then it hit me. Instead of a British Richard, I could have Ricardo. I snapped my fingers. "I got it. He'll be Spanish and be Ricardo."

A couple of years ago, I went to Costa Rica with my parents and Adam. There I met Ricardo, a dreamy Spanish male. I thought I was in love with Ricardo, but then I loved everyone in his family. Life was relaxed and different there from living in Park City. Dating a foreigner with black hair and a dark complexion seemed very romantic.

Angie handed the toy to Connor. "That's right, you thought about staying in Costa Rica to be with him."

I sighed. "Sometimes I miss dating Ricardo. We didn't have much in common, but he was sweet."

"Have you talked to him lately?"

I shook my head. "It's been a few weeks. I told Jake he wouldn't know my boyfriend since they didn't travel in the same circles, so this will be perfect. And I won't be lying as much since Ricardo was my boyfriend."

"And he wanted to be more than that."

"I was stunned when he gave me a diamond on New Year's Eve. We'd only known each other for seven months. And he was hurt when I gave it back to him after wearing it for only a month."

Angie squeezed my shoulder. "I'm glad you aren't living in Costa Rica. You won't have to make up an occupation and you can tell Jake about the family business. Ricardo and his family have a banana empire, right?"

I shook my head. "They raise coffee. I did tell Jake I had a date with my boyfriend on Friday, but I'll just say some important business came up and he had to cancel."

"You could explain Ricardo's absence at the party by saying he couldn't book a flight in time."

I thought for a moment. "Maybe Ricardo will want to come to the party. I'll call him soon."

Angie laughed. "I know. You break up with a guy, and you end up having another phone buddy."

I knew she was thinking how Sean called me a lot even though we broke up months ago. The bad thing was he calls me at two or three o'clock in the morning after he's been out drinking. Lucky me, having drunk Sean calling to tell how lonely he was without me.

"Ricardo got his pilot's license a couple of months ago, so he can fly his dad's small plane. I can see him flying here for it." I picked up my purse and slung it over my shoulder as I stood. "I think I know the perfect costume for the Halloween party."

I went early to Mom's coffeehouse to wait for Adam and Tracy at a corner table. As I walked inside, I smelled cinnamon and realized coffeecake or muffins were probably baking.

Mom and Dad had bought a quaint house two years ago and completely restored the original pine floors. Leslie's Coffee Shop was the name they decided on. She'd created a warm, relaxing atmosphere for her customers, where they could converse with close friends or sit on comfy upholstered chairs in solitude, studying or reading the paper. A rocking chair sat in front of a fireplace. Her menu included various coffee and tea drinks, fruit smoothies, scones, muffins, coffeecakes, cookies, ice cream, cheesecakes, egg salad and tuna salad sandwiches. She had a small section displaying local authors' books for sale, and welcomed book clubs with their weekly discussions.

She liked to encourage young talent and tonight a guitarist played in the background. He was in one of Dad's math classes at University of Cincinnati.

Mom set a basket of my favorite blueberry muffins on the table. She looked pretty in a black and white shirt with black tapered pants. Her dark brown hair flipped at the ends. She wore a pearl necklace and earrings given to her by Dad last Christmas. I smiled, recalling how she clipped out pictures of pearl earrings and necklace sets on sale and put them where he could see them. I loved Dad, but sometimes he was clueless what to get Mom.

I hoped my future husband would surprise me with wonderful gifts. If ever the right guy happens along, that is. I wasn't taking Angie's suggestion of settling just to have a husband. Too bad Brian didn't have a brother. And especially one with perfect vision. I didn't want my children to have to deal with glasses or contacts. Mom and Dad were both nearsighted, so that meant their children inherited the same vision deficiency. Adam and I both wore contacts because we were afraid of having laser surgery to correct our vision.

Mom smiled at me. "You have to come on Thursday night. Your old English teacher, Dale Jansen, is coming to read his poetry. He published a collection of his poems. After his reading, he's going to do a book signing."

Mr. Jansen might know something about Max and Mrs. Connelly. But first I needed to ask Mom what she knew about Max. "Mom, sit down. I need to talk to you about M—."

Mom interrupted me and said, "A man. I'm ready to hear about the new man in your life." She grinned and sat in a chair across from me. "I hope it's Jake."

I stared at my mother, wondering why I'd ever started telling her about all my dates. Big mistake. Now she was constantly asking me about my love life. As if there was any, right now. "Mom, sorry, I was about to say Max, not man. Although...I guess man is in his last name."

She leaned forward, looking puzzled. "You mean Max Hartman?"

I nodded.

"Poor Max dying like that. Such a terrible accident."

"It might not have been an accident. Adam and Tracy should be here in a little bit to shed some new information on that closed case."

After I filled her in about what Tracy had found in her mother's closet, she said, "Oh my, I think I might have started all these questions about Max's death."

"What do you mean?"

"I called Tracy and asked her to look in her mother's closet for a bag of clothing Karen wanted to give for our annual clothing drive. Before Karen left, she called me and wanted me to come over, but I was too busy here. She said she was leaving them in her walk-in closet."

I'd forgotten Karen and Mom had worked together on a few charity committees. Here I was only thinking of asking her questions about Max. How could her charity work with the mayor's wife slip my mind? Gee, I was young yet. What was my memory going to be like when I was older? I could blame my memory lapse on Jake. Backing me against the wall and kissing me was enough to make any woman forgetful. I thought he was a heartthrob in high school, but now he seemed even more attractive than ever.

"Hi, Catherine," Miranda Carter said, interrupting my thoughts.

I smiled at Miranda, a sixteen-year-old who had brown eyes and brown curly hair. She was proud of the perm she recently got in her chin length hair. She was one of my favorite people in the world. Mom hired her to work a few hours in the coffeehouse after school. Miranda was born with Down syndrome and was one of the best workers.

"Hi. How are you?"

"Fine." Miranda looked at my empty coffee cup. "Would

you like a refill?" At my nod, she carefully poured coffee.

"If you aren't busy Sunday afternoon, we could go to a movie together."

"I'd like to go to a movie with you." Miranda gave me a broad smile. "Is it okay if I bring my boyfriend?"

I laughed. "You have a boyfriend and didn't tell me? Did you two just meet?"

"No. He goes to my school and he's in classes with me. I like Kevin a lot. He didn't know if we should be girlfriend and boyfriend until I told him. Do you have a boyfriend?"

I shook my head. "Not right now."

Miranda frowned. "You need a boyfriend. Maybe you should get on the TV show where you give a rose to the guy you like."

"That's a good suggestion. Maybe I'll try to get on *The Bachelorette* show and get a boyfriend."

"I agree with you, Miranda. Catherine does need a boyfriend." Mom patted my arm. "I better get back to work."

Miranda looked down at the coffeepot in her hand. "I should go and refill more cups. Call me sometime about the movie."

As I watched Miranda chatting and pouring coffee, I thought how great it was that Mom hired people with disabilities. Unlike some small business owners, she didn't mind doing the extra book work required by the government. Unfortunately, other businesses didn't keep the disabled people once their job coaches left, since the managers never bothered to get to know their special employees. Mom's customers loved Miranda with her outgoing personality and eagerness to please.

I was enjoying a muffin when I saw Adam and Tracy

walk in. I waved to them. Tracy wore black cropped pants with a shrunken jacket and both pieces had pink piping trim. She looked great in the suit with her thin, tall frame.

After they both sat, Tracy said, “Thanks for meeting us.”

“How many muffins have you eaten already?” Adam asked. “Don’t tell me your usual four. I don’t know how Mom makes a profit with you eating so many muffins.”

I rolled my eyes, wishing he wasn’t right in his guess. I couldn’t help myself when it comes to blueberry muffins. “What about you? Mom says she sees you every morning when you pick up breakfast.”

Tracy grinned. “You’re adults and your mom should charge you both.”

“Hey, we’re free labor when she needs us,” Adam said, grabbing a muffin from the basket.

“That reminds me, I might help out on Thursday night. Mom said Mr. Jansen is going to be here to do a reading. I’ll ask him questions about Max and the fire.”

Tracy tucked a strand of auburn hair behind her ear. “Maybe you should wait to investigate Max’s death until after the election.”

“Hi, Tracy. Do you want coffee or...” Miranda stopped speaking when her hearing aid whistled. She pushed her hair out of the way and pressed on her ear mold. “I hate wearing hearing aids.”

I noticed her ear molds were red and pink striped instead of the usual clear or neutral color. “Pretty snazzy colors for ear molds. They look cool with your red aids.”

Miranda smiled. “Thank you.”

Adam and Tracy ordered drinks and cheesecake and Miranda left.

I figured Tracy wanted to talk to her mother before I started asking people about what happened so I asked, "When's your mother coming home?"

"Next week. She's going to as many cities as possible to campaign before November." Tracy leaned closer to me. "After I talked to Adam the first time, I found an old calendar planner in the box." She opened her purse and took out the calendar. After she flipped to May, Tracy said, "See, maybe Mom and Max were going to tell me something after my high school graduation."

I looked where she pointed and read aloud, "Tell Tracy."

Tracy's eyes filled with sadness. "Max died before I was told anything. I'm afraid someone tried to shut him up so I wouldn't learn the secret."

Chapter Three

Could I wait until next week to start investigating what happened to Max? Once I decided to right a wrong, I loved to snoop and to expose the bad guys. I understood how Tracy wanted to talk to her mother first, but then why did she involve me already? True, Karen Connelly's explanations to Tracy's questions would be beneficial when I tried to discover what happened to Max in the boiler room. And my gut told me it was murder. Someone didn't want Max as a custodian any longer at Park City High School. Maybe he knew something illegal was going on and had to be eliminated before he told the police.

Or maybe his death had everything to do with his love for Karen.

Adam told Tracy, "I doubt if Catherine can wait for your mother's return. Once there's a mystery, she's off searching for clues, collecting data and interviewing people."

"How do you know me so well?" I asked.

"Hey, we started off close." Adam grinned. "You wanted a piece of me when I was a baby."

I frowned. "Mom never should've told you."

"Okay. Fess up," Tracy said. "What are you two talking about?"

"While Mom was breastfeeding me, my darling sister became jealous and bit my little toe."

"I was only two years old," I said in an indignant voice. "And I was jealous of all the attention you were getting."

Tracy gave us a humorous glance. "I'm glad you two moved on from your childhood." She handed me the paper with the harsh message on it and said, "I appreciate you taking a look at this note I found."

I studied the handwriting for a few minutes. "Is it okay if I make a copy of it tonight?"

"Sure. I just want it back when I ask Mom about it." Tracy paused for a moment. When she spoke again, her voice was barely a whisper. "I was so heartbroken when Max died. He'd been a wonderful friend to me since elementary school. I was happy when he switched schools my sophomore year."

"He might have switched so he'd see your mother when she volunteered at school," I said.

"I imagine he might have left St. Christopher for money. I'm sure the public school paid Max a lot more to be a janitor," Adam said.

Adam, Tracy and I went to the Catholic elementary school, but Park City never had a parochial high school. Until Tracy had brought it up, I hadn't thought too much about Max switching schools. "I can't remember what year Max started working at St. Christopher. Do either of you remember what grade you were in?"

"First grade." Tracy moaned, hiding her face behind a menu. "Dana Tucker just walked in. She's obsessed with my father and acts like I'm her best friend."

Turning my head, I saw the blonde-haired Dana walking toward our table with Miranda right behind her. "I think she already saw you. Doesn't she work for your dad?"

Tracy put the menu down and shook her head. "Not any longer. He moved her to the city sewer department."

Why had the mayor gotten rid of his very beautiful administrative assistant? Was there too much temptation there for him to be unfaithful? Or had there been an affair that turned sour on his part?

Miranda set blue cups of coffee in front of Adam and Tracy. "I'll be right back with your cheesecake."

"When you bring their cheesecake, please bring me a cup of coffee," Dana said, grabbing a chair from a nearby table. "Tracy, you haven't returned my phone calls. Has your dad been keeping you busy at City Hall?"

"I'm in law school. In my free time, I help Dad with running for Grandpa's seat."

"I guess I better be careful what I ask you about your dad's campaign," Dana said.

With raised eyebrows, Tracy asked, "Why do you say that?"

"I meant because we have a reporter sitting right here from *The Messenger*. Let's not give her any ammunition to use against Pat."

I felt uncomfortable, remembering disagreeing with Mayor Connelly on certain issues. I was in a tight spot but felt compelled to speak up. "Tracy understands I need to cover the news, but she knows I'm having a private conversation with her and Adam. I wouldn't think of reporting anything said here in an article."

Tracy cleared her throat. "I'm not worried about discussing the campaign in front of Catherine. I respect her integrity as a reporter. She's always responsible when she's critical of some of my dad's policies and shows both sides."

"Hey, I was just joking." Dana smiled, but Tracy didn't return her smile. "You didn't get your dad's sense of humor. I'm sure anything we say at this table is off the record."

Dana must have seen another side to Mayor Connelly than I did. I'd never noticed him having a sense of humor.

Adam asked Dana, "How do you like your job?"

Dana shrugged. "It's a job I hope I won't have forever. I've applied for a job in Cincinnati. I live there, anyhow."

"I didn't know that," I said. "Where in Cincinnati?"

"I bought a condo in Hyde Park."

How could Dana afford housing in an elite neighborhood?

While Miranda brought the cheesecake and Dana's cup of coffee, my cell phone rang and I saw it was Jake calling. I answered with a "hey".

"I'm at your apartment," Jake said, "and since you aren't here, I've been stood up."

"We didn't have a date."

"Sure we did."

I decided to get away from listening ears. I walked over to stand by the window. Looking out into the street, I said, "You're just trying to act like we're even now and it's not going to work."

"Okay, you got me. But I promise if we go out, we'll have a great time."

"Remember Ricardo."

"Who's Ricardo?"

That's right. I'd never given him the name of my boyfriend. Two slip-ups in one day with my memory. "Sorry, I forgot I didn't tell you my boyfriend's name."

"That's right, the one I won't know. I'd like to meet Ricardo. Is he coming to the Halloween Party?"

"He wants to, but it might be hard."

"Why's that?"

I paced in front of the window. "He lives in Costa Rica."

Jake laughed. "You have to be kidding me. I guess he's flying in on Friday for your date."

In a huffy voice, I said, "I don't see why that's funny. He has his pilot's license and a small plane. I met Ricardo when I was vacationing in his country, and of course he flies here to see me." This conversation needed to end. Ricardo had flown to United States twice to see me, but I hated giving the impression he still did and in a plane he didn't have when we were dating.

"I have to go," I said in a firm voice.

"Did you tell Ricardo about our kiss?"

"Our kiss? You kissed me."

"Catherine, you kissed me back."

"I don't remember that part." Another lie, but I didn't want to give Jake the satisfaction of knowing I liked his kiss.

"Ricardo or no Ricardo, I'm not giving up on you. I blew it in high school, but things are different now."

"Yes, it's different now. Have a good evening."

"It'll be hard, but I'll try."

"You do that. Bye, Jake."

"Wait."

I sighed. "What is it?"

"Wear the famous belt skirt tomorrow to work."

"Who told you about it?"

"Tim mentioned how great you look in it."

I swallowed hard and felt relieved it wasn't Brian making

a comment about me. But Brian had never shown any interest in me sexually, so I always felt comfortable around him and enjoyed his and Angie's friendship. I didn't like it that Keith hit on me when Hilary wasn't present. Tim did, too, and his wife Susanne could be in the same room. It was depressing and enough to make a girl not want to get married.

"It's not something I wear to work." I paused for a moment. "I'm surprised Tim even mentioned it to you. You and Tim must've been talking about me."

Jake sighed. "Okay, you're right. I told some of the guys I like watching you get drinks at the water fountain."

I was flattered, but didn't want to tell Jake. "Thanks for calling, but I need to go. Talk to you later. Bye."

I dropped my smartphone in my bag. What if Brian or someone else mentioned to Jake how Ricardo and I were no longer an item? I could say we broke up but got back together. And since Ricardo and I did call each other every couple of months, it wasn't such a big lie.

As I walked back to join Adam and Tracy, I smiled, thinking how my plan to get to Jake was working. He noticed me in a big way.

"Dana left when you did," Adam said. "I guess Tracy and I were boring without you at the table."

"I've changed my mind," Tracy said as I sat down. "I want you to go ahead and ask Mr. Jansen questions about Max. Just don't mention my mom. I need to talk to her first."

I nodded. "Okay. I won't say anything about her."

"Sorry I keep changing my mind." Tracy took a deep breath. "I'm glad Adam arranged for us to talk about what I found. I was upset when I first saw some of Max's items in the box and realized Mom kept her past love for Max a secret.

And with Dad running, I'm sure she won't want it to get out now."

I patted Tracy's arm. "I understand."

"We showed the note to Mom to see if she recognized the handwriting," Adam said. "She's not sure but she thought it looked like Miss Kent's writing."

"Miss Kent never liked Max," I said. "I wonder where she lives and I'll try to get a writing sample."

"Just go to the high school," Adam said.

"I thought she retired a year ago," I said.

"When I did the blueprints a month ago for the school's new addition, she was there. She's filling in since the other secretary's on maternity leave."

"I'll go tomorrow before I go to work. I'll try to get other samples too. Since your mom helped out at the school, someone from there might have sent her the note."

Tracy leaned toward me. "It might be hard to grab anything."

Adam grinned. "How are you going to do that, sis?"

"Easy. I'll ask Miss Kent to send my transcript some place and while she's looking for it in the file, I'll get a sample."

He shook his head. "She'll send you to a guidance counselor."

"You're right." What excuse should I use for bothering Miss Kent? "I'll say I need facts for a story about something at school. Like the number of free lunches this year."

"That should work," Adam said.

Tracy sipped her coffee. "I wonder if Dad even knows about Mom being in love with Max at one time."

That was something I wanted to find out. Had he seen

the calendar with the note to tell Tracy? Maybe he had and never wanted Tracy to know the truth. Or maybe he wanted her to know something, but Max dying had changed everything.

Max and Karen obviously had never gotten over their love for each other. He moved to Park City to be close to her. A love like that never should have been denied.

The next morning, I met with Miss Kent. She looked different to me with her short blonde hair. When I was in high school, she had dark brown hair with a little gray in it. She must have gotten grayer and decided to go blonde.

While she spoke on the phone, I glanced around the school's front office. I saw the clipboard on the office counter with student sheets to sign in and out when arriving late in the morning or when leaving school early. Everything looked the same from when I went to school, including the camera aimed at the counter to tape anyone entering the office. A TV anchored on the wall above Miss Kent's desk shot images every few seconds of various classrooms. I walked closer and peered at the screen. Nothing going on—just empty classrooms.

Glancing at Miss Kent's desk, I saw a phone message from her to Principal Hudson. I picked up the paper, noticing Miss Kent's handwriting reminded me a little of the writing on Tracy's note in my purse. Strange, she printed the first letters of some words and used cursive for the rest. I needed to compare the writing to see if Miss Kent could've given the note to Karen Connelly.

Before I could seize the memo, Miss Kent ended the call. She snapped, "Why are you reading Mr. Hudson's message?"

I smiled at her. “I was just going down memory lane, realizing how many things seem the same as when I was in high school. Remember how I stopped in here to get admittance slips from you?”

Miss Kent nodded. “You always timed it when I was too busy to ask you a lot of questions.”

“I have a question for you now. I hate to bother you, but I need some facts about the number of free school lunches for a survey I’m doing.”

“I’ll get it. Mr. Hudson keeps that in his office.” She left to retrieve the information in the other room.

Bingo. I got the sample plus a bonus. I slipped them in the back of my legal pad.

She handed me the papers. A big diamond ring caught my attention as Miss Kent brushed a lock of blonde hair away from her face. How could a school secretary afford a diamond that size? Or was it a diamond? Zirconia, maybe. “Your ring’s beautiful.”

She glanced at it. “It was a gift.”

Or maybe she bought it herself with the blackmail money from Karen. I’d think more about this possibility later. “Do you have a minute to answer a couple of questions about the government food program?”

“Sure.”

I sat down in a vinyl chair, held my pen over my pad and waited for her answer.

“I can’t believe you’re going to write down what I say in longhand,” Miss Kent said, staring at my pad. “I wouldn’t have expected that.”

“You’re observant. Reporters still might grab old-fashioned paper for our interviews. Sometimes I use my iPad but I also like to use pen and paper too."

A few questions later, I knew I could leave without making her suspicious. As I was about to leave the office, a short man with bushy eyebrows and thinning gray hair said hello to me and I greeted him back.

"Catherine, this is Ralph Tindall," Miss Kent said and continued her introduction, "and Catherine Steel is a reporter for *The Messenger*. Ralph's our custodian."

Recognition was in his eyes as he looked at me. "I read your stuff all the time."

I was pleased we now knew each other. Although Ralph hadn't been working at the school when Max was there, I knew I might want to talk to him in the future. Ralph might be able to tell me more about the boiler room where Max had been found dead on the floor.

I drove my red Honda Civic to the newspaper office. Smiling to myself with a new success, I turned into the parking lot next to *The Messenger's* building. Once inside the office, I pulled out the papers I'd swiped off of Miss Kent's desk. Mr. Hudson's handwriting looked nothing like the threatening note. I doubt if a principal would stoop to blackmail. I stood in front of the copier, staring at the probable blackmail note. Miss Kent had tried to disguise her writing. I was sure of it. Although the letters on the note were carefully slanted, the handwriting still resembled Miss Kent's. All the words were written in cursive except for one letter. It was printed. I didn't need to get more samples. I had the writer of the blackmail note.

My thoughts drifted to Max and how Miss Kent hadn't liked us dedicating the yearbook to him. Maybe there was a deeper reason she'd belittled his value to the school.

And Miss Kent might not just be a blackmailer. She could be more dangerous. She might be a murderer.

Chapter Four

After work on Wednesday, I returned the note to Tracy and showed her Miss Kent's phone memo.

"If Miss Kent wrote it," Tracy said, "I wonder if Mom was having an affair with Max. That'd definitely be something to blackmail Mom with."

I nodded, relieved she brought up that her mother possibly had been unfaithful to Mayor Connelly. "Soon, you'll talk to your mom and find out what it was. I have to admit I'm thinking that's what happened."

We chatted for a few minutes, then I left to go to a Halloween costume store. I'd seen a couple of costumes I liked online. I wanted to check out what was available in a store, then I wouldn't have to worry if an Internet purchase would arrive in time, or if it would be exactly what I wanted. I decided against having Angie make my costume. She had enough to do with Connor, a dress to finish for one of her regular customers and getting costumes ready for her and Brian.

Driving to nearby Cincinnati was a possibility, but I knew I might find my costume at a small Halloween shop at our mall. During fall, the store had costumes, then switched to other saleable items during different holiday seasons. Since it was still a week and a half until Halloween, I was surprised to see so many shoppers rifling through the costumes.

As I walked to the adult section of the store, I saw a small girl with her mother looking at a Dorothy costume from The Wizard of Oz. I remembered one Halloween when I was about that size. I was Little Bo Peep who lost her sheep. Mom made the dress and bonnet and I even had white pantaloons to wear. After Mom finished sewing my costume, I'd modeled it for Dad.

His eyes had narrowed as he stared at me. "Something's missing here." After a few seconds, he said, "You need a staff to carry as little Bo Peep."

He made me this awesome shepherd's staff, and Mom put a yellow ribbon around it to match the ribbon ties on my bonnet.

And here I was twenty-five years old and still excited about dressing up for a Halloween party. Now I needed to see if I could find the super villain costume, which I knew would be sensational. I shuffled through stacks of costumes in clear plastic bags and saw nothing. Instead of ordering online or going to Cincinnati, why not make it myself? I'd need a red wig so I picked up one.

I groaned a little when I saw the long line in front of the only register. As I stood waiting to pay for the wig, I looked out into the mall and saw Dana Tucker leaning against a man. I squinted, trying to see the man better. It was Mayor Connelly's campaign manager, Fred Newman. Fred didn't have the mayor's good looks, but he was attractive and charming, his dark hair making a nice contrast to Dana's blonde beauty. He definitely was making the correct choices in running the mayor's campaign and wanted his man to get to the House of Representatives. He kissed Dana before they walked away together.

I moved a little closer to the register, making a mental note to tell Tracy how I saw Dana with Fred.

Well, waiting in line wasn't my favorite thing, but at least tantalizing smells were coming in the store from a nearby Cinnabon restaurant. I loved their cinnamon rolls topped with cream cheese frosting. Almost as much as blueberry muffins.

Finally, the cashier with mousy brown hair and big glasses scanned the wig price and added the tax. "It's eighteen, eighty-six please."

I handed her a twenty and smiled at her. "I bet you'll be glad when Halloween's over. You're so busy, and working by yourself makes it rough."

She took the twenty, put it in the drawer and gave me the change. "You're right. I'll be glad when Halloween's over. In fact, I hate Halloween."

Panic rose in my heart when I saw her holding my bag with the wig in a clenched fist. Why did I open my big mouth? Obviously, I said something to set her off in a bad mood. I stared at the plastic card pinned on her orange top. It read Maggie. I reached across the counter for my bag. "Thanks, Maggie."

"Do you want to know why I hate it?" Maggie didn't wait for me to answer. "I live in an old Victorian house and all the neighborhood kids think it's haunted so every year they do all kinds of stuff. They throw shelled corn on the porch, hide in the tall bushes, toilet paper the yard and bang on the door before they run away. One year they blew up my mailbox with firecrackers."

"I'm sorry."

A woman in line shouted, "Hey, I'm tired of waiting. Stop the chit chat."

Maggie tossed my bag to me and glared at all the customers behind me. "Guess what? I don't care. I'm taking a break."

I heard a low chuckle. I turned and saw Jake behind the line of angry people. I had to do something here or I'd have a riot on my hands. I moved quickly and put my hand on Maggie's arm. "Please, I'll bag for you and later, I'll treat you to a cinnabon or something."

She looked at me like I was the crazy one, but my body relaxed as she nodded. After fifteen minutes of Maggie scanning the purchases and me bagging, it was Jake's turn. He had a Caribbean pirate's costume complete with shirt, pants, vest, belt with sash and a bandana. I grinned as I stuck his costume in a bag. "It looks like you have everything you need."

"What are you wearing with the red wig?"

"It's a secret."

Jake gave me a broad smile. "You seem to have a feel for bagging. You might want to work here part-time to fill your lonely hours with Ricardo so far away."

I extended his bag to him and he grasped my hand firmly. I looked directly into his eyes. "I'm not lonely." I saw a flicker of disappointment in Jake's brown eyes.

"Is Ricardo coming to the party?"

"I'm not sure."

I gave him a surprised look when he squeezed my hand before taking the bag.

"I have boxing tonight so..." He hesitated for a moment,

then said, "I better get out of here."

"Hey, Jake, wait," I said as he walked to the entrance.

"What?"

"Don't take too many punches. I don't want our sports editor to get beat up."

After he left, Maggie said, "I don't know what this Ricardo looks like, but Jake's handsome and definitely into you."

During a lull, Maggie and I straightened up the store. The customers had tossed costumes and accessories where they didn't belong. As I put a princess costume in the children's section, I noticed it was eight o'clock.

I glanced at Maggie and said, "The mall closes at nine. I better go now and get our cinnabons."

"Okay, thanks." Maggie waved her hand around the store. "And when you come back, I'll give you an employee's discount on any costume here. You were nice to help me."

I smiled. "Thanks, but I'm thinking of making my costume."

An hour later, I was home in my one-bedroom apartment. Before I moved in, Angie had gone with me to check out the apartment building. She took one look at the hardwood floors and in a teasing voice had said, "You have to rent this place. You can spill milk and it won't soak into the carpet."

I gritted my teeth because I hated to be reminded of what had happened to our carpet when we were roommates for a year during college. We were moving in when I set a gallon of milk on the carpeted floor. I went back out to get more stuff out of the car and with a stack of clothes in my arms, I accidentally kicked the gallon over. It took me forever to get rid of the rotten milk smell.

Hardwood floors weren't the only reason I signed a lease. When the manager told me the toilet needed to be replaced with a brand new one, I was elated. Hey, I wouldn't have to put my butt where strangers' butts had been. I'd be the first person using it. Mom loved my walk-in closet, especially since she didn't have one. I wanted to move to a bigger place some day because I got claustrophobia in the kitchen. Ever since I was small, I've hated being in small, tight places. My kitchen fit this description.

I grabbed a pair of comfortable blue flannel pajamas off my bed and found a pink T-shirt to pull on too. After a few minutes of searching in the bathroom, I found an elastic band and pulled my hair back into a ponytail.

Glancing at the wall clock, I saw it was nine-thirty. The *CSI* I liked watching on Wednesday night didn't come on until ten. I had thirty minutes to wait. Since I didn't see anything else I wanted to watch before *CSI*, I realized it was only seven-thirty p.m. in Costa Rica. I chewed on my bottom lip, thinking it might be a good time to call Ricardo about the Halloween party. Even though I didn't expect him to fly in for the party, I wouldn't be fibbing to Jake about asking Ricardo. And it'd be good to talk to him again. The last time we talked had been a couple of months ago.

I could speed dial Ricardo's number since I had him on my contacts. After two rings, he answered in his adorable Spanish accent and his voice sounded sexy. My insides stirred at the memory of his passionate kisses. Just because I was a virgin didn't mean I was a prude when it came to making out. I rested my head against the sofa. "Hi, it's Catherine. I've missed talking to you."

"I'm glad you called."

Good, he missed me. Maybe he'd go with me to the party. I had the perfect costume in mind for him. "How've you been?"

"My life's been great. I started a letter to you, but never finished it." He sighed. "I need to tell you something very important."

A letter. Why had he started writing me a letter? That didn't sound good. Oh my God, he had a terminal disease. He couldn't bear to write and tell me he was dying.

"Catherine, are you still there?"

I'd take some time off and fly to Costa Rica to be with him. That's what I'd do.

"Yes, I'm still here. What's wrong?"

"I met a beautiful woman, and we're getting married soon."

I straightened my back, leaning forward a little. How could this have happened? I took a deep breath. My Ricardo had gotten engaged. I didn't want him to marry someone else. Why hadn't I grabbed him? And why hadn't he mentioned her to me before?

"How long have you known her?"

"A short time, but I feel like I've known her forever. Anita's incredible."

"I'm glad you're..." I swallowed, then said, "Happy."

"You don't sound like it."

"I guess I hadn't entirely ruled out that we might get married someday. When you asked me, I was only twenty-three years old. How old is Anita?"

"She's twenty."

"That's young." Gee, she was ten years younger than Ricardo.

"She's definitely not too young for me. Anita's a real woman and she makes me feel like a man."

What the hell had I made him feel like? A child?

"Congratulations to both of you."

"Thank you. Why did you call? Any big news in Park City?"

"I was going to invite you to an awesome party, but it sounds like your partying days are over."

Ricardo laughed. "Anita loves to party, but she's not into sharing me."

"I didn't expect you to come now." Or want you to, I felt like saying. It wasn't just Ricardo I'd miss, but his family. "Give my love to your parents and the others."

"I will. Tell your family I said hello."

I wanted to say more, but knew if I did, I'd start sobbing into the phone. You see, I have this problem. I can't let go of people. At high school graduation, while we stood outside in the hallway waiting to walk in to take our seats, I started crying. One moment I was laughing and talking to my classmates. Then suddenly it hit me how our high school days were over and all of us would go our separate ways and life would never be the same. The tears had poured down my face, and poor Angie had to do fast damage control to my makeup.

"Well, I guess it's time to say goodbye."

"Catherine, wait."

My heart instantly felt lighter. He changed his mind and wanted me in his life instead of Anita. "Yes," I said in a hopeful voice.

"Have fun at your party."

I murmured thanks, said a quick goodbye and closed my cell phone. I felt like shit. Ricardo and I had just broken up a year ago. I definitely didn't want him to marry this bimbo Anita. Sure, things changed between us when I gave his engagement ring back. We tried dating for a few months after the broken engagement, but Ricardo continued asking me to marry him. I wasn't ready. I thought I loved him, but couldn't commit to marriage.

I checked the time to see if it was too late to call Angie. It wasn't ten yet so I speed dialed her number and when she answered, I said, "Another eligible bachelor is no longer available."

"Don't tell me Sean's getting married."

"Nope, it's not Sean. I called Ricardo about the party, and get this, he tried writing me a letter to tell me he's getting married."

"Who is she?"

"Her name is Anita and she's only twenty years old. And he had the nerve to tell me she makes him feel like a man."

I walked to my computer desk and looked for my tissue box. I found it after lifting some books. I pulled out a tissue and blew my nose.

"Don't cry. You didn't want to marry him anyhow."

"I'm not crying. I just have the sniffles. I wish he'd waited until I got engaged. And I'm thinking maybe I should've married him. Like you said, I'm too picky and I should've settled for Ricardo."

"Catherine, it's going to be okay. You two didn't have much in common except for being Catholic. You would've been miserable with Ricardo after a few months. And he was anxious to get started on having a family so that's probably another reason for his rush. When Connor was a newborn, Ricardo mentioned how much he wanted to have a son."

I sighed. "I guess now that he's out of the picture, I keep thinking about the good times we had together."

"You were a cute couple. I wonder what Anita looks like?"

"She's probably beautiful and they'll have beautiful children together." I paused for a moment, visualizing little boys looking just like Ricardo.

"I wonder if he gave her your ring."

"That'd be crappy if he did. I should've kept it."

After we finished talking, I stood in my tiny kitchen, thinking how I chose this life over having a life with Ricardo. Living in beautiful Costa Rica wasn't good enough for me.

As I took a glass out of the cupboard, I realized I'd wasted my time dating Sean. Ricardo was so much nicer to me than Sean ever was. I opened the refrigerator and took out a bottle of margarita. Why didn't Ricardo have his pilot's license and a plane when we dated? It would've made everything easier on us.

After I poured a glass of my favorite drink, I held it up and said, "To you, Ricardo and your future wife. And to me, no Ricardo to have my secret sexual fantasy with."

We never made it that far. Our timing was just off. Really off.

Chapter Five

I walked into Mom's coffeehouse on Thursday night wearing an awesome black skirt with black knee high boots and a cream colored sweater. Mom was beside me instantly and gave me a hug.

"You look terrific," she said, wearing a black skirt herself and a pink sweater with her pearl necklace. Her hair was pulled back in a chignon. She smiled. "We were thinking alike except your skirt shows more."

I returned her smile. "We both have impeccable taste." I took a quick glimpse around the room. "Looks like you have a nice crowd for Mr. Jansen's reading."

"I hope they buy his poetry book. Would you like coffee?"

"I'd like a cappuccino."

While Mom got cappuccinos for both of us, she said, "Let's sit down and chat. I haven't talked to you since Tuesday."

We sat at an empty table with orange and yellow mums in a vase with a yellow ribbon around the base. I leaned over to sniff a fat orange candle. "It smells like pumpkin pie."

Mom nodded. "I wanted to set the right atmosphere for Dale's reading, and I'm going to dim the lights when he starts. He has a few Halloween poems about ghosts so I decided to put orange candles on all the tables."

"That's cool. Did you tell Mr. Jansen I'd like to talk to him tonight?"

"I did. He's glad you're interested in finding out more about Max's death. I guess he tried to tell the police he didn't think it was an accident. Dale knew Max better than I realized. He said they were good friends."

"Max touched many lives with his kindness. If he was murdered, I want to catch the killer and get him or her behind bars."

Mom sipped her cappuccino. "I liked Max and want to find out what really happened. If you need my help, you have it."

I cringed inside at Mom's suggestion, remembering the last time I was investigating a big story and she went with me. We carefully dodged the surveillance cameras and snuck into a building where I needed to find information to prove what I suspected about a prominent CEO. Keeping hidden was crucial, so when Mom's ankles made a cracking noise as we tiptoed around, I lived in fear the security guards might hear us. It was so bad that I wondered if she had a calcium deficiency. That's right... I meant to pick up some calcium tablets for her and never did.

And I also realized why Dad never takes her fishing with him. She can't be still for more than a few minutes.

I knew better than to get into a discussion again about why she shouldn't go with me if I did some undercover sleuthing. She'd say, "What should I do in my spare time? Knit booties for grandbabies I don't have?" On second thought, she'd only said that once. She doesn't knit. But she frequently has talked about me meeting the right man and getting married.

Thinking of babies and marriage reminded me of Ricardo so I told her, "I talked to Ricardo last night and he's getting married to a girl named Anita."

Mom raised her sparse eyebrows. "I bet that was a surprise. How do you feel about it?"

I noticed she'd gotten better at coloring in her brows. When they first were thinning, she told me how intimidated she felt using makeup and hated that she no longer had nice, full brows.

"I was sad when he told me. I still have strong feelings for him. And Angie's told me I'm too picky when it comes to men. She didn't mean it about Ricardo, but just in general, and I started thinking how Ricardo did treat me well and we had fun together."

"I know you two did have fun. Your dad and I liked Ricardo a lot."

I shrugged. "I guess I had my chance to marry him. I shouldn't whine now about losing him. It's just that I might not meet anyone as good as him."

Mom patted my arm. "It's going to be fine. You'll meet someone you love and want to marry." She grinned. "And you won't have to settle. Anyhow, you're not the type to settle."

"I like being single except when I see Angie so happy with Connor and Brian, then I start thinking how nice it'd be to have a husband and a family."

Mom's blue eyes brightened. "I have a stipulation. Your future husband should live close enough or move here. Then when you have a family, I can help you out when you need me to. It's best to live close to the wife's mother."

I knew why Mom said that. Her family lived a few hours

away, but my dad's family lived in Park City. When Adam and I were small, Grandma Steel said, "I already raised my family so don't expect me to help with your children."

I grinned. "I guess Costa Rica wouldn't have been close enough for your help with the grandbabies."

"Not in a million years." Mom stood. "I better get this show on the road."

I watched her talking to Mr. Jansen. He hadn't changed much since I attended Park City High School. His thick hair was still brown and his clothes looked like what he wore when I was in his advanced literature class. A white shirt, gray pants, navy blue jacket and no tie. He still had dark circles under his eyes. I recalled him having lousy eye contact in class. When Mr. Jansen talked to his students, he looked to the side or down at the floor. Sometimes he raised his gaze to the ceiling while speaking. Now, that was distracting. Hopefully, while doing his poetry reading, he'd make eye contact so the audience would feel involved in his selections.

I bit my lower lip as a thought occurred to me about Max and Mr. Jansen. Both men were single, so they probably had a lot in common. I wondered if they'd ever gone to bars together. Or sat in front of the TV to watch football games or other sports.

That's one thing I didn't like about being single. I had no friend to just hang out with or to go clubbing with me. Angie and I had a blast before she got married. We went to bars, loved to shop together, rented movies, or went to our Showcase Cinema when we could afford the steep prices to see a new movie. I needed to find another single woman to do stuff with, but couldn't think of anyone. All my girlfriends were married or in relationships.

"Could I have your attention please?" Mom said, standing in the front of the room. She smiled and continued, "Good evening. Thank you all for coming. I'm happy to have Mr. Dale Jansen here tonight. He's a published poet and we're fortunate that he's going to read several selections. When he's not writing poetry, he's a teacher and is head of the English Department at Park City High School. Let's welcome Mr. Dale Jansen."

Mom started clapping and everyone joined in as Mr. Jansen walked across the room. "Thank you, Leslie." He glanced at the audience for a moment and made eye contact with us. "I see many familiar faces, and I appreciate you coming to support me."

He sat on a high stool and opened his book. He cleared his throat and said, "The first poem I'm going to read was inspired by the students in my classes. The title is 'A Lonely Heart'."

His voice was a tad shaky with the first stanza, but then his body relaxed and his voice became firm. As I listened to his words about loneliness, I wondered if he'd ever shared his writing with Max.

Maybe he'd talked to Max about his author aspirations. He might've been in the boiler room the night Max died. I took out my pad and jotted down a few questions to ask Mr. Jansen. I looked up and tried to listen, but thoughts about their relationship took over. How close were the two guys? Was there a special interest they shared?

Forty minutes later, after I snapped a few pictures of Mr. Jansen autographing books, I decided that was enough to choose from to accompany the article I was writing for *The Messenger*. Feeling nauseous, I touched my stomach and hoped I wouldn't do something embarrassing like belch loudly. Why did I pig out on cookies and ice cream? I won't mention the other stuff I ate since Ricardo's announcement.

If I kept up this disgusting eating, my Halloween costume would have to be something other than the sexy one I wanted to make.

Before asking Mr. Jansen's questions about his writing and about Max, I decided to get something to settle my stomach. When I stood next to her, I whispered, "Mom, I need something for my upset stomach."

She gave me a worried look. "I hope you're not getting the flu."

I shook my head. "I think it's a combination of not sleeping well last night and eating too much junk food."

"I have Tums in the kitchen, but nothing else."

"I'll take some Tums." I followed her into the kitchen and watched her get the antacid calcium out of the cupboard. "You should take them for your calcium needs."

"I do." She handed the bottle to me. "I hope this helps, but they don't last long."

I unscrewed the lid on the bottle and took out two berry flavored Tums. After I chewed both, I said, "Thanks, Mom. These taste better than the white ones."

My phone rang. It was Angie. "I did get that dress done for my customer today. If you want me to help you with your costume, I can help you this weekend. Brian offered to watch Connor."

"That's great. Thanks."

Mom said, "I'll check to see if Dale is ready to talk to you."

I gave Mom a nod while Angie said, "You never told me

what your costume is going to be. Just that you bought a red wig. Are you going to dress as Mary, Queen of Scots?"

"No, I won't be Queen Mary."

"I can see you as an adorable Raggedy Anne."

"You're not even close." Setting the bottle back on the shelf, I said, "I don't think Raggedy Anne would be considered a sexy costume."

"I was kidding. Come on, tell me what you decided."

"I'm going to dress up as Poison Ivy. Instead of buying a costume, I thought about making it by using a body suit." A stack of dirty cups and plates sat by the sink, so I opened the dishwasher and started putting cups on the top rack. "I'll glue silk ivy leaves on it and wear light green tights and put ivy leaves down the sides of the legs."

"Awesome. I love it. And we can make an ivy leaf necklace. You should wear boots and maybe a cape." Angie laughed. "I feel sorry for poor Jake. He doesn't have a chance."

I glanced to see if Mr. Jansen was still occupied and he was. "I hate telling Jake already that I don't have a boyfriend. I was planning on telling him eventually that Ricardo and I broke up, but I'll probably need to tell him now."

"It'll be fine. I think he'll be relieved you aren't dating Ricardo."

"It was a relief he was out of the office today and not asking me more questions about Ricardo. I'd have blurted the whole thing to him. He was in Cincinnati playing with the Bengals. Can you believe it?" I was a bit envious. I know I couldn't practice with professional football players, but I'd love to do something really big and write a fab story about it.

"I've heard all about it from Brian, and he's excited

Jake's going to practice with them and that he gets to write an article about his experience." Her tone was apologetic. "I'm not telling you anything you don't know. You probably already knew about his article."

"I'm jealous. What a blast for him." I thought for a moment. "If I tell him now Ricardo's no longer in my life, I won't have an excuse not to go out with him and he's been coming on strong about us going out. Do you give jerks a second chance?"

"Maybe you should give him a chance. I bet you two could have lots of fun together."

"I think he's more interested in me because I'm playing hard to get. If we go out then I won't be a challenge, and he'll dump me. I don't want to get hurt again. Remember how excited I was when I found the perfect prom dress at that rural formalwear shop?"

Mom had driven an hour and half to this store called Hilltop Designs perched on a hillside on a rural road across from a goat pasture. I was excited after Mom bought me a pale blue dress with wonderful detail and exquisite beading. The following year Mom took Angie with us so she could get her prom dress there.

"I remember," Angie said, "and you wouldn't wear it your junior year because you still had the bad memory of wearing it and waiting for Jake."

"I thought it might happen again. You know...always destined to be stood up on prom night, but I tried to reduce the probability by not accepting a prom date from another track athlete." I sighed. "I couldn't believe Jake told me to go ahead. He had the tickets plus I was only a sophomore. That would've been terrible to have driven there and then have to stand outside because I couldn't get in to the prom."

"Just see what happens when you go to his Halloween party. If he hits on you, just go with it." Angie continued in a teasing voice, "But I don't know, Hilary might be more his type."

I chuckled. "Then Jake can use his pirate sword when Keith gets angry at him for taking his woman."

"Pirate sword? What are you talking about?"

"When I got the wig, he was in the store buying a complete pirate's costume." I edged closer to where Mom and Mr. Jansen were chatting. "I better go. I need to talk to Mr. Jansen yet."

"Good luck. Let me know what he tells you about Max."

After I joined Mom and Dale, she escorted us to a secluded spot by the fireplace. "You two should be comfortable here." Mom looked at Dale and said, "I meant to tell you earlier that you did an excellent job reading."

"I can't thank you enough. I sold fifteen books tonight. I'm very happy with how everything went."

We sat on a small red sofa. I flipped my pad open. "Congratulations on your book. Your poems are insightful."

"Thanks. I enjoy your newspaper articles." He smiled.

I asked him when he started writing poetry and how he found time for his second career. After I jotted down his answers, I asked him a last question. "What do you hope your readers will get out of your poetry?"

"Just that they read them with an open mind and see how our lives are intertwined. Each person needs to find his purpose in life." He paused for a moment. "And in our small corner of our world, we can make a difference."

After I got it down quickly, I said, "I like that. I'll quote you and have it in bold print with a box around it to make it stand out in the paper." I saw him looking over my shoulder, trying to read what I'd written. "Don't worry, I'll get it right. I've developed my own way of getting stuff down by using shorthand for some words."

"She taught herself using my old shorthand book." Mom sat on a chair opposite us. "I'm tired. I need to rest these old legs."

He gave Mom a broad smile. "I bet you're glad Catherine became a reporter instead of a CIA agent."

She nodded, looking at me. "Honey, you did worry me when you talked about how you just had to be a CIA agent. I'm thankful you got over that stage. Although investigative reporting isn't without danger. I never knew so many things in Park City needed solving until you started working at *The Messenger*."

I still wanted to be a CIA agent someday. I'd be good at it, but why bring it up now when Mom was obviously trying to give me the lead I needed to talk to Mr. Jansen about Max.

"Speaking of solving stuff, I'd like to ask you about Max Hartman's death. I've been wondering if the boiler room fire was an accident. Do you think Max was careless with the equipment?"

Mr. Jansen shook his head. "Never. He inspected on a regular basis, and he was careful about start-up and shutdown of the equipment. He had the procedures written down very clearly so everything was simple and straightforward. I was in the boiler room a lot and saw how he took care of everything. That's what I told the police, but they didn't buy it."

"Do you know of any enemies Max might've had?"

He shook his head. “I can’t think of anyone not liking Max. The students and teachers all thought a lot of him.” He turned to look at Mom. “Remember, Leslie, how he made coffee in the teacher’s lounge in the morning? And when Miss Pierce’s mother was ill, Max took a cup of coffee to her each morning for several days and asked about her mother.”

Mom raised her eyebrows. “I think he realized that was a mistake because she started going to the boiler room to see him. She was infatuated with him.”

“I didn’t know that about Miss Pierce,” I said. “I just recall her being weird and sitting on the floor when she taught geometry. Were there other boiler room visitors?”

He nodded. “When I was on my way to see Max during my planning period, the principal was leaving and he looked agitated. It was a few days before Max died.”

I twisted a strand of hair around my finger. “I wonder what that was about. I better talk to Mr. Hudson.”

Jansen gave me a worried look. “Don’t mention me.”

“I’ll keep you out of it. Did Max have any interests outside of school?”

“Max was a certified electrician. He had big plans to quit that summer. He told me he’d saved a great deal of money so he could open his own small electrical shop. He planned on selling ceiling fans, chandeliers and other lighting fixtures.” Mr. Jansen smiled. “He said I could be his first customer.”

“I read the old newspaper article again,” I said, “and the fire chief said a gas leak caused the explosion, probably due to human error. Did you talk to the chief about Max being careful?”

Mr. Jansen nodded. “I did. And he said it only takes one mistake.”

Mom said, "If I remember correctly, it seemed the police decided quickly it was Max's fault."

"I did go more than once to talk to the police and they always tried to intimidate me and acted like I didn't know what I was talking about." He crumpled his napkin. "It was unbelievable how one day Max was alive, asking me if I'd be the best man at his wedding and then only a few days later, he was dead."

"Who was he going to marry?" I asked.

"He said he'd tell me as soon as she was divorced." He straightened his shoulders. "Max said for years he'd loved her and he could wait a little longer because she was worth waiting for."

I felt like he wanted to tell me more. "I think you know the woman."

He sighed. "I always thought it must be Karen Connelly. I only saw them together maybe two times, but it was enough to see how much they meant to each other."

I drew a heart on the side of my paper. "If Karen Connelly was the woman in his life, I wonder what stopped them from getting married in the first place?"

"Probably a lover's quarrel," Mom said. "Your dad and I broke up three times before we got married."

"Mayor Connelly might have gotten his wife on the rebound. I wonder how he felt about that." I looked at both Mom and Mr. Jansen. "Are you two thinking what I am?"

Mom raised her chin. "I'm afraid so. The police are on the city's payroll, so if the mayor had the explosion eliminate Max from Karen's life, he could've made sure the police closed the case quickly. As Marcellus in Hamlet said, 'Something is rotten in the state of Denmark.' "

"You got that right." I hooked my pen onto the outside of my pad. "Something is rotten in Park City."

I could definitely wait to be a CIA agent. There was enough drama and crimes to solve right here to keep me busy.

Chapter Six

On Friday morning, I sat at my desk, wearing my favorite pair of jeans with a raspberry colored, single-button shrug sweater and a white top underneath. The vibrant raspberry was enough to brighten anyone's work day. While leaving my apartment, I'd slipped on a comfortable pair of loafers and was happy to leave the stiletto heels at home. My feet needed a break from walking back and forth in high heels in front of Jake. I wondered if he'd miss me wearing a short skirt today.

I didn't have to wonder for long.

"Are you working on your romance article?" Jake said, standing next to me.

I turned away from the monitor screen to see him grinning at me. He wore jeans and a shirt with the Bengals' Tiger logo on it. I shook my head. "No, I'm finishing up the interview I did with Mr. Jansen last night about his new poetry book." My eyes widened as I gazed at Jake. "I guess the Bengals didn't sign you."

"Even if they could add me to their roster mid-season, I couldn't leave the newspaper and miss seeing you parade up and down the hallway to get your water."

"I better get a water bottle so I don't distract you from

your work."

"I like the distraction." He leaned closer. "And you look great in jeans and that..." He stopped to take a better look at my shrug. "That little sweater and tight top."

Glancing down at my chest, I said, "It's not tight, just slightly fitted."

"How's the absent Ricardo? Is he going to make an appearance at the Halloween party?"

It was time to tell Jake that a Spanish girl had taken Ricardo's love away from me. No, I couldn't say that. It wouldn't be wise to mention I was jilted for another woman. And really I wasn't, since I broke up with Ricardo first, but still I hadn't anticipated him finding someone to take my place in his heart. This stretching the truth a little bit—okay, a lot—was making my life too stressful.

I looked Jake straight in the eye. "We broke up."

His eyebrows shot up in surprise. "I'm sorry."

"I don't like speaking Spanish anyway."

"Doesn't he speak English?"

I nodded. "It was a joke. Ricardo speaks better English than I do. But his family talks in Spanish most of the time." I wondered if Anita realized what a great family she was marrying into. Probably not.

"You better still come to the party."

That's all he had to say. What happened to hitting on me and asking me out for tonight? It was Friday, after all, and I was definitely free now. "I'll be there. Have you talked to Brian? Is everyone going to McFadden's tonight?"

He shrugged. "I haven't heard. But I'm leaving this weekend to cover the World Series."

This was why being a couple would never work for us.

One of us would always have a story to cover, but still it was funny that he wasn't all over me. What happened to him trying to convince me to give him another chance? It couldn't just be because he was leaving for the World Series.

I mean, he could've mentioned going out for a drink before he left. That was it. We could go out for a nice drink after work, and it'd be fun to be the one to suggest it. "Let's go out for a drink tonight."

He shook his head. "I don't think that's wise."

I tapped my fingers on the desk. "What's going on here? You just said the other day how much you wanted to go out with me and I could even stand you up since I missed the prom. Then we'd move on. What gives?"

His expression grew serious. "I think the biggest mistake single women and men make is to bounce from one relationship to the next without evaluating what went wrong. I know you really don't want to use me to help you get over Ricardo. And I don't want you to date me on the rebound. That's unfair to both of us. My policy is to wait a month after a breakup before I date someone new."

"So you want to give me a month after my breakup with Ricardo before we date?"

"Or longer."

Now that Jake knew I was available, he wanted to wait before going out with me. Unbelievable. When I decided to take a chance on him, he was indifferent. I thought there were sparks between us, so why was he pulling back?

He was only interested in the chase. That had to be it. That was what I'd feared.

Something wasn't right here and I thought for a moment, giving Jake a weak smile. Then it hit me how his words sounded so familiar. Shit, he was playing me. His whole rebounding theory was taken from my magazine article, “Catherine’s Ten Simple Dating Rules”.

I glared at him. “You read my dating article.”

He grinned. “I thought you’d catch on. And a drink tonight sounds good.”

It turned out to be more than a drink.

He grabbed me at four o’clock and pulled me to my feet. Handing my purse to me, he said, “We’re leaving now to get our drink and something to eat at a nice place.”

I was thrilled he was anxious to spend some alone time with me in a romantic setting. Okay, maybe a bar-type restaurant isn’t romantic like my secret sexual fantasy, but it sounded like fun to spend some time relaxing over a drink and chatting. But then I didn’t want to be too submissive. I stood still. “What’s the rush?”

“Because I’m not taking a chance of something happening in Park City that you’ll decide needs investigating and you’ll disappear.” He took a quick breath. “Also I’m starving. I missed lunch.”

I laughed. “I did too.”

Five minutes later, we were in the parking lot.

Jake put his hand on my arm. “I’ll drive. My car’s over there.”

“We can both drive.”

He looked down at me. “We should go to a fun spot like the Mt. Adams Pavilion for our drinks. Parking’s a pain there. We should just take one car.”

“I wish they still served food in October.”

“We can first go some place to eat. It’ll only take us about thirty minutes or a little more, depending on traffic."

He was a guy after my own heart. I loved Mt. Adams. The Pavilion was nestled high above downtown Cincinnati and the Ohio River. There was a spectacular view of Cincinnati's skyline and the Pavilion got packed on the weekends with a trendier crowd.

I beamed at him. "It's such nice weather today that we can sit outside on the deck at the Pavilion and enjoy the view. With the autumn leaves, it'll be fantastic."

He opened the door of a black convertible Mustang for me. "Would you like the top down?"

"If it's not too much trouble."

"It's not and there won't be many warm days left like this to have it down."

I quickly got in while he put the top down. "Thank you. Riding in your convertible and going to the Pavilion is so cool." I threw my shoulders back. "I feel so free after being in the office all day."

He nodded. "I like getting out of the office to report on the sport news." As he turned the key in the ignition, he said, "My new Mustang has a lot of horsepower with the EcoBoost engine."

I grinned. "I might have to borrow it then when I'm doing my investigating and time's essential to nailing the criminal."

He grinned back at me. "Only if you take me along."

"This car's loaded." In a lower voice, I said, "And I'm glad it's not a Jeep."

"Pardon me?"

I've dated two guys who drove Jeeps. Both of them said they were in love with me and suddenly, both times, Matt and

Sean decided they needed their space and stopped seeing me. So I was drawing the line at dating any guy who drove a Jeep. They aren't mature enough for a girlfriend.

I took my gaze off the dash to look at him. "Sports editors must make more than investigative reporters."

"I don't know about that, but I'm two years older than you."

I didn't want my hair whipped around my face. I looked for something in my purse to pull my hair back. In the midst of gum wrappers, makeup, tissues and loose change, I was in luck when my fingers lifted an elastic band. While pulling my hair back, I asked, "So why did you leave a bigger newspaper for *The Messenger*?"

"Jane talked to me about her plan to expand the sports section as one way to increase circulation, and she needed another editor."

"Are you glad you made the switch?"

He stopped at a red light and his gaze was irresistible. "I am now."

I ignored the intensity in his brown eyes. "I guess in your spare time you read women's magazines."

The light changed to green and his foot hit the accelerator. "I read your articles in Angie's magazines yesterday while I waited on Brian to get ready. He went golfing with me." As Jake shifted into third, he said, "You're a prolific writer. Let's see, you pretty much write investigative articles full-time, human interest stories occasionally, and you even freelance for women's magazines."

I nodded. "Never a dull moment."

"So how about Rule One?"

"I don't know what you mean."

"In your Ten Dating Rules, you tell in Rule One, never have sex on a first date. Have you ever broken that rule?" He studied my face.

I moved my head to watch the road ahead. Another red light. Where had all the traffic lights come from? I didn't remember having all these when I drove to Cincinnati. Shouldn't we be getting to Interstate 75 South? I took a deep breath, not because I'd broken Rule One, but because I was shocked he'd asked. Jake was definitely not the high school boy I wanted to go to the prom with in my sophomore year. Back then, he focused on running for a track scholarship. His focus seemed to have changed a lot.

He was now a grown-up male with sexual needs.

Several reasons occurred to me why he wanted to know how I'd act on a first date.

a) He hadn't had sex recently and he was horny. He couldn't wait and wanted to have sex on our first date so he was asking to see if I was a willing woman. Or I was so hot, he didn't think he could resist me. And he wanted to know now so he could stop and get condoms.

b) Or he really liked and respected me too much to make me feel used, and didn't want to feel disappointed in me if I jumped into bed with him on the first date.

c) And oh dear Lord, was this our first date? I thought we were just going out for a drink.

Why did I ever mention going out for a drink?

"I didn't mean to give you a tough question to answer," Jake said.

"It's not and I've never broken Rule One. I didn't answer immediately because to tell you the truth, I was trying to analyze why you asked."

He squeezed my knee. “Sorry. It just popped out of my mouth. And it was in bad taste. Will you forgive me?”

In spite of the green light and the driver behind us beeping his horn, his gaze met mine for a moment.

I nodded. “I forgive you, but if you don’t get the car moving, the people behind us won’t be in a forgiving mood when the light changes back to red.”

As we sped away toward the ramp for Cincinnati, he said, “With the top down and going faster on 75, it’ll be too noisy to talk.”

Glancing at Jake’s profile, I said, “Okay.” No talking was fine with me because I needed time to refresh my memory about the rest of the rules for dating I’d written in my article. I didn’t want to be caught off-guard again by Jake’s questions.

Once in Mt. Adams, we did street parking and went to Mt. Adams Bar & Grill. After we ordered fried jalapeno ravioli for an appetizer and beer, Jake said, “You did a great job on that article last week about hiring disabled people.”

I fingered the button on my shrug sweater. “I’m hoping more business owners will hire people with disabilities. Recently, Target hired a young man to get the carts out of the parking lot, Kroger has three people bagging groceries, and my mom has a teenager, Miranda, born with Down syndrome, working in the coffeehouse.”

The waiter set napkins and beer in front of us. I murmured a thank you, and Jake said, “I think I saw Miranda the other day when I ordered take-out. She’s a cute kid.”

“She’s adorable. Once the employers realize how reliable handicapped people are, I’m hoping more will be hired.” I sighed. “Another problem is transportation. Many times it falls on the parents’ shoulders.” My cell phone rang and I took it out of my purse. “Excuse me, I better get this. It’s my dad.”

“Hi, sweetie,” he said. “I’ll be able to change your oil tomorrow.”

“Thanks, Dad. I’ll bring it over before I go to Angie’s.”

Dad always changed my oil for me. I didn’t like taking it some place to have it done. Once in a while he griped, though, and said I should have a boyfriend to do it for me. Maybe I’d watch him on Saturday. I should learn how to do it myself, which might turn into a story. I could write about how any woman can change the oil and replace the filter, or how to pick a trustworthy garage to avoid scams.

“I have the type of oil your car uses, but you’ll need to get an oil filter.”

“I bought a filter and oil the other day.”

“Your mother tells me you’re investigating Max Hartman’s death to see if it was murder instead of an accident.”

I glanced at Jake to see if he was listening, but decided I’d tell him about my suspicions. He could have some information about Max that might be valuable. “I just started digging around. I don’t know too much yet.”

“You be careful and don’t trust anyone. If it was murder, you might be in danger.”

While Dad and I chatted, the appetizer arrived. I said goodbye and put my phone away. I asked Jake, “What do you remember about Max Hartman?”

“I knew him a little from St. Christopher’s, but he wasn’t at the high school when I was. Mom cut out the newspaper clipping when he died and sent it to me at college. So what’s this about?”

I swallowed a bite of the filled ravioli and liked the hot

peppers. "That's right, he came to the high school when I was a junior, so you wouldn't have been there." I sipped my beer. "I can't go into all the reasons right now, but I don't think the boiler room fire was an accident. I think it's possible Max was murdered. And Mr. Jansen, the English teacher, was a good friend of Max's, and he said Max was always careful with the equipment. He tried to tell the police and the fire chief he believed Max was murdered, but they wouldn't listen and they closed the case."

Jake wiped his mouth with a napkin. "Sounds like there was something to hide. When I get back from covering the World Series, I can help you with your investigation."

"I haven't talked to Jane yet about it because I'm waiting for some more information."

While the waitress placed Jake's order of pasta and grilled chicken and my cheeseburger in front of us, I observed all the memorabilia surrounding the antique bar. "This is definitely a *Cheers*-like atmosphere."

"Do you like it?"

"No."

"Sorry. I was hoping you'd think it was cozy."

"I was kidding. I love it."

An amused expression crossed his face. "You've changed since high school."

"How's that?"

"You've grown into a confident, exciting woman."

"Keep the compliments coming and I might go out with you again."

Outside the pub, Jake put his arm around my waist, giving me a squeeze. We grasped hands to stroll through the romantic neighborhood with tiny lights illuminating the walkway to the Pavilion. Happiness oozed through my body because I noticed how we had a smooth walk together. No jerkiness, no stumbling, just a pleasant rhythmic flow. "We walk nicely together."

He kissed the top of my head. "We'll have to go on lots of walks."

Once at the Pavilion, we sat at one of the four outside decks. While looking at the Ohio River, I could see into Kentucky and said, "It's neat how you can see Newport on the Levee from here."

"Sometime we can go to one of their restaurants and a movie."

My phone rang again and it was Adam

"Tracy called her mom and Karen came back early. Since it's almost closing time, Tracy and I are going to the coffeehouse. Could you meet us there?"

"I'm at the Pavilion right now with Jake. What happened?"

"A lot," he answered in a tense, clipped voice. "Tracy's been crying. She's had a big shock."

Chapter Seven

Jake and I drove straight to the coffeehouse. I mentioned getting my car, but he said, "You're not ditching me yet. We'll get it later."

Miranda saw us enter and when I saw a hopeful glint in her eyes, I knew what she was thinking.

"You got a boyfriend now." She smiled at Jake. "You're cute."

I rolled my eyes. "He's not my boyfriend. We work together at *The Messenger*."

Miranda shrugged. "That's too bad. You should have a boyfriend."

Didn't Miranda and I have this boyfriend conversation recently? And she'd keep on me until I told her I've got a boyfriend. I moaned. "You've been talking to my mother again."

"You're twenty-five." Miranda fingered a tea towel in her hand, eyeing my ancient face, probably looking for wrinkles. "I have a boyfriend and I'm sixteen."

Jake winked. "I agree with you, Miranda. Catherine should have a boyfriend. And I'm sure she will soon."

"My boyfriend Kevin and I want to double date, so I hope it's soon. He can't drive."

Jake pushed his hands into his pockets. “Would you and Kevin like to come to my parents’ house for a Halloween party? It’s next Friday night.”

“That’s not trick or treat night, is it?” Miranda asked.

I recalled how she’d talked about going out on Beggar’s Night. Wearing a costume and walking around her neighborhood was a big deal to her since her mom had said this was her last year to go. “It’s not on Friday. If it’s okay with your mom, I can pick you and Kevin up for the party.”

“I’ll ask her when she picks me up.” Miranda smiled at both of us. “Thank you.”

I scooped out chocolate chip cookie dough ice cream for Jake and, of course, for me while we waited for Adam and Tracy.

An hour later, Mrs. Carter picked Miranda up and gave permission for the Halloween party. After the last customer walked out the door, Tracy and Adam came in.

Tracy noticed Jake and seemed uncomfortable. Adam asked her, “You remember Jake Michaels, don’t you?”

She put an arm around Adam and looked at Jake for a moment. “You’re the one who made Catherine throw up on prom night.”

Jake narrowed his brown eyes. “I didn’t know you got sick.”

I was embarrassed he knew now I was ill when he never showed up. “I was just a little queasy.”

“I came here to tell you what I learned today, but maybe this isn’t a good time,” Tracy said.

Her being uneasy to share her news with Jake present made me realize she needed to keep her news private. Oh no, it must be pretty bad. “I was out with Jake when Adam called to tell me to come here. You can trust Jake. He won't tell anyone if you want to talk about what you learned today."

"It's okay," Jake said when Tracy remained quiet. "I'll leave and you can call me when you need to go get your car."

Tracy shook her head. "It's okay, since Catherine trusts you. But none of what I'm about to tell you can be repeated until Mom and I talk to Dad. We need to decide when the best time is to tell everyone. It's just hard with the election coming up."

Mom finished in the kitchen and joined us. "Let's sit down. Tracy, did you want something to eat or drink?"

"A glass of water, please."

After Mom got the water, we followed her to the front room and she closed the blinds. Adam pulled Tracy next to him on the loveseat. I sat in a blue flowered upholstered chair across from Jake. Mom moved a small padded chair closer to mine.

Tracy exhaled a deep breath. "I'm sad about what I found out today. Mom stunned me when she told me the truth."

I said in a gentle voice, "It has something to do with Max, doesn't it?"

She nodded. "He was my father. Mom and I went to Columbus today. I wanted to see where he's buried and pay my respects. I knew him for years and never suspected the truth."

Adam reached over and held her hand. "I can't believe it either. But that explains why he was interested in you all the time."

"It's so unfair I didn't know about Max being my father before he died. I guess he saw I was happy and decided not to complicate my life by telling me when I was little." She glanced at the others. "And I love Dad. He raised me. But I should have been told the truth years ago and now Max is dead. I feel cheated and sad. And I don't think the fire was caused by his carelessness."

I nodded and mentioned what Mr. Jansen had said about the whole fire incident. "And he said Max mentioned getting married."

"Mom and Max were planning on getting married as soon as she divorced Dad." Tracy sipped her water and went on, "And I've been right in not liking Dana. What I suspected about her having an affair with Dad did happen, but it was brief. She knew I was Max's daughter."

"I'm surprised she kept the secret," I said.

"I met Max's sister Gwen while we were in Columbus. She thinks Dana didn't want to share Max's affection with his real daughter. Keeping quiet suited her purposes."

"Wow, so now you have an aunt," I said, thinking how much Tracy had learned in one day about her biological father, an aunt, and why Dana disliked her.

Tracy nodded. "It was sad seeing her. You can tell Gwen was his sister. There's a strong family resemblance. It'd been nice to had her in my life while I was growing up." She paused for a moment. "It was weird seeing school pictures of me on her mantel. Of course, Max had given them to her."

"I'm so sorry, honey," Mom said. "Does Gwen have a family?"

"She had a son, but he died in Iraq. She has a husband." Tracy leaned against Adam. "Gwen said Dana loved Max and thought of him as a father figure even though he never adopted her. Her own father had deserted her, and Max tried to be a father to her. But Gwen said Dana's mom, Elaine, knew Max was still in love with my mom and that caused problems in their marriage. When Max learned I was his daughter, he left Dana and Elaine."

"After all these years, Dana probably blamed you and Karen," Mom said.

"Maybe she was trying to break up your family by having an affair with your dad," I said.

"Obviously I never had what I thought I had. Both of them kept my real father's identity a secret for years." Tracy frowned. "They planned on telling me everything after graduation. Mom wanted me to know earlier that Max was my father, but he wanted to wait. He was going to open a store and quit his custodian job. He'd made an offer on Nolan's Hardware Store."

Mom raised her eyebrows. "I'm surprised Mr. Nolan was going to sell it. His son's been running it for years."

"Max made so many plans for his future with Mom. He never stopped loving her." Tracy sighed. "And Mom loves Dad, but I think deep down Max was her real love."

Mom leaned over and squeezed Tracy's shoulder. "I'm sorry they didn't have a chance at happiness."

"But why didn't they get married in the first place?" I asked.

"After their graduation, Mom and Max had a fight because he wanted them to get married and leave on his motorcycle for their honeymoon. She hated his cycle and they got in a stupid fight about it."

Tracy went on, "And she knew her parents didn't like Max and wanted her to go to college. He left and said he was going to travel throughout the states on his motorcycle. After he left, Mom realized she was pregnant with me."

"I guess she never told him she was pregnant," Adam said.

"She didn't know where he was. She called Gwen a few times but never told her she was pregnant. All Gwen knew was that he'd been at Niagara Falls. He had a little tent with him and he was camping out as he traveled."

"I'm surprised Max didn't call your mother," I said.

"Gwen said he did call, but my grandparents made sure Max never talked to her. Even when Mom told my grandparents she was pregnant, they never mentioned that Max had called. They didn't think Max was right for her."

"I can't imagine them not liking Max," I said.

"I think they just wanted their only daughter to marry rich. My grandparents were wealthy and involved in politics. Grandpa Connelly was campaigning and brought Dad with him for a big fundraiser."

Mom nodded. "I remember Karen telling me once that she met your dad at a fundraiser. She said it was love at first sight."

Tracy shrugged. "It wasn't for Mom, but Dad fell in love right away, and she told him she was pregnant."

"He must have loved your mother a great deal to marry her when she was carrying another man's child," Mom said.

I leaned forward and asked, "What did your mom say about the note?"

"You were right in suspecting Miss Kent." Tracy pushed a lock of auburn hair away from her face. "She was blackmailing Mom about her second affair with Max. Miss Kent didn't know about their past high school relationship. She'd threatened to ruin Dad's political career. She wanted money to keep quiet. Mom had forgotten she kept the note and this is going to sound crazy, but she ended up loaning money to Miss Kent. She needed money for medical expenses for her mother."

"Why didn't your mom tell you Max was your father after he died?" Had Karen decided since he was dead, it was better not to say anything? Or was she afraid Max died because someone didn't want Tracy to know the truth about her real father?

"At first, she was too upset at losing Max to deal with telling me the truth, and later she thought maybe it was better I didn't know. Mom and Max didn't sleep together again until Dad had the brief affair with Dana. She was surprised Miss Kent found out about them."

"School secretaries always seem to know what's going on," Mom said.

I stared at Tracy for a moment. "You look so much like your mother. Did your dad know Max was your biological father?"

"He knew and didn't want to lose her and me to Max."

"Does your mom think Max was murdered?"

"She thinks it's possible, but that wasn't the question I expected you to ask. I bet you're wondering if she suspects that Dad killed Max and maybe part of her is afraid he did. But I know he didn't."

I rubbed my forehead. "If Max was murdered, what was the motive? Was it to stop him from marrying your mother? Or was it something entirely different?" I thought for a moment. "Mr. Jansen said he saw Mr. Hudson leaving the boiler room in a rage once. I wonder if Max knew something that got him killed."

Ninety minutes later, Jake and I were back at the parking lot outside the newspaper building. I hit the automatic button on my keys to unlock the door of my car. Jake stood near to me and said, "I'll follow you back to your apartment to make sure you get home safely."

I smiled up at him. "I'm a good driver and the one beer I had was hours ago."

"I don't doubt you're a good driver, but with you investigating Max's death, you might be putting yourself in danger."

"Few people realize I'm looking into what happened."

"Someone might be watching Tracy and see her talking to you. And there seems to be a lot of conspiracy surrounding Max's death. Lots of unanswered questions." Jake clenched his jaw. "If there's a murderer and he finds out you're investigating, he might need to stop you."

I wrinkled my nose at him. "Okay, you win. Follow me."

Jake kept right behind me during the fifteen minute drive to my apartment. There was a vacant parking spot right next to the door. Just as I climbed out of my car, he pulled in. I was surprised to see him walk toward me instead of driving away. "I live in a very safe building. You have to have a key to the outside door to get in." I saw his grin under the security light.

"You didn't think you'd get rid of me that easily, did you?"

He pulled me into his arms and his kiss was demanding. But I had no trouble kissing him back. The touch of his lips sent off wonderful shivers through my body. When we stopped kissing, I said, "That month of not starting a new relationship went fast."

"I couldn't help myself. You make an adorable reporter."

"Thanks for driving to Mt. Adams. I had fun."

"I did too. I better go. I have an early flight."

"Are you flying out of Dayton Airport?"

He nodded. "And I better leave before I cause you to break your number one rule."

"That won't happen." My eyelashes fluttered against his cheek. His breath was warm and moist against my face. "I didn't know this was officially a first date."

"Hey, Steel, it was definitely a date."

He put a lock of hair behind my ear and my heart raced at his gentle touch. I was ready for another one of his sweet, passionate kisses. Instead, he surprised me with a chaste kiss on the cheek. That Jake Michaels knew what he was doing. He was going to leave me wanting more, hoping I'd wonder what could have been.

"You better get to bed. I know you have a busy morning tomorrow too." He gave me a broad smile. "You get to watch your dad change oil in your car."

I laughed and went up the one step to the door. "I'm going to do some hands-on work with Dad and learn how to change the oil myself."

"I probably won't get to see you again until the party."

I slid the key in the lock and before opening the door, I winked at him. "If I don't get my costume done, you might not see me."

"Hey, I'm not worried. You already committed to bringing Miranda and her boyfriend."

I waved goodbye and went inside my building. After I ran up the stairs to my apartment door, I slid the key in. Once inside I shut the door and locked it. I kicked off my shoes and tossed my purse on the small table in the kitchen before opening the refrigerator. My gaze stopped for a second on a bottle of white wine on the top rack, but then I decided on orange juice and poured it into my favorite Scooby Doo glass. When I was little, I loved watching Scooby Doo cartoons every afternoon.

With my pajamas on, I knew what I needed to do. I sat on top of my bed and put my laptop in front of me. Since I hadn't written anything down when Tracy told us about Max, I wanted to update my notes. I drank juice while I waited for the Max file to open. I read over the questions I'd listed after I talked to Adam the first time and concentrated on the last two.

Was Max murdered?

If so, what was the motive?

Well, assuming Max was murdered, and it certainly looked like he was, I knew that focusing on the motive was crucial. I decided to make a list of suspects.

1. Miss Evelyn Kent

—Definitely didn't like Max. Didn't want the yearbook dedicated to him.

—Tried to blackmail Karen Connelly.

2. Mr. Hudson

—Jansen witnessed Hudson's anger at Max about something.

—What was his secret that he didn't want Max to expose?

3. Mayor Connelly

—Probably wanted Max out of his wife's and daughter's

lives—but would he kill Max?

4. Fred

—Not likely that five years ago, the mayor's political career caused him to kill Max—find out where Fred worked five years ago.

5. Dana

—Appears she's been jealous of Tracy's life and felt she lost Max as a father figure because of his love for his real daughter.

—In her situation, Max alive would have been the best scenario so Karen C. would divorce the mayor so he'd be free to marry Dana.

—Maybe Dana was bitter & wanted revenge for being dumped by the mayor and hoped he'd be blamed.

I couldn't think of anyone else to put on my list so I saved it. As I closed the laptop, my cell phone rang. I saw it was Jake. "Hi. Didn't I just see you?"

"I'm calling to apologize before I leave."

"I forgive you for not taking me along to San Francisco. I could've shopped while you covered the World Series. Maybe next year the World Series will be somewhere again that I haven't been."

He chuckled. "That's not it, but you're a quick one. I'm sorry you got sick while waiting for me to show up on prom night. I never thought the track meet would last so long, but it was wrong of me to keep you waiting. I bet you were beautiful in your dress."

"I did love the dress. I wore it my senior year."

"I guess the guy showed up and wasn't a jerk like me."

"He did, but then he wasn't a track star."

"If you learn anything about Max's death, give me a call."

That was nice he was interested enough to want me to stay in touch. "On Monday, I'm going to talk to Jane about investigating his accident."

Chapter Eight

On Saturday morning, Brian kept his promise and took Connor away to play in a park while we worked on my Halloween costume in Angie's sewing room.

After they left, I told Angie, "Tracy blurted out to Jake how I threw up when he didn't show on prom night. He apologized."

"You might've lost your virginity if you'd gone out with Jake that night," Angie said, touching a corset on a dress form.

"Ang, why would you think that?" She should remember that wasn't in my prom plans.

Angie glued more leaves onto the corset. "I bet lots of kids in our class lost their virginity on prom night. Remember, Hilary said her parents let her get a hotel room for the night."

"I remember she said that, but she lies so much. I'm not saying her parents never did, but I bet they didn't get Hilary and her boyfriend a room when she was only fifteen." I shrugged. "Jake and I were going to the After Prom with no overnighter planned in a hotel room."

"Now don't you think using this steel-boned corset is better than a body suit?"

I nodded, looking at the stiff garment covered with hundreds of individual silk ivy leaves. “Thanks for suggesting it.”

She grinned at me. “And I won’t have to charge you for it since Mrs. Daniels decided to give it to me.”

“I can’t believe the stuff Mrs. Daniels tells you to order. Then she changes her mind and she still pays for everything.”

“And this corset was over a hundred dollars.” She turned away from the costume to watch me gluing leaves on the panties. “The panties are looking good.”

I sat in a comfortable, low-armed chair where Angie usually did hemming and any hand-finishing stuff. Brian mounted a shelf on the wall for a TV and a DVD player. He bought both for her birthday to speed up these chores. Next to the chair was an oak stand with a lamp on top, and the shelves underneath were filled with sewing books.

Since she had several regular customers, her room had a separate entrance. Next to the door, she had a huge window with a scenic front view of the tree-lined street. Not only did Angie live in this lovely brick two-story house, but five minutes away was a family-owned Mexican restaurant with the best tasting enchiladas. I glanced toward the window, thinking maybe Angie and I could go there for lunch.

I asked her, “When we’re done here, do you want to get something to eat at El Cholo’s? My treat.”

“Sure. I think Brian’s taking Connor to McDonald’s anyhow.” She put down the hot glue gun. “Let’s work on the tights while the leaves dry.”

I took off my jeans and pulled on pale green tights, and Angie gave my legs a long stare. “What’s wrong? You always said I had good legs.”

"You don't have good legs. You have fantastic gams."

"Did you change your mind about putting leaves on the tights?"

With a thoughtful expression, she held a couple of leaves against my leg. "I'm trying to figure out how to get the leaves to lay the right way. I want to run a line of leaves down the outside of both legs. I'm thinking maybe I'll have to hot glue them on while you have the tights on."

I ran my finger across my lip. "I guess the glue won't go through and cause the tights to stick to my legs."

"I don't think stitching them on will work."

"Not to change the subject, but this reminds me of when we used to work on our 4-H sewing projects together."

Angie nodded. "Your mom was sweet helping us with our projects. She put lots of miles on her car driving us to meetings, camp and the fair. I don't know what I'd done if it hadn't been for your mom."

Angie's mom always said she was too busy to drive her places because she had to work all day. I thought it was sad that Mrs. Yates never made time for her only child. "And look at you and Mom with your own businesses. I'm so proud of you both."

"I think we better try the corset on and see how it looks now with the attached leaves." Angie removed the corset from the dress form and continued, "Talking about businesses gives me an idea. I'll have Brian take photos of you in your costume. He does a better job than I do with the new digital camera."

I remembered she wanted to get the costume job for the next Park City Playhouse performance. "I'll take shots of you and Brian in your costumes to show too."

She stepped next to me with the corset in her hands and after I pulled my sweater over my head, I removed my bra. After the corset was on, Angie kept tightening the strings. While I stood in front of the full length mirror, I felt the laces cinching. I'm not a small-breasted woman and wear a C cup, but what I saw in the mirror amazed me. My cleavage looked like a D cup. "I love the feel of this corset. I feel so feminine and incredibly sexy, yet powerful at the same time."

Angie laughed. "That's good. Poison Ivy uses her sex appeal to her advantage." After she tied the strings, she turned me around to face her. "This could be too much for Jake. You might lose your virginity on Halloween night."

"I don't want that to happen. I guess you could add more leaves."

"I don't think more leaves will help."

Connor burst into the room and ran to Angie. "Mommy, Mommy," he said as she bent down to scoop him up.

Brian followed Connor. "This is the most energy he's had. He acted tired at the park, but here I couldn't stop him. He had to see Catie and Mommy and he..." Brian stopped and his jaw dropped as he looked at me. "Angie, you better make a Poison Ivy costume for you too. Catherine looks great in hers."

Angie wrinkled her nose at Brian. "I don't think Catherine will want me to go as Poison Ivy to Jake's party."

"You can wear my costume when you take Connor out trick or treating," I said to Angie, knowing Brian wouldn't go for my suggestion.

"No way," Brian said. "I don't want the neighborhood men ogling her."

While still in Angie's arms, Connor leaned over and

pulled a few leaves off my corset. "Pretty," he said.

Brian chuckled. "Looks like Connor likes your costume. He knows a good thing when he sees it."

As Connor lifted off another leaf, Angie said, "Connor, stop it. Catherine's wearing this for Halloween."

I held Connor's hand and kissed it. "I need my leaves, but if there are any left, I'll give them to you."

Since she noticed Brian's gaze lingering on my costume, Angie muttered, "I changed my mind. I'll take the pictures of you."

I was desperate on Saturday night. I couldn't find one single female to go clubbing with me. I wanted to go to this trendy place called McFadden's in Cincinnati. I'd gone once with Sean and loved the lively atmosphere and how mostly young professionals my age were there. Even though it was like a New York Irish pub, they had something like fifty televisions so everyone could watch a game. But if there was no game on, there was a DJ. I loved dancing to their party music.

The problem was Angie and Susanne were my closest friends in college, but now they were married. Since I didn't want to sit around on a Saturday evening, I called the drama queen, Hilary.

"Sure. That sounds like fun," Hilary said. "Keith's not doing anything so he can go with us."

No, I said to myself, not Keith. He was the most boring man ever, but even if I could stand his dull personality, I really hated it when he hits on me. Hilary could be a few feet away, and he'd tell me how great he was in bed and what I was missing. It was getting old when I'd turned him down countless times. And even if I could stand Keith, I'd never do anything with him behind Hilary's back.

Why couldn't she do anything without the creep? Now I'd be the third wheel again. No, I was not going to spend a disastrous Saturday night with Hilary and Keith. Hilary alone was drama enough. "I have another call. I'll call you back in a few minutes."

Of course, I didn't have another call, but I needed to figure out how to get out of spending the night with those two. I'd never call Hilary again to do anything. I called my mom at the coffeehouse. When she answered, I said, "Mom, I'm so depressed. I have no girlfriend to do something with me tonight."

"You have so many friends. There must be someone."

"Nope. Everyone's married or in relationships."

"What about the girl at the costume store? Maybe she'd like to do something tonight."

"That's a good suggestion. I'll give Maggie a call. And if she's busy, you can go clubbing with me."

Mom laughed. "Yeah, right. I'm sure you want me along. I have to get back to work. Are you coming over tomorrow?"

Leslie's Coffee Shop was closed on Sundays. Adam and I went home sometimes on Sundays and ate one of Mom's home-cooked meals. "I don't know yet. Miranda and I might go to a movie sometime in the afternoon."

After I finished talking to Mom, I tried calling Maggie. The line was busy at the store. I couldn't think of another unattached girlfriend to call so I got on my laptop to see what new DVDs were out. Renting some movies might not be so bad. I could get out my margarita glasses, a gift from Ricardo, and drink while watching a movie. Or I could go over to

Angie's and take my bottle and movie with me. I sighed, remembering they were going to Brian's parents' house to celebrate all the October family birthdays for the month. I could crash their party to see if an available guy was present.

Or I could go to the coffeehouse tonight. No, I was just there Thursday.

Or I could put on my Poison Ivy costume, drink my margaritas and watch Batman movies. I wonder if Jake would like my costume. Brian sure did and he'd never paid any attention to what I wore.

Wait a minute. I shouldn't give up getting hold of Maggie. The line might be free now. She could want to go with me after she closed the store.

Saturday night might be saved after all.

Maggie wanted to go home first to take a shower. A child had messed with a bottle of Halloween makeup in the store and had accidentally squirted it all over her. I drove to Maggie's old Victorian house since I was the designated driver for the night.

After Maggie opened the door, she asked me, "Does this look okay?"

I nodded. "You look cute in it." She wore a nice pair of black pants with a pink sheer lace top complete with a cami.

She smiled at me. "I wouldn't go that far."

"You do look good. Here's my sweater to wear with it," I said as I handed it to her.

"I just hope it fits."

"I'm sure it will."

"I need to finish putting on my makeup. If you don't mind, you can follow me upstairs."

I followed Maggie upstairs to her bedroom, and she sat on an oak bench upholstered in a soft floral fabric.

"I love your vanity table. I should get one."

"Thanks. I don't take time to put much makeup on for work, but I'm excited about tonight. I'm going all out here." She gave me a worried glance. "I was a little surprised you asked me. I guess none of your friends could go with you."

"I'm happy you can go with me." I sat on the edge of her queen-sized bed. "My friends are married or in relationships. This will be fun for me too." I didn't mention how I almost got stuck with Hilary and Keith. Fortunately, I didn't have to cancel on them. Keith decided he didn't want to go to McFadden's, therefore, Hilary was going wherever he went.

When I'd called Maggie at the store, she'd said no, but when I told her I'd tell what I say to guys that gets their attention, she changed her mind.

She smiled. "I can't take the suspense any longer. What's the great pickup line you use?"

Maggie's probably going to be disappointed when she hears the short phrase but hey, it works. "Okay, here's the pickup line. I just look the guy directly in the eye and say, 'You're hot.' And they're shocked because it's unexpected for a girl to go to a guy and say that. A lot of times, he'll give a big grin and start talking to me."

Maggie finished curling her eyelashes and twisted her body to look directly at me. "I don't know. You could say anything or nothing and still have guys come on to you."

I shook my head. "No, I've been rejected. But you can't let the fear of rejection stop you from making contact. Sure, it hurts but each time it gets easier."

Maggie's hazel eyes widened. "Maybe men don't like

women to approach them."

"I've asked men, including my brother, and most of them love women to make the first move. I mean, think about it, all their lives they've been under pressure to make contact and then they're rejected. They love it when a woman does the approaching. And if you're rejected, it has nothing to do with you being a forward woman, but just because they don't like you." I was glad to see Maggie brush some peachy blush on her pale cheeks.

She stopped applying her makeup. "That doesn't sound hopeful."

"You aren't attracted to every man you meet, and it's the same with men. One way to find out if a guy's interested in you is to make eye contact when you see one you find attractive and smile at him. If he returns the smile, go ahead and start a conversation."

"About what? How I work in a store at the mall?"

"Sure. Ask him if he has his costume yet for Halloween and tell him you can help him choose one in your store if he doesn't." I saw she wasn't keen on the Halloween theme. "Something else I do is give compliments. Like I might say, 'You look great in that sweater.' Guys love being the recipient of honest flattery."

"How about if tonight I observe you in action?"

"That's cool." I grinned. "I hope your Mr. Right won't be there tonight since you're just observing."

At ten-thirty, Maggie and I were at McFadden's eating a shared order of cheese sticks. I decided to drink a second light beer with the food and knew we'd probably stay until closing at two so it'd be okay. But that would be my limit. Like most women, I can't drink too much since my body absorbs the alcohol more quickly than a guy's.

While dipping a stick in marinara sauce, I said, "See that group of good-looking women against the wall over there?"

Maggie turned her head to look where I pointed. "Oh no. I don't have a chance with so many of them here."

"But you do. They're so busy talking to each other they won't be trying to meet new people, and men aren't going to approach them. Men have a hard enough time approaching a woman if she's alone. "

Maggie gulped her beer while staring at an attractive man by the bar counter. "I can't believe he's here."

"Who is he?"

"He's a lawyer, and he came to talk to one of my paralegal classes."

"I didn't know you were going to college."

Maggie nodded. "I went for a year to NKU, then dropped out because I had no clue what I wanted to do. Then I decided to be a paralegal. I've been taking classes at UC for a year."

I rubbed my thumb over my frosty glass of beer. "Perfect. You should go over and tell him how much you enjoyed his lecture."

She shrugged and wiped her mouth with a napkin. "He won't remember me."

"He doesn't have to. Go talk to him."

Maggie grinned. "You just want to eat the rest of the cheese sticks while I'm gone."

As she slowly walked to the lawyer, it hit me that I forgot to tell her to check for a wedding ring. I studied him but his left hand was stuck in his pants pocket. I saw him smile at Maggie. After they chatted for a few minutes, Maggie's body relaxed.

Okay, now it was my turn. I glanced around and saw a drop dead gorgeous man. I drew in a long breath. He was so good-looking that I wondered if he was out of my league. He had black hair and he reminded me of the movie star, Henry Cavill. As I continued to stare at him, I figured he was in his early thirties. What should I say to him? I had to think of a fresh line for him.

I couldn't initiate contact with him. With his looks, he probably has women chasing him all the time. Something different needed to be done to get him to notice me. He could be my Mr. Right. With a thumping heart, I decided to walk by him and go to the rest room. After all, I wore my belt skirt with my sparkling shirt. He might stop me and ask me to dance.

As I walked past him, I swayed my hips. I don't know how I made it to the bathroom without looking to see if he even noticed me. Once in there, I exhaled a deep breath, leaning against the wall.

A woman standing in front of a mirror stopped brushing her long blonde hair and stared at me. "I love your skirt. Where did you get it?"

"My friend made it for me."

"I'll buy it from you."

"It's not for sale."

She took a piece of paper and pen out of her purse. "In case you change your mind, here's my name and phone number."

I thought of giving her Angie's phone number so she could get her own skirt, but I don't want her to have one just like mine and have us at the same places wearing belt skirts.

With the paper in my hand, I read Regina. It occurred to me how Angie never makes duplicates. "I'll do better than that. I'll give you my friend's name and number." I tore a piece off the bottom of the paper and used her pen to write down Angie's business information. "She's a designer and she doesn't make copies, but give her a call. She's very creative."

Before Regina left, she tried again and said, "We can switch skirts. I think we're about the same size and I'll pay you a hundred dollars."

I shook my head and she left. I touched up my makeup and brushed my hair before I followed her. As I exited the bathroom, I ran into a hard chest. I looked up and my jaw dropped. It was the hot guy.

I muttered, "Sorry, I didn't see you."

He put his hands on my waist and smiled. "I started thinking you drowned in there."

"A woman tried to grab my skirt off me." When I get nervous, I tend to blurt out anything.

He gave my skirt an appreciative, long look. "Did she have great legs too?"

I shrugged. "I didn't notice."

"I imagine you have things happening to you all the time."

His hands were still on my waist, making me feel crazy inside. "Why do you say that?"

"The first time I saw you tonight I thought you looked like trouble."

That comment threw me for a moment. How did he mean that? Trouble because he had a girlfriend or fiancée but was attracted to me? "It depends on what you mean by trouble."

"I just bet you're a handful." He smiled and held my chin in his hand. "I want to kiss you."

At McFadden's, kissing someone you just met happens a lot, so I wasn't all that surprised. Hopefully, he hadn't made some bet with a guy that he'd kiss me. No, he was too mature for that. "I object since we don't know each other."

"My name's Scott."

"I'm Catherine." I smiled at Scott. "Now that we're on first name basis, you may kiss me."

While we kissed, my cell phone rang and I was startled at the sound. Scott stopped kissing me and asked, "Did I make the earth move for you or did your cell do that?"

"On a scale from one to ten, I'd give your kiss a seven."

His lips parted in surprise. "Only a seven?"

"I'm sure with practice, it'll go up to ten. Why don't you join me at my table?"

While easing between people, I noticed Maggie was still talking to the lawyer. Scott pulled my chair out for me. I slid the small clutch purse off my shoulder and took out my smartphone.

Scott's eyebrows flickered a little. "I hope that's not your boyfriend."

I shook my head when I saw it was Jake. I'd call him back later. I turned off the phone before putting it back in my purse. Scott's eyes were dark brown and fringed with thick, long lashes. I wish I had eyelashes like that. "So Scott, what's your last name?"

"Michaels. I live in Florida, but I came home to visit my parents." He paused for a moment. "I just thought of something. They're having a Halloween party next Friday. Why don't you come to it?"

It couldn't be. I mean, could I have kissed Jake's older brother? I remember there being three sons in the family, but only knew Jake's younger brother, Chad. I never knew the oldest son. "Do your parents live in Park City?" At his nod, I continued. "I work at *The Messenger* with a Jake Michaels. Is he your brother?"

"He sure is."

"Jake already invited me to your parents' Halloween party."

Scott grinned. "So my little brother's interested in you. We have excellent taste. But I was never good at sharing."

Chapter Nine

After talking and dancing for a few hours, it was closing time. Scott kissed me again in the parking lot.

"I wish you hadn't done that." I couldn't shake the feeling Scott and I shouldn't kiss. I was afraid Jake would be hurt if he knew I'd kissed his brother.

"It's okay. You said yourself that you and Jake only went out once. He doesn't own you."

I gave Scott a weak smile as I leaned against my car door. "I have a problem. Jake's wanted to take me out sooner, but I gave him a hard time because of something that happened in high school."

"What happened in high school?"

I sighed. "It wasn't entirely his fault because he was at a track meet, but I was his prom date and he never showed up. And he broke a date on another occasion." I didn't want to go into details and thought I summed it up pretty well.

"I don't see how he could've done this to you twice. I don't blame you for giving him a rough time." He drew me into his arms and his demanding lips caressed mine.

Even though the touch of his lips was a captivating sensation, I pulled away from Scott slightly. "I plan on dating him later."

"I understand." A flash of humor crossed his face. "You can punish him by dating me."

"That doesn't seem fair to either one of you."

"Was it fair how Jake treated you in high school?"

"I was hurt, but I understand now how the track meet was important for his scholarship. And I was attracted to you right away, but that was before I knew you were Jake's brother."

"So if I wasn't Jake's brother, we wouldn't be having this conversation?"

I shrugged. "Probably not."

"I've enjoyed spending time with you tonight. I want to see you tomorrow. Or I mean later today."

"I don't know." Would it hurt to date Scott while he was in town for the week? Jake was at the World Series and we weren't boyfriend and girlfriend anyhow.

"How about we do something fun later today and take it from there?"

I sighed. "Don't hate me, but I'm attracted to you and to Jake."

"But Jake's not here."

"You're right. I'd like to see you again today." Then I remembered my tentative plans with Miranda. "I might be doing something with a friend in the afternoon, but give me a call."

Scott put a lock of my hair behind my ear. He leaned down and his lips pressed against mine, then gently covered my mouth. Maybe it was a bad move on my part to allow it because now I was confused. I'd been in love with Jake during high school and still had a thing for him, but kissing Scott was so enjoyable.

When he released me, I said, “I can tell you and Jake are brothers.”

“Why do I feel this is like a joke with a punch line? But okay, I’ll play. How can you tell?”

“You’re both good kissers, but there’s a difference in your technique. Jake shoved me against a wall and kissed me, while you were a gentleman and said you wanted to kiss me before you did.”

“Who did you like better?”

I shrugged. “Both. But you and I need to take our kissing down a notch. We just met tonight so I want to slow it down.”

“I was thinking of taking it up a notch. Or two.” He gave me a boyish grin. “But hey, you’re the boss.”

The boss. I liked that, but I squinted at Scott, thinking he was teasing. I bet he wanted to get in my pants. And that might be a dilemma. I didn’t know what I want from Scott. I just knew I was attracted to Scott...and to Jake.

I glanced at McFadden’s door and said, “I wonder what happened to Maggie. She said she’d be right out.”

Scott fingered a leather belt on my skirt. “I love this skirt on you.”

My heart accelerated. Could he tell how he was affecting me? “I’m glad I wore it then so you noticed me.”

He stared at me. “You could’ve worn anything, and we’d still be standing here together.”

A few minutes after two a.m., I saw Maggie with several other patrons leaving McFadden’s. Maggie walked toward us. I pulled my keys out of my purse and Scott said, “I can’t let you leave without a goodbye kiss.”

Maggie said, “That’s not fair. My guy didn’t kiss me.”

I grinned. “It’s the skirt. I always get attacked when I

wear it."

Scott frowned. "Were you wearing it when Jake kissed you?"

I shook my head. "He never saw me wear it."

"Good. Maybe you should retire the skirt."

Scott kissed me before I climbed into the car. Part of me couldn't figure out why he was kissing me so much and another part wanted more. He was one hot guy and a good kisser.

Maggie slid into the passenger seat. I put the key in the ignition and started the engine. With my window down, I said, "That'll be hard to do." I drove out of the parking lot before he could say anything else and waved to him. How could I stop wearing this skirt? It makes me feel sexy and obviously Scott was teasing me.

Maggie looked pleased with herself so I said, "I guess you hit it off with the lawyer."

"Thanks for taking me with you tonight. Greg's going to call me."

"I'm glad."

While I drove, I started thinking I hadn't played hard to get. But then Scott was only in town for a week so the rules could be bent. I was definitely attracted to him, but I didn't plan on getting too involved with him in a week's time. I was upfront with him about Jake, and one of my rules was never to stop dating others after a fantastic first date. Of course, that was assuming Scott and I even had a first date. Too many women (and sometimes men) stop dating others after an awesome first date. Getting too involved too soon with one person could be devastating if it ended up being the wrong one. If you were dating more than one person, you needed to be honest with everybody. I should tell Maggie not to always be available.

"So who's the movie star clone?" Maggie asked. "He resembles Henry Cavill from *Man of Steel*."

I glanced at her while we stopped at a traffic light. "I know. He's a dead ringer for Cavill. And I'm sorry I forgot to introduce you to him. His name is Scott Michaels. Do you remember Jake from the night I helped you bag in the store?"

Maggie laughed. "When I got upset and told you how I hated Halloween...sure, I remember him. He bought a pirate costume. I thought he'd make a perfect pirate. But what does Jake have to do with Scott?"

"I didn't know Scott before tonight and when we were talking, I found out they're brothers."

"Wow, that's something, but what's the problem? You never went out with Jake, right?"

"We knew each other in high school and we were supposed to go to the prom, but we didn't." I explained the whole situation to her about Jake, and how I didn't have any qualms dating both except for one problem—the brother thing.

"It doesn't seem right to date both at the same time, regardless of them being brothers."

"It's better to date more than one guy in the beginning instead of always being available, plus you might decide later you don't like the new guy enough and you'll regret not going out with someone else. And also you have more leverage in the relationship if he knows you're still dating others. He'll take more care of his appearance when he knows there's competition and just be more considerate when he makes dates with you."

"I'll be happy to have one guy in my life."

"I told Scott how I plan on dating Jake, and I'm going to be honest with Jake." I glanced in my side mirror and changed lanes. "Since Scott's not staying longer than a week, I'll probably only see him a couple of times before Jake gets back."

Maggie got a pack of gum out of her purse. "Would you like a stick of gum?"

"No, thanks." I sighed. "Dating can be so much fun, but sometimes it's such a hassle."

"I wouldn't know. I haven't dated for a long time."

"I have a list of ten dating rules. My mom gave me some of them, and I added to her list for an article I wrote. If you want, I can email the rules to you." I decided I shouldn't start shooting my mouth off about what to be careful about and etc. I didn't want to insult Maggie. This way I was giving her a choice if she wanted to see them or not.

"Yes, please email them to me. I can use help."

On Sunday afternoon, Miranda called and canceled on me. She and Kevin needed to shop for their Halloween costumes instead of going to a movie. Before Miranda hung up, she asked me, "Do you have a boyfriend yet?"

This girl doesn't give up. "It's okay, Miranda. I have two boyfriends."

"I don't know about having two. I think one is better."

"One's a spare." I laughed. "It's okay, I'm kidding. I do like these two men, but I wouldn't call either one my boyfriend yet."

"When we go to a movie, are you taking both of them?"

"That's a good question, but it shouldn't be a problem.

The one guy doesn't live around here, so I'll ask Jake when we go."

After I finished talking to Miranda, I got my laptop out to work on my investigation of Max's death, but got sidetracked when I checked my email. I saw Maggie had emailed, asking me to send her my dating rules. Since it'd been some time since I'd written the article, I decided to look them over. I read.

Catherine's Ten Simple Dating Rules

1) *Never have sex on a first date.*

If the guy really likes you, he'll wait. And the truth is men sometimes hold a double standard. He might feel disappointed if you have sex with him on the first date. And if you decide to go ahead and never hear from him again, you'll feel used. Avoid alcohol so you'll have more control and keep the first date short.

2) *Never give your home or work address on a first meeting.*

It's good to be friendly and to initiate conversations at singles events, but play it safe and don't give personal information on a first meeting. If the first date doesn't go well, you don't want this person to show up at your home or work place. Agree to meet in a public place and take your cell phone. I actually do this on the first few dates. Tell another person your date plans. And don't leave your beverage unattended. If you have to leave, order a fresh one when you return. Being cautious will prevent having someone slip you something. The best thing is to not have alcoholic drinks because drinking might relax you too much and you might not catch small clues that this person might not be right for you.

3) *Successful dating depends on you getting off your butt.*

Guess what? You won't meet Mr. Right sitting on your butt and staying home on a Saturday night. You need to go where you'll see eligible guys. Take charge of your life and go to parties, dances, and volunteer for social events. For example, there might be a fundraiser for something like heart disease and if you volunteer, you have a good chance of increasing your chances of meeting Mr. Right. Another way to meet a guy is to think what men love to do. For example, men go to gyms to shoot hoops, so go there. If you don't want to play, you can go to the gym to watch. Go to almost any sporting event to meet single men. Home Depot is another good place to see guys. This way you know they have homes and know how to fix things. Another way to meet a guy is to go out on blind dates and don't be afraid of your friends fixing you up with someone. Be sure they know what qualities are important to you in a man. Even grocery shopping can be productive if you go to a store where a lot of single men do their shopping. Don't be afraid to ask an attractive guy about something he's buying.

4) *When you go places, don't always be part of a group.*

Guys are afraid to approach you if you're part of a group. I think women have a tendency to drag their friends with them when they go to any social event. A guy is already scared of rejection and when he sees you in a group, he'll wait for you to be alone or for a break in the conversation before attempting to talk to you. Since this might never happen, go by yourself or just take one friend.

5) *Be bold.*

Think of a good pickup line you'll feel comfortable saying

to a stranger. Or give a compliment and say something like, "That's a great looking shirt on you." Guys love hearing something positive about how they look. I know what you're thinking. Men are turned off by forward women. Wrong! You making the first contact relieves some of the pressure off them. And if you get rejected, so what? Women reject men plenty of times. Before you say hi or use your pickup line, make eye contact with someone you think is attractive and smile at him. If he returns the smile, then initiate conversation with him.

6) *Encourage the person to talk and be a good listener.*

Don't ask personal stuff when you first meet someone. It's okay to talk about boring things the first few minutes. People don't want to share feelings and personal stories until they feel it's safe to do so. Keep it superficial and maybe five or ten minutes later, both of you will start talking about more individual things. When you ask questions, show an interest in what he's telling you. He'll be flattered if you encourage him to talk. Alert: I have a tendency to talk too much and too fast if I'm nervous. Try to avoid talking all the time because this seems to turn guys off fast.

7) *Make sure you both follow through.*

You hit it off with this guy, and you can tell he's interested in seeing you again and the bar closes at two a.m. Be up front and find out if you both want to see each other again. Remember some guys are just flirting and aren't planning on going out with you. Women do the same thing. Don't leave and just say, "I had a nice time. See you again, I hope." Set a time and place to meet again. Exchanging phone numbers is good, but understand if both of you've drunk a lot, you might not remember the next day what a great time you had with him.

8) *Don't stop dating others after a terrific first date.*

Women are notorious for not dating others after a great first date, and a few months later, they feel stupid for getting too involved with the wrong person. It's okay to not always be available to one person. Just be truthful about it to everyone. No one should expect total commitment in the early months of dating.

9) *How does he act on dates?*

There's no excuse for bad behavior. Does he call you when he's going to be late? Does he ask you what you want to do? Is he critical of you? Is he cheap on dates? Don't marry the first man you're attracted to and who's considerate about calling you on Tuesday for a Friday date. Marry a man you love and can live with.

10) *Don't do rebounding.*

Wait around a month or longer after a breakup before you see someone new. So many times women want to get over some guy and will go from one relationship to the next with no alone time in between. Don't start a new relationship to help you get over someone else. It's unfair and it's just not a good idea. And what will probably happen is you'll choose the wrong person again.

After I finished reading my rules, it occurred to me how I always Google any future boyfriend to see if I can dig up any dirt on him before committing myself to a new relationship. But did I need to Google Scott Michaels? I mean really, he was Jake's brother. I probably should sometime add that to my list of dating rules. Something like saying, find out as much as possible about the new man you're interested in by Googling him. And look for him on Facebook. A girl couldn't be too careful in today's world of weird people. Not that Scott was weird. He was perfect.

I sighed. So many things to consider when dating. Maybe an arranged marriage was a good way to go. It'd take the pressure off me and put it on my parents.

I shook my head at the thought of my dad selecting a husband for me. I don't know if I'd ever be happy with his choice. Mom might be able to handle it.

Searching the Internet about Scott better wait. My love life was important, but finding out what happened to Max needed my immediate attention.

Chapter Ten

Tracy called me Sunday afternoon while I stood in front of my closet looking through clothes for something to wear for my date with Scott. He'd just called from the golf course and wanted to take me to dinner and a movie after he finished. I couldn't see a thing I wanted to wear. Maybe I could make a quick trip to the mall.

"Are you busy tonight?" she asked.

Now I really wanted to go out with Scott, but I had a feeling Tracy needed to talk to me. "I have plans, but I can change them if necessary. What's up?"

In an excited voice, Tracy answered, "Dad wants to give you an interview about our family and how he knew Mom was pregnant when he married her. And he's not talking to any other reporter until after your interview is in the paper."

What a shocker. First, that Mayor Connelly wanted to give me an exclusive interview. And second of all, why now before the election? Did Connelly think he could win votes since he married a pregnant teenager? And had it occurred to him the voters might question his motive for revealing it after all this time? And did this mean he hadn't been involved in getting the police and fire department to list Max's death as an accident? My gut feeling was that it was a ploy to get sympathy and votes. Or was he smart enough to realize it could come out anyhow before the election and thought he should be the one to break the news?

"Yes, I want to interview your dad. I appreciate him giving me the interview first."

"Could you come tonight to our house at six?"

"I'll be there. Thanks, Tracy."

I moved away from my closet and glanced at the clock on my nightstand. It was two and I hated to call Scott on the golf course, but I didn't want to put it off, either. Would he understand I had to do this interview? As a newspaper reporter himself, Jake definitely would. He knew the story had to come first.

I walked to an accent chair in the corner of my bedroom. While I waited for Scott to answer, I glanced at the vase of silk flowers on a small table by the chair and remembered how Sean had given me the flowers. I'm not especially keen on fake flowers, but I'd appreciated his gift.

"Hi, beautiful," Scott said. "What's up?"

"I'm afraid I need to cancel our date. I'm really sorry, but Mayor Connelly is going to give me an interview and it has to be tonight."

"If you need to interview a celebrity, I know someone you can interview. He's bigger than the mayor."

I guess Scott could be telling me the truth. He was a lawyer and might have handled some cases for celebrities in Florida. "I'm interested. Give me a name."

"He's a famous lawyer."

I laughed. "Would this celebrity lawyer happen to live in Florida?"

"You got me. And I understand how it's important for

you to interview Mayor Connelly with the election so close."

I was relieved he was okay with me canceling and decided further explanation wasn't needed. I wasn't about to tell Scott how it wasn't just about his candidacy, but instead an announcement he wanted to make about Tracy not being his biological daughter. "Thanks. And I better let you get back to golf."

"Wait, we can still do something after the interview. Just give me a call when you're finished."

I sighed. "I'd love that, but after the interview, I'll have to get it done tonight. I'm not sure, but Jane will probably want it to run first thing in the morning."

"I can come over and help you."

His offer was tempting, but I couldn't see him being much help with the actual writing. He'd be a distraction. Even so, I did want to spend time with him. Maybe I could get the article done before it got too late. "I'll call you and maybe we can get still get something to eat."

I called Jane, but she didn't answer. I left a message on her voice mail. I poured a glass of iced tea and carried it to the table. While sitting and staring at my iPad, I sipped my tea. Not sweet enough. I should drink unsweetened tea, but for now I needed more sugar. I got up and opened the silverware drawer to get a tablespoon out. I took the lid off a blue Lennox sugar bowl designed with poppies and thought of Angie as I scooped out a heaping spoonful of sugar. She'd bought the bowl for me for babysitting Connor. Like I really wanted a gift for watching my precious godchild.

As I sat down at the table to organize my thoughts for the interview, I stirred the tea for a moment. While listing a few questions on my pad, I chewed my bottom lip, thinking how it'd be great to share the interview news with Angie and Mom. And they didn't know yet about Scott. I'd wanted to tell Mom during Sunday dinner, but before I got to, Adam announced he was going to propose to Tracy.

My little brother would be getting married before I did. That just didn't seem right. I should be first. Besides, he was too young. What was his rush?

My cell phone's ringtone interrupted my thoughts of Adam's engagement plans.

It was Jake. At first, I felt guilty I hadn't returned his phone call. But I'd been busy meeting Scott, going to Mass in the morning and enjoying Sunday dinner at my parents'. "Hey," I said into the phone.

"You didn't return my phone call so thought I'd check to see how you're doing."

"You miss me already?"

"Yeah, you grow on people."

"I'm impressed. For a sports editor, you're such a slick talker. You know just how to make a woman feel special." Jake definitely needed to take lessons from his brother Scott. Oh crap, should I mention Scott to him?

"So what's up? Anything exciting?"

Well, here was the perfect opening I needed to tell Jake I'd met his brother at McFadden's but I decided it could wait. "I have something pretty cool to tell you. Guess what happened?"

"Give me a hint."

"It's about Mayor Connelly."

"He decided not to run so you're going to run for the House."

I sighed. "You're not a good guesser. That's not it."

"It'd be bad if you ran anyhow."

"Hey, I've thought about running for political office someday. Why do you think it'd be bad to have me represent the people?"

He laughed. "You'd drive all the men in Congress wild wearing your belt skirt and heels. With you around, nothing would get accomplished. "

"I wouldn't dress in my belt skirt in Congress," I said. What was Jake thinking?

"I'm hoping to see this famous belt skirt soon."

"I did wear it on Saturday night, and a woman wanted to buy it from me."

"Where'd you go on Saturday night?"

I just had to open my big mouth, didn't I? "McFadden's. Remember Maggie from the Halloween store? She went with me."

"Did you have a good time?"

What Jake especially wanted to know was if I'd met any guys. It might be fun to mention I met a guy, a dead ringer for the actor Henry Cavill. Would Jake even realize I was referring to his older brother? I wondered how close the two brothers were. Scott had said he wasn't into sharing when I'd mentioned Jake wanting to date me. Did they talk about their girlfriends to each other? Doubtful, I realized. Guys don't chat about new women in their lives until it's serious.

"I did, but I wanted to tell you my big news, remember? I'm interviewing Mayor Connelly tonight and it's an exclusive. He wants to talk about how he knew Karen was pregnant when he married her."

"That's a surprise."

"What, that he knew or he's giving me an interview?"

"I'm wondering why he wants to talk about Karen being an unwed pregnant teenager before the election. I guess it'll cast him in a good light. How does Tracy feel about the interview?"

I swallowed my tea. "Tracy called me to set it up and she seemed fine about it."

"I wonder if Mayor Connelly knew Max was Tracy's father."

"That's going to be one of my questions."

"Are you going to ask him if he killed Max?"

"You can read my interview online."

Never broadcast ahead what you're writing—especially not to another reporter. Okay, Jake was a sports editor, but he didn't need to know what questions I'd be asking. What was I thinking? I didn't know for sure what direction the interview would go. Although I hadn't been given a list of questions allowed, I had a feeling I'd be limited to one topic. I bet they'd just want the public to know Max was Tracy's father and nothing more.

I exhaled a deep breath. "I'm not sure if it'll be in Monday or Tuesday's edition. I haven't talked to Jane."

"No doubt she'll want it in Monday."

At five-fifty, I pulled into Connelly's driveway behind Drew, the newspaper's photographer. It was a wonderful that Drew was available when Jane called him. I could've taken pictures with my iPad, but when Jane returned my call, she said I shouldn't have to snap photos and do the interview.

After I shut the door, my car beeped as I pushed the button to lock it.

Drew grinned at me. "Do you think someone might

break into your car in the mayor's driveway?"

"My dad taught me to always lock your vehicle." I walked to where Drew stood. He wore jeans and a T-shirt. He needed a haircut with his blond hair looking long and shaggy. "One time he didn't lock his car in high school, and his seat was slashed."

Drew nodded. "You can't trust anyone. Especially a politician. Why do you suppose Mayor Connelly asked for this interview?"

"He has some big news to share." I touched Drew's shoulder. "We better get moving before he changes his mind."

Before I could ring the doorbell, Tracy, in black straight-leg pants and a printed top, swung open the door and smiled at me. "Hi. Thanks for coming this evening."

It hit me right then how it would be great having Tracy for a sister-in-law. Not just because the mayor might get elected to the House of Representatives and I'd have the inside scoop, but because I liked Tracy a lot. "Hi. You've met Drew, right?"

Tracy gave a quick nod, her wavy auburn hair moving gently around her face. "Yes, I have. It's nice seeing you again, Drew."

Once inside, I saw a huge vase of flowers sitting on a round cherry table in the foyer. A throw rug was underneath the table and behind I saw a spiral staircase. Since there was a cathedral ceiling, I looked up at the windows along the wall at the top of the stairs. "That's a beautiful staircase."

"It's so pretty during the day with the sunlight streaming in. Mom told the architect how she wanted lots of natural lighting." Over her shoulder, Tracy said, "Follow me. Mom and Dad are in the living room."

Upon our entrance, Mayor Connelly stood and shook my hand. "It's good to see you, Catherine. Thank you for coming."

As always, the mayor looked handsome in a dark suit. Karen Connelly wore a dark gray one button jacket with an ivory blouse and black pants. She surprised me with a hug and asked, "How's your mother?"

"Her coffeehouse keeps her busy, but she loves it like that. She just had Mr. Jan…" I stopped myself just in time, I hoped. I didn't want to mention Mr. Jansen to her right now. It just seemed like poor timing since he'd been Max's friend. Karen had already dealt with a lot in the last twenty-four hours.

Karen said quickly, "I read your article about Dale Jansen. I'll have to buy his book."

I decided to jump right in. "Mr. Jansen thinks Max was murdered."

Tracy's eyes narrowed. "I think the focus should be that Dad wants everyone to know my biological father was Max Hartman. We should avoid discussing how Max died."

"We were hesitant to do this interview before the election because we don't want the subject of Max's death to be brought up," Karen added.

Tracy looked at Drew. "Would you like to take your pictures first? It might be good to get them out of the way."

While Drew positioned them on the dark blue sofa with Tracy in the middle, I sensed a certain uneasiness. Looking at them, I suddenly realized Tracy had been the one wanting this scheduled interview. The mayor hadn't requested it and Fred wasn't present. Tracy had always been a persuasive person. I bet she influenced her parents to consent to my interviewing them. Would I go so far as to call her a manipulator? I believed so, but a very charming manipulator. Maybe that's why I respected and liked her so much. She decided what needed to be accomplished and got it done.

Too bad she hadn't known Max was her father before he died. Max thought he was protecting his daughter from knowing her biological father was a janitor while growing up, but that wouldn't have mattered to Tracy at all. Of course, it wasn't just the job but the fact the mayor and his family were so wealthy. Max must've felt he couldn't compete with that. But Tracy would've loved Max, regardless of the position and financial differences between her two fathers. If given the chance, Tracy would've found time for father-daughter relationships with both Max and Mayor Connelly.

If it hadn't been kept a secret for years, would Max still be alive?

After a few shots, I sat in a high back chair and flipped open my iPad. Drew pointed to the door and I gave him a quick nod. "Thanks, Drew." I was happy I had an app that would record audio, and sync the audio with the pace of my notes. It is instant annotation. It was cool I'd end up having an audio and digitally written record of an interview. As I stared at Mayor Connelly, I asked, "How do you feel now that Tracy knows you're not her biological father?"

"I'm glad she finally knows the truth." Mayor Connelly held Tracy's hand in his. "When you love your child as much as I do, you want the best for them, and Karen and I wanted to tell her years ago."

Karen nodded. "Max didn't want her to know until after she graduated from high school."

Tracy had never mentioned to me how Max learned about her in the first place. I wondered if Karen had felt guilty and decided to tell him. I asked her, "When did you tell Max he had a daughter?"

Karen sighed. "I tried to contact him when I first realized I was pregnant, but I wasn't able to get hold of him. I talked to his sister a few times, but I didn't mention my pregnancy. Five years later, she happened to mention to Max how I'd called and wanted to talk to him."

"Why didn't she tell him that you called earlier?"

"I guess because I was married by the time Max came back from his motorcycle trip. He never mentioned to Gwen how he was disappointed I hadn't responded to his letters or telephone calls. He didn't realize I hadn't gotten any of them. Then Max got married. Gwen probably forgot about it until she realized how unhappy Max was in his marriage. I don't know."

"Did Max contact you then?"

Karen nodded. "He called me and we talked for a few minutes. I didn't tell him about Tracy. I thought I was doing the right thing and thought it would only hurt him."

"How did he find out?"

"He called again on Tracy's birthday, and I was busy with the guests. The housekeeper told him I couldn't come to the phone because of my little girl's birthday. He started thinking how I must have called Gwen because I wanted to tell him I was pregnant."

"Mayor Connelly—"

"Please call me Pat."

I grinned. "Does this mean since we're on a first name basis, I have to be nice when I write political articles about you?"

Pat smiled back at me. "Of course. Especially since your

brother loves my girl here."

"And I can see why he does. We all love Tracy."

"It's mutual." Tracy leaned back against the sofa. "I think a lot of the Steel family."

There was a question I hadn't asked that needed to be asked. "Pat, did you always know Max was Tracy's father?"

He nodded. "Karen told me his name before we were married."

I shifted my gaze from my pad. "When did you realize he'd moved to Park City and taken a job at Tracy's school?"

Pat glanced at Karen. "I don't remember exactly. Do you?"

"I told him as soon as I knew Max moved here." Karen rested her chin on her hand. "I think it was when Tracy was in first or second grade."

"It was first grade," Tracy said.

I wanted to ask Karen if the affair had really started then, but decided to learn Pat's reaction to Tracy's father moving to Park City to be close to her. "That must have been upsetting to you both to have Max in the same building with Tracy. Were you worried he'd eventually want to claim her as his daughter and maybe share custody?"

Karen shook her head. "I knew he wouldn't do that."

"Pat, did you hate Max for trying to be so close to Tracy?"

"I wasn't thrilled he came to Park City, but at the same time, I felt sad for him. If circumstances had been different, he'd have married Karen. But instead, his life had been changed forever when he left on his trip and left Karen behind."

"I can understand you feeling sympathy for him, but

didn't you worry Max might eventually decide to go to court?"

Pat shook his head. "It'd never have gone to court. We'd have worked something out. We all loved Tracy very much and would have settled it somehow out of court."

I chewed on my lower lip, thinking how Tracy would hate me for asking the big question, but I might as well get it over with. "This is off the record and I'll honor your request to not mention murder in my article, but when you found out Karen planned on leaving you to marry Max, did you want him dead?"

"I didn't want to lose Karen to Max, but I never wanted him dead. This is off the record too." Pat's voice faded, losing its steely edge. "Karen was faithful to me until I had a brief affair with another woman. It was my fault Karen turned to Max when Tracy was in high school."

"I believe I know the person you're referring to and won't mention this to anyone, but why did you just move her out of your office?"

"I moved her right away out of my office to another floor. I waited to move her out of the building because she was so unstable."

Karen sighed. "You must think we're terrible with both of us being unfaithful in our marriage, but in a way, I think our affairs ended up making our marriage stronger now than ever. We've had to overcome a lot."

I shook my head. "I don't think you're terrible." I turned to Pat. "Did you put pressure on the fire chief to say the boiler room fire was an accident?"

Pat frowned, his eyes level under drawn brows. "Of course not. He thinks it was definitely an accident and wasn't murder."

“In my senior year, we voted to dedicate the yearbook to Max. He was one special guy, making a difference in so many lives.” I paused for a moment, giving a thoughtful glance to all three. I decided not to say how Tracy had brought all this to my attention when she showed me the note and told me about the high school pictures. “I owe it to him to find out what really happened. I believe he might’ve been murdered, so I’m going to investigate his death.”

Karen was quiet, but Pat immediately said, “If I can be of any help, please feel free to call me at any time.”

“You can answer another question for me, Pat. Where were you the night Max died?”

“I was at my dad’s house. Ironically, I was telling him Karen wanted a divorce.” His eyes narrowed. “Am I on your list of suspects?”

I nodded. “I’m afraid so, but you aren’t my number one suspect.”

He didn’t give me a politician’s confident smile, but just a tiny controlled grin. “Well, that’s something.”

Chapter Eleven

I had a page done on my interview, but I didn't want to call Scott yet. I flexed my fingers and looked away from my laptop, contemplating what I should write next when my cell phone rang. I glanced to see who was calling. It was Angie. "Hi," I answered. "Boy, do I have news for you—"

"Connor's sick and he's in Cincinnati Children's Hospital," Angie said in a panic-stricken voice.

"Oh no, what happened? He was fine yesterday." I remembered him pulling my poison ivy leaves off my costume and how happy he was when he came back with Brian from the park.

"I saw a lump on his leg last night when I got him ready for bed. It was red and hot when I touched it. I took his temperature and he was running a fever. It went up to one hundred four degrees this morning. I called the doctor and she was nice and opened up the office to see him. After she examined Connor, she wanted us to take him to Children's Hospital for x-rays of his leg and blood tests. She said it might be cellulitis."

Cellulitis sounded like cellulite, but I knew it wasn't that. "What's cellulitis?"

"Connor's physician said it's a bacterial infection of the

skin that spreads. It usually occurs after some type of trauma causes an opening in the skin."

I heard her blow her nose. "Are you okay?"

"Yes. I'm trying not to cry. On Friday a little boy bit Connor on his leg."

"Poor Connor." I could only imagine that at his age he must be frightened to be seeing all these strangers and getting jabbed for blood samples. "How is he now?"

"He keeps crying and right now they're taking the x-rays. I thought I'd hurry and call you. I just can't believe this could happen. Brian's worried too."

I'd canceled my date with Scott for an interview, and now I couldn't finish writing the article until I saw my godchild for myself. And I wanted to be there for Angie and Brian. Big problem, though. The article needed to be written tonight. Jane had requested it as soon as possible. I'd just have to work on it in the hospital and email it to her.

"I'll leave right now for the hospital."

"Thank you, Catherine. I was hoping you'd say that. I called Mom, but she's out with a new boyfriend. She can't be bothered."

I heard the hurt in Angie's voice. "I'm sorry."

"The hospital is close to the Cincinnati Zoo. You turn down Burnet Avenue and—"

"I remember where it is. I did a story once on The Jane and Richard Thomas Center for Down Syndrome." I did a whole article about all the disabilities the hospital served in their Division of Developmental Disabilities. Because of personally knowing Miranda, I remembered best the Down syndrome information.

"Okay, but be sure to call if you get lost."

I was glad that after I had arrived home, I'd changed out of my suit into comfortable jeans and a long-sleeved white top. I might have a long night ahead of me at the hospital, but I hoped Connor would be discharged and could sleep in his own bed.

Grabbing a navy blue jacket off the bedroom chair, I shoved my arms into the sleeves. Should I take my laptop with me so I could finish my article in the hospital? After a moment's thought, I decided I'd better since I didn't know how long I might stay. I might even want to email my article to Jane from the hospital. I put my laptop in its zippered case and put the strap over my shoulder before I rushed out of my apartment into the parking lot. As I unlocked the car, a horn beeped and I jumped at the sharp sound. Within seconds a dark car pulled up beside me. The automatic window went down, and I saw Dana's face.

In a knowing voice, she said, "I saw you were at the mayor's house."

"Hello, Dana. Tracy invited me over this evening." I wasn't about to tell Dana I did an interview with the whole family present.

She gave me a twisted smile. "Did Tracy invite the photographer over too?"

"Since you obviously were on the street watching, why didn't you invite yourself in?"

"What kind of dirt did our dear mayor give you about me?"

"Nothing I didn't already know." With an impatient toss of my head, I said, "Dana, don't worry, you won't be in my article. I have to go now."

"You better watch yourself."

"Why's that?"

"Pat will try to seduce you too." Dana winked at me. "But I bet you already know how good he is in bed. Do you really think you're fooling anyone with all your negative comments about his job? And now you go to his house to do an interview. I knew you were sleeping with him and that's why he dumped me."

I shook my head. "Dana, get real. I don't have a thing for the mayor. I've never slept with him and never will." I opened my car door, hoping that would end the conversation. "Bye, Dana."

"Wait, please. I'm glad you aren't having an affair with Pat. I had to be sure before I told you something." She stuck her head out of the window. "I can see you're in a hurry," she lowered her voice, "but I need to talk to you soon about Max's death."

Although I hated the thought of spending time with Dana, I definitely needed to talk to her about Max's murder and realized she knew something about the mayor. Why else would she want to make sure I wasn't sleeping with him? She wanted to know she could safely confide in me. What did she know about Mayor Connelly, or should I refer to him as Pat? "I don't think tomorrow will be good, but how about we meet on Tuesday?"

She nodded. "That's fine."

"I'll call you tomorrow about the time and place."

Before getting on the hospital elevator, I called Scott and explained what had happened to my godchild. When I told him our date was definitely off, he said not to worry, he understood and hoped Connor would get well soon. I got off the fifth floor and found Connor's room. He wore a hospital gown with *Sesame Street* characters on it and was curled up against Angie. He looked miserable. Normally, when he saw me, his face broke into a big smile, but not tonight.

I leaned down and kissed his forehead. "Hi, Connor. I have something for you." Fortunately, a few days ago, I bought Connor a book and had never taken it out of the car. This was a good time to give it to him, to cheer him up a little. He loved books. I opened the book to show how lifting the flaps on each page revealed what the trucks carried in their beds.

"What a cute book," Angie said as she lifted a flap and pointed to a truck loaded with monkeys. While Connor lifted another flap, she said, "His blood work is all done for now. He does have cellulitis, and the doctor wants him to get started on antibiotics soon."

"Is he spending the night then?"

Angie nodded. "He'll be hooked up to an IV to get his medication."

"Where's Brian?" I asked.

"He went outside to make a few phone calls."

A young woman with short black hair entered the room. "Hi, Connor. I brought you something you might like." She held up a Disney movie, *Frozen*.

"He loves that one." Angie smiled at the woman. "Thanks."

"If you think of any other movie or toy he might like, I'll be here for another hour in the playroom." The young woman said, "Bye, Connor. Hope you feel better soon."

Connor got to watch a few minutes of his movie before a nurse jabbed him several times trying to get an IV in his small arm. When Brian came in, he hugged me. “Thanks for coming.”

“You couldn’t keep me away.”

Brian reached his hand over the bed railing and gave Connor’s shoulder a slight squeeze. “Hey, little guy. Jake said to tell you hi.” Brian glanced at Angie. “I told Jake about Connor. He said Connor’s in his prayers.”

“Too bad he’s at the World Series. I bet he’d be here,” Angie said, sitting on a small pink vinyl couch.

Brian nodded. “He wanted to know how long Connor will be here. I told him as long as it doesn’t spread to his bone, he should get home in two to three days.”

Angie said, “Did you tell him we might have to forget about the Halloween party?”

“He hopes Connor will be fine and we can still go.”

“I don’t know. Maybe.” Angie paused and grinned at Brian. “If we should go, you can go as Robin Hood.”

Brian shook his head. “I’m not dressing up as Robin Hood and wearing tights.”

“Well then, I can't be Lady Marian." Angie frowned. “We'll have to think of something else for our costumes.”

It was obvious Angie wanted to be Lady Marian, and I stopped listening to their conversation about them attending the party dressed as Robin Hood and his fair lady because the whole topic reminded me that Scott and Jake would both be there. Could I spend time with each and have a great time? I could see me dancing with Scott, and Jake getting pissed about it. After all, the first invite came from him.

Good thing I saw the costume Jake bought, so I’d know which brother will be the pirate. I’d have to ask Scott about his costume. I could see him dressed as Superman, Batman,

Captain America or some kind of super hero.

Spending time with both a pirate and maybe Superman was definitely my kind of Halloween party.

I managed to finish my article while Angie and Brian took turns comforting Connor. After I proofread it, I emailed it to Jane. At ten o'clock, I took over while they went to get something to eat in the hospital. The LaRosa's Express where they served pizza was open until eleven p.m. Before they left, I went to the small refrigerator on the floor where they kept milk, juice, and pop for the young patients. I got Connor apple juice and a small package of crackers.

"While Mommy and Daddy get something to eat, you can eat too," I said to Connor as Angie and Brian walked out of his room. They'd mentioned bringing breadsticks back for us, but I wanted to keep Connor's mind off them leaving. A snack might help.

After he slowly nibbled on a cracker and took a few sips of juice, I read the truck book. I was surprised he was still wide awake, but realized he probably missed his own bed at home. I glanced around the room to see what else I could do to relax him. My eyes rested on a bottle of lotion. "Would you like me to rub some lotion on your arms and legs?"

"Yes, Catie." He watched me carefully as I squeezed lotion on my hands, and then I rubbed them together.

With my hands up in the air, I wiggled my fingers. "Connor, I'm going to give you a great massage. Ready?"

He gave me a small grin. I gently massaged each limb except for the arm with the IV and avoided the sore bump where his infection started. He dozed off for half an hour, but his eyes opened when Angie and Brian came back. Angie carried a small box and smiled at Connor. "Would you like a breadstick?"

Sniffing, Brian said, "Connor, you smell like a girl. What did Catie do to you?"

I laughed. "He doesn't smell like a girl. You exaggerate. I used the hospital's bottle of lotion and gave Connor a relaxing massage so he could sleep."

Brian grinned. "It looks like it worked all right."

"He did sleep a little."

Angie split the breadstick in half for Connor and offered me a piece of pizza to eat. I murmured thanks, but shook my head. I couldn't afford to gain a pound with my Poison Ivy costume being a tight fit. While Connor ate, Angie converted the couch into a single bed since she was spending the night.

After Connor finished his breadstick, Brian changed his diaper. We watched the news and Connor fell asleep. I noticed Angie looked tired, so I said, "I'm going to leave, but I'll come back tomorrow to give you a break."

Angie shook her head. "You don't need to do that. Brian's going to work in the morning and then he's coming in the afternoon to relieve me." She gave Brian a quick kiss. "You better get going and get home. You can walk Catherine to her car."

After I pulled out of the parking garage, I drove a couple of blocks with my window open because I felt tired. I wanted the cool air blowing in my face to keep me awake. That was okay until something got into my eye. I wiped around the corner, trying to remove it when my eye started burning. *Great, I must have lotion under my nail from when I put it on in the hospital room.*

With blurry vision, I pulled over in a parking lot. I took a case from my purse and popped out the one contact lens to clean it. Suddenly a face appeared at my window and startled me so much that I dropped my bottle of contact solution. He said in a gruff voice, "You didn't see a thing, did you?"

No gun was pointed at me but I didn't want to find out if he had one. In a shaky voice, I said, "You got that right. I can't see anything. My contact's dirty."

Should I mention I was in the process of cleaning it when he interrupted me? Probably not a good idea.

He stared at me for such a long time that I agonized over a terrible possibility. He might not believe me. Maybe he was considering shutting me up for good. Peeling out of the lot could save my life.

Fortunately, I didn't have to resort to any grandstand heroics, because finally in a mean voice, he said, "You better get the hell out of here now."

I choked out a yes and slammed on the accelerator. As I drove away, I glanced in the mirror and with my one good eye, I saw a group of men looking like they were conducting business in a rundown neighborhood. Unbelievable, I was in the middle of a drug deal. And then I saw the guns.

For a very, very brief moment, I wanted to know what was exactly going on. I sensed a story for me to report, but decided I'd take the stranger's advice and get the hell out of there.

Chapter Twelve

My article with the news that Tracy wasn't the biological daughter of Mayor Connelly appeared in the Monday edition of *The Messenger*. Jane wanted me to get busy interviewing people and work on my investigation of Max's death. Although I was sure the Connelly family wouldn't approve of my investigating right before the election, I'd be discreet. Let Pat Connelly have his election. Jane said if I didn't have time to write my weekly column, old columns could be used. I knew I was onto something big because Jane always avoided using previously published material.

Jake called from the airport while he waited for his flight to San Francisco. The first two games of the World Series had been in Missouri with the next ones scheduled in San Francisco. He complained about having no game to go to on Monday and wished he could come home for a day.

"But you need time to do your interviews."

"I'll have some free time, though. I don't suppose you'd want to fly to San Francisco and do a little sight-seeing with me?"

His sexy voice was doing things to my thought process and I almost murmured a yes. But then I remembered his brother Scott and using this time to see how things worked out between us. I also thought about Connor being in the hospital, but knew Angie would tell me to go to San Francisco instead of helping her with him.

"As tempting as it is, I can't. I don't have money to fork over for an airline ticket."

"Maybe we can get the paper to foot the bill. You can help me cover the World Series."

I laughed. "I don't see Jane approving that request."

"She should be pretty pleased with you right now. Your Connelly article is well-written. You did a terrific job, and I'm sure many reporters are jealous you got the scoop."

"Thank you."

"Since it's not in your article, I'm assuming none of the Connellys wanted to talk about Max's death."

"Right. The focus was on Tracy's news and nothing else. I brought it up, but the discussion about a possible murder was off the record. And I'm okay with that."

"Do you think Mayor Connelly killed Max?"

"As I told him, he's on my list of suspects, but he's not my number one suspect now."

"Who is your first suspect?"

"You are."

"Come on, stop kidding."

"That's right. It can't be you. You were away at college when Max died."

"Why did you bump the mayor down on the list?"

"I asked him if he'd wanted Max dead, and Connelly seemed sincere when he said he hadn't."

Jake chuckled. "And you believe a politician?"

I hesitated, thinking about Dana wanting to talk to me.

"This time I do except..."

"Except what?"

"When I was leaving to see Connor, Dana stopped me in the parking lot and said she wanted to talk to me about Max's death."

"But why did she wait five years? Unless she wants you to expose something about the mayor so he'll lose the election."

"I don't know, but she wanted to be certain it was safe to talk to me. She suggested I was having an affair with Pat to see how I'd react."

"Whoa, Pat. He's Pat now to you," Jake said.

"He told me to call him Pat since Adam and Tracy are in love. And I'm not having an affair with him."

"I knew that."

"That's a relief. I don't want you to think badly of me."

"I could never think badly of you." He paused for a moment, then continued. "What do you think of me?"

"I think you're incredible and a man of great strength."

"Okay, what do you want me to move for you?"

I laughed. "Nothing. I wish you'd been with me last night when I was in the middle of a drug deal. I was terrified, especially when I was afraid the guy had a gun."

"Are you crazy? You better be more careful. Don't tell me you stopped to interview the drug dealers."

Monica Osborne's squeaky chair gave her away. Turning, I saw the food editor leaning over her arm rest. Because she gave me an embarrassed glance, I knew Monica had been listening to my phone conversation. One of these days, she was going to fall on the floor.

After every weekend, Monica wanted to know what I'd

done. She informed me how she had to live through my adventures and dates since she was married and had kids. I'd have to tell her about meeting Scott. She'd love it. Sometimes I envied her. She didn't have to look for Mr. Right. Monica was at a good place in her life, being thirty-three, married with two adorable kids, attractive, and having a career she enjoyed.

I grinned at Monica while she sat up in her chair. She ran her fingers through her naturally curly brown hair. To Jake, I said, "I'm not sure it was a drug deal, but I think it probably was. I got something in my eye and pulled over to clean my contact so I could see when this man appeared by my car."

"I take it that your window was down and probably your door was unlocked..."

I sighed. "I wasn't thinking. I told him I didn't see a thing and he said to leave. I saw they had guns as I drove away. I called the Cincinnati police when I got home."

"Were you able to give a description?"

"Not really. He wore a cap with the visor pulled down on his face."

"Let's hope the dealers didn't get your license plate number."

I groaned. "Oh, thanks. I never thought of that. But having this happen reminded me of something about Max."

"I'm sure Max didn't do drugs."

"He didn't. When I was a senior he turned a group of boys in to the police. Their parents were pretty upset Max didn't go to them first about their kids' drug problems."

"I'm surprised Max didn't go to Mr. Hudson."

"I remember the boys were in Adam's and Tracy's class

so they were seniors when Max died. Do you think they had something to do with Max's death for revenge?"

"They could have been angry enough to mess with the boiler."

"I'll have to add them to my list of suspects."

"And here I thought while I'm away, you'd be curled up with a hot romance novel and missing me, but instead you're getting chummy with the mayor, accused of having an affair with him, and get yourself in the middle of a drug transaction."

"That about sums it up."

"Good. I was afraid there might be more."

I realized there was more if going out with Scott tonight was included.

"So how is it covering the World Series?" I asked.

"Great, except I want it to be over soon so I'll get home, and we can go out to maybe dinner and a movie." He gave a nervous laugh. "Can you fit me into your busy schedule?"

I sat up straighter. Unreal. He'd rather spend time with me than extra games at the World Series. "As long as I don't have another date, I'd like that."

"Don't tell me. You might hook up with the drug dealer."

I laughed. "That's a possibility."

"I remember one of your rules was about not expecting total commitment in the early months of dating. You said not to stop seeing other people because you might get stuck with a loser."

I chewed on my bottom lip. Why did he persist in throwing the rules up to me? "Sometimes I wish you hadn't read my dating rules."

"Sometimes I wish you hadn't written them."

One of Jake's reporters stopped by my desk and asked in a low voice, "Is that Jake?"

I nodded. "Austin wants to talk to you. I'll put him on the phone."

After handing the phone to Austin, I went to Jane's office. Since the receptionist was away, I peeked in the doorway. Jane looked up from her desk and smiled at me. "Come on in."

I pulled the door shut. No eavesdropping employees in the newsroom needed to hear my plans to visit the boiler room at Park City High School. I stared at Jane and thought how lucky I was to have such a dynamo for a boss and mentor. Both Jane and her husband had improved the layout of the paper plus increased the number of readers in the thousands. This had been no easy task with the dwindling number of subscribers. She was dressed in a pink blouse with three-quarter length sleeves. With her sitting behind her desk, I couldn't see her legs but knew she always wore pants to the office. Even though Jane's only in her forties, she refuses to color her white hair. I agree. She has beautiful hair and wears it short.

"Catherine, I was just thinking about you." Jane grinned. "What, no skirt and heels today?"

"It seemed like a pants day." I didn't want to take time to tell her the reason behind the skirts and stilettos. Today I wore a bright blue jacket with a silky white top and gray pants.

"You look great in skirts, but I like what you have on today." She looked at my shoes and said, "I love your red loafers. Go ahead and sit down." She exhaled a breath. "If I could have had a daughter, I'd want her to be just like you."

I wondered why she hadn't had children since she definitely loved them. She'd made a fuss over Connor when he was in the office a month ago with Angie. I bet she'd waited because of her career. "Maybe you could still have a child. Women have children in their forties."

She shook her head sadly. "We can't have children. Years ago, we found out we aren't compatible. George's sperm and my eggs just can't get it together to conceive. We tried to adopt twice but both times the birth mothers changed their minds and kept the babies."

"I'm sorry."

"It's okay." Jane gave me a small smile. "The newspaper is my baby now. And I do have my sister's precious children to spoil."

"Well, they're lucky to have you for an aunt."

"Sorry I dumped on you. When I took my morning jog, I saw the cutest baby girl," she sighed, "and it started me thinking what we missed by not having kids."

"Maybe you could try adopting a special needs child or one from another country."

"We did go to a meeting about Chinese baby adoptions and we're considering that possibility." She threw her shoulders back. "Enough baby talk. Please tell me you're digging today."

I nodded. "Big time digging. I'm hoping to call you one of these days and shout, stop the presses."

"Now that's the kind of stuff an editor likes to hear." Jane frowned. "I do have a concern, though."

"What's that?"

"I'm afraid you might not play hardball because of Tracy being your friend."

"She wants me to find out if Max was murdered. In order to do that, I have to expose the truth, whatever that might be."

"Good. You'll have to be tough. I'm hoping if Max was murdered, you'll get enough evidence that the police will reopen the case."

"I'm hoping I'll catch the killer."

"You don't have to be that tough."

I knew I better change the subject before Jane started telling me how I needed to be cautious. "Oh yeah, I came in to tell you I talked to Miss Kent and she gave me the go ahead to see Mr. Hudson and the school janitor, Ralph Tindall." I glanced at my watch and saw it was ten. "I'll need to leave soon to see them."

Jane grinned. "You get to have all the fun. What about Dana Tucker?"

"I talked to her again and I'm going to her condo tonight after I visit Connor." Jane knew about my godchild's illness from an earlier morning chat.

"Give Connor a hug for me."

I fingered a lock of my hair and said, "Get this. She lives in an expensive condo in the Hyde Park area."

"How can she afford that on a secretary's salary?"

"That's what I want to know." Angie and I had looked at small apartments in the much desired Hyde Park when we were college students, but realized that even with splitting the rent, we couldn't afford the neighborhood.

Apparently, Dana had a huge cash flow coming from somewhere other than her job in the sewer department.

I looked from wall to wall in the janitor's room outside

the boiler room, trying to find Max's collage of pictures. Whenever students had given him their school pictures, he'd put them up on the walls and some on his desk. Tears filled my eyes. He was one of the good guys. I heard Ralph's voice and wiped my eyes before turning to face him. "I was just looking for memories from my high school days. Max used to put up school pictures. I'd given him a senior picture."

Ralph shook his head regretfully. "Sorry, the wall was empty when I got the job."

"Max didn't put it on the wall. He told me that the photo of a future editor-in-chief of *The New York Times* should have a place of honor. And I teased him that I was going to be a CIA agent."

"You should stay with reporting. I look forward to reading your articles."

"Thank you. I came down here a few times to complain to Max when Mr. Hudson told me some of my articles weren't appropriate for the school paper."

Ralph raised his bushy eyebrows. "Oh, you were a rabble rouser."

"I got so upset about my stuff being cut that I thought about starting an underground paper." I smiled. "Fortunately, Max discouraged me and said he'd hate for me to get expelled."

"I never knew him, but I heard how everyone went to him with their problems. He's a legend around here."

I nodded. "Max was really special and loved children. I think he'd be happy I'm writing this article about school safety."

Since I was going to ask Ralph and Mr. Hudson questions about the boiler room, I hadn't wanted it to appear that I was investigating Max's death as a possible murder case. I wanted them to think I was totally interested in what was being done presently in the school system to keep the students safe from any explosions and gas leaks. Jane had agreed I should visit a few schools and talk to their custodians.

Our cover story had worked when I explained to Miss Kent that parents have a right to know how safe their child's school is. She was eager for me to visit Park City High School and bragged how Mr. Hudson devoted a great deal of time to keeping the school safe. She reiterated how Max's accident was an isolated incident and nothing like that had happened again.

"I'll show you the boiler room." Ralph opened the door and said, "It's too bad Max was in here when the explosion happened. With the concrete walls, the only damage was contained in here."

Once inside, I nodded. "Probably having the boiler room in the basement helped prevent other injuries."

Ralph told me how he was properly trained to safely operate the boiler system. He answered my questions about inspections and said how important it is to check the units regularly to make sure the equipment is in proper working condition. Maintaining heating equipment annually can save injuries and lives.

"What if you do all this and still something happens?"

Ralph said, "Most explosions are due to human error."

Upon examination of the boiler, I said, "Do you think Max made an error that cost him his life?"

"I'm not positive, but according to the fire chief's report, Max didn't catch a faulty gas valve. Mr. Hudson has the report in his file if you want to see it."

I lifted my arm to look at my watch. "Speaking of Mr. Hudson, I have an appointment with him next." I shook Ralph's hand. "Thank you for taking time out of your day to answer my questions. I'll let you know when it'll be in the paper."

"Feel free to use my name in your article."

"Okay, that's good to know."

As we left the boiler room, Ralph said, "I saw your article on the front page this morning. Too bad Tracy didn't know her daddy before he died."

I walked to an old ugly brown couch by the door and ran my fingers over a cushion. "I see you kept Max's couch."

Ralph nodded. "It's comfortable and still in good shape. They don't make couches like this anymore."

Ten minutes later, I was seated in Mr. Hudson's office. The principal, a tall man in his forties with black wavy hair, looked impeccable in a black suit with a white shirt and a red patterned tie. He was a handsome man except his eyes were too big and bulged a bit. "Thanks for seeing me so quickly," I said.

He stood to greet me. "It's always a pleasure to see you, Catherine. I read your article this morning with great interest. I never suspected Max was Tracy Connelly's biological father."

I nodded. "It was a surprise."

"Miss Kent said you want to talk to me about what we do to keep the children safe from fire and other disasters while they're in school. Have you talked to other school principals about school safety?"

"Not yet." I sat in the chair opposite his desk. "I thought

I'd start with my favorite principal. And with school just underway, I thought it'd be a great time to get the facts about how safe schools are. Parents will be reassured to know what's being done to prevent any accidents from occurring."

"With good maintenance of school boilers, annual inspections, and the appropriate training, we keep the school safe."

He said exactly what Ralph had said. Did they read the same script? "So you feel comfortable that what happened to Max won't transpire again?"

"Even under the best conditions with safety inspections and taking diligent care of the boilers, accidents can happen." He took a paper out of a folder on his desk and handed it to me. "This is the report from Max's accident. What happened to him shouldn't have taken place, and both the boiler inspector and fire chief stated a faulty valve controlling the amount of natural gas fueling the boiler probably caused the incident. Max must have missed it. The boiler with the problem only had one gas valve, and it allowed too much gas to build up, so when the boiler flame ignited the gas, the explosion occurred."

I read over their report. "It's good no one else was hurt or killed."

Mr. Hudson nodded. "The explosion was so strong it blew the door off the hinges. That night Max went to the boiler room after the boys' basketball game. He loved basketball and went to most of the home games."

"Did you and Max have a disagreement about the boiler needing a replacement valve or maybe other new parts?"

Mr. Hudson shook his head. "No, we never did. What makes you ask that?"

"Because someone saw you leave the boiler room looking angry shortly before Max died. And I know some school administrators are on a tight budget, so maintenance of school boilers gets low priority."

"As a school administrator, I make sure there's money for the upkeep of equipment." He picked up a stack of papers before he continued. "The person was mistaken. I don't remember getting angry at Max."

I cleared my throat. "Maybe it had nothing to do with the boiler and the equipment. Just think back to five years ago, maybe there was another school issue you two had a disagreement about...like he was socializing too much with the students or something."

He placed the report into the folder and looked up at me. "It seems like you're pretty interested in Max's life. Which story is it? Max or school safety?"

"School safety, but I'm asking questions about Max to see what kind of frame of mind he was in the night he missed the faulty gas valve."

"There wasn't any argument between us before he died."

I didn't believe him because I didn't see why Dale Jansen would lie about what he saw.

And Max knew Hudson had a secret. Had Mr. Hudson known how to tamper with the valve to cause an explosion, so Max would be out of the way and his secret would be safe?

Or was Max simply the victim of a tragic accident?

As I left Mr. Hudson's office, the bell rang and students spilled out into the hallway. Miss Pierce stopped by me in the hallway. "Good morning, Catherine."

I turned to look at her and said hello. "How's Geometry?"

Miss Pierce wore a brown skirt and a brown patterned blouse, similar to the drab clothing I remembered her wearing when I was in her Geometry class. She still wore her hair in a long braid—the only difference was that it was gray now instead of brown. "I'm not teaching it this year. I'm teaching Pre-Calculus, Algebra 2, and Trig. I like it except now I have to do more preparations with teaching three subjects."

I wondered if she still taught some days from the floor. It was strange having to peer down at the teacher. "Do you have a class now?"

She shook her head.

"Could I talk to you for a moment?"

Her eyes darkened. "I read *The Messenger* in the library, so I'm not interested in buying a subscription from you."

"You're safe. I'm not selling subscriptions."

"Good." An annoyed expression crossed her face. "I remember you asking me to buy magazines, Christmas paper and cards when you were a student here."

"You have a good memory. We were doing lots of fundraisers in my junior year to pay for the prom."

"Since you aren't selling anything, I have a moment. We can go to my classroom."

Even though she taught different subjects now, she was in the same classroom where I had Geometry. It was across the hallway from Mr. Jansen's room, and he stood outside his classroom, greeting students as they walked through the doorway. When he glanced at me, I waved at him.

Miss Pierce waited for me to enter the room. Then she pulled the door shut. "It's so noisy out there."

Even though I'd never cared for Miss Pierce as a teacher,

right at this moment I felt compassion for her. Obviously, she was concerned about money since she didn't want to be asked to buy a newspaper subscription. Maybe she could do some grading for Dad. He'd been complaining about the assistant who worked for him at UC.

"I don't know if you have any free time, but my dad could use someone like you to help with grading his midterms at UC. I'm not sure how much it'd pay." I took a business card out of my purse. I held it out to her and said, "Here's his business card. If you're interested, you can give him a call."

Miss Pierce studied the card for a moment. "Thank you, but I'm too busy with my own workload." With raised eyebrows, she asked, "What brings you to Park City High?"

I explained my safety article to her and ended with how there hadn't been an accident since the one in the boiler room. "Did you know Max very well?"

A look of tired sadness passed over her features. "We were very close and he distanced himself from me when he became involved with a married woman. I think he was under so much stress with her in his life that it was an error on his part in the boiler room."

Talk about delusional. I thought Mom was right that Miss Pierce read more than friendship into those few cups of coffee Max took to her.

"It seems to be the consensus that it was an accident. I just can't imagine Max being careless. He was so conscientious. The woman in his life must have been something else." I dropped my gaze for a second, then widened my eyes. "Did you know the woman?"

"I confronted Max about how I knew he was having an affair with Karen Connelly. He didn't deny it. Of course, I didn't know until today's article that he was Tracy's dad." In an angry voice, Miss Pierce said, "She didn't even have the decency to include him in their daughter's life. I told him Karen was just playing with him and that a woman like her wasn't interested in a real relationship with a janitor."

"How'd he take that?"

"He said he wasn't going to be a janitor much longer." She exhaled a breath. "And he was right, he died soon after."

Chapter Thirteen

Angie's rocking motion relaxed Connor and he slept against her chest with his IV stand right next to him. He was still hooked up to get medication through his vein.

She said quietly, "I don't know what I'd do without this rocking chair. Last night he woke up several times and I rocked him back to sleep."

I'd picked up Angie at home to go to the hospital. She wore gray warm-up pants with a drawstring and a loose-fitting slipover top. She planned on sleeping in her clothes again and spending the night at the hospital.

"Connor certainly likes his mommy to rock him." I frowned. "I don't know if I want to have kids. This is so stressful with Connor being ill."

"You better have kids someday so we can be mommies together." Angie stopped rocking. "You look cute," she said, eyeing my denim skirt, red sweater and black boots. "What are you doing after you see Dana?"

I shrugged. "I don't know yet." I knew I was meeting Scott at McFadden's for a drink after I left Dana's condo, but I didn't want to tell Angie I had a date with him. And since we were going to decide then what to do with the rest of the evening, I wasn't completely telling a lie.

Funny, I'd originally meant to tell her on Sunday and hadn't gotten a chance. Maybe in my subconscious, I don't want to tell her because of Jake. If she knew, Angie might say I was trying to punish Jake by going out with Scott. Even if I said, "I was attracted to Scott before I knew he was Jake's brother," it wouldn't make any difference to Angie. I just knew my friend too well.

Or she might try to make me feel guilty. But I wasn't doing anything wrong. I wasn't two-timing them. Scott knew my history with Jake and that I planned to also date his brother. And obviously, I'd tell Jake when he returned to Park City how I met Scott.

"Have you heard from Jake recently?" Angie asked.

I wasn't surprised she asked about him. She mentioned him frequently to me and I knew why. With Brian and Jake being best friends, we could have fun doing stuff as couples.

I nodded. "He called and we might go to dinner and a movie when he gets back."

I didn't get to say more because Brian returned from the gift shop, carrying a helium balloon for Connor. It was six o'clock, so I decided to leave and call Dana on my cell phone outside the hospital, thinking I should have heard from her.

Dana answered right away and apologized for not calling me from work. "I had to finish a stupid report and the traffic was bad. I'm home now so you can come any time."

I left the hospital in a hurry, anxious to find out why Dana had said what she did about Mayor Connelly. I was positive she wanted to tell me a lot about her affair with him. And I bet she knew something about Max's death.

I was relieved that I didn't get lost and arrived at Dana's

condo in twenty minutes. What a lovely spot, I thought, as I glanced at the trees and quiet street.

Dana opened the door as I reached the porch and said, "I timed that right. I was just coming outside to watch for you."

She wore low-rise jeans with a skin-tight light green sweater, and I wished my abs were as flat as hers. Did she do those exercises in magazines that say something like "Have a flatter belly in fifteen minutes of exercise"? Or I bet there was a fitness facility for the condos' residents.

I followed her up the stairs. Over her shoulder, she said, "There are four condos on the first floor and two on the second."

"How long have you lived here?"

"Two years." She opened the door to her condo and once inside, Dana asked, "Would you like a tour?"

I nodded, knowing she wanted to show me how nice she had it and I didn't blame her a bit. There were two big bedrooms, two baths, a kitchen with beautiful granite countertops and stainless steel appliances, a dining room and a covered deck. And the living room had a wood burning fireplace.

After I admired everything, we both sat on her red leather sofa. Dana pushed her long blonde hair away from her face. "Would you like something to drink?"

I shook my head. "No, but thank you. Do you have a second job to afford all this?"

She frowned, biting her lip. "I might as well tell you how I was able to buy this. Max had a life insurance policy, and I was his only beneficiary."

"Were you surprised?"

She shook her head. "He'd told me about it once when I

was in high school, but I hadn't really thought much about it. I mean, he wasn't old and he was in good health."

"He loved you a lot to make you his beneficiary." Why hadn't he included Tracy?

"When Max and Mom got their divorce, I was crushed."

"Right after the divorce, did he have any contact with you?"

"He came to visit me once or twice a month until I graduated from high school. But it wasn't enough. I hated it when he moved. I was only ten years old and it was awfully hard."

"I'm sorry."

Obviously, she loved Max a lot, but was it possible her love of money was greater? Did she know Max wanted to tell Tracy about her being his daughter? Was Dana afraid Max would change his life insurance policy to include Tracy so they would share the money? Or maybe he'd have wanted Tracy as the sole beneficiary. How much did Dana know about the impending marriage?

Dana glanced out the front window. "Most of the leaves are off that tree by the building. Max loved fall."

I smiled, thinking about his pumpkin dish filled with candy. "He definitely loved Halloween. He must've spent a small fortune on the Halloween candy he gave to the students." Max had lived life to the fullest, making the best of a situation he couldn't have been happy with.

"I was pretty much out of it after Max died. I didn't have sex for a long time."

I wondered what a long time meant to Dana—a week, a month? "Did you and Mayor Connelly break up before Max died?"

She nodded. “And that’s what I need to talk to you about. Pat said he was wrong in having an affair with me, and it was his fault Karen wanted a divorce. He said she had an affair with Max to get back at him.”

I shook my head. “Your affair might have pushed her into Max’s bed, but I don’t think she ever got over her love for him and wanted to marry him, regardless of Pat and you having an affair.”

Dana looked down at her manicured nails. “When Max died in the boiler room, I just assumed it was an accident. I mean who would want to murder Max? But with Pat running for the House of Representatives, I started thinking how determined he was about not losing Karen. And then I remembered what he said.”

Okay, don’t leave me hanging here, Dana. “What did he say?”

“He said he wanted Max out of the picture, and he would rather die than see his wife married to the janitor.”

“So you think Pat might have had something to do with Max’s death?”

“I hope not because if he did, I’ll kill him.”

She could just be saying that so I wouldn’t suspect her being involved in the murder. “Why did you wait to tell someone what Pat said?”

“I didn’t think Max was murdered or that Pat would kill him.” She pulled on her sweater sleeve. “I guess if there’s a possibility Max was murdered, I wanted someone to know what Pat said.”

“There’s something I’m very curious about. Did you ever think of telling Tracy that Max was her real father?”

“Not really. She already had the perfect life and perfect

family. She didn't need a second father. Besides, Max asked me not to."

"Before Max died, someone saw Mr. Hudson leave the boiler room, looking very angry. Did Max ever mention anything to you about Mr. Hudson? I don't know if you know him, but he's the principal at Park City High School."

"I met him when I went to visit Max at school. Max never said anything about having words with Mr. Hudson." She chewed her bottom lip. "I'm still in love with Pat...unless he had anything to do with Max's death."

Something might have occurred between the two. Max could have uncovered dirt about Hudson. Different scenarios ran through my head. Hudson embezzled money from the school, or he did something else illegal, or Hudson lied about something to the school board members that could hurt the students. I wondered if Mr. Hudson knew how to tamper with gas valves.

Jake might be right that Dana wanted me to expose something about the mayor so he'd lose the election. I bet she didn't want Pat to leave Park City. "Dana, since you told me that Pat wanted Max gone, are you hoping I'll mention the scandals involving you and Pat, and Max and Karen so Pat won't be elected to the House of Representatives?"

"That thought entered my mind that you'd leak what I said in *The Messenger*, but I was telling you the truth about Pat saying he'd rather die than lose Karen to Max." She sighed. "I'll never get Pat back if he leaves Park City. I moved here hoping he'd miss me and feel freer to see me here. But instead I got transferred to a different building at work."

I recalled how Fred and Dana had been seen together. "I'm sorry. But you and Fred make a cute couple."

"I'm just seeing Fred so I can keep tabs on Pat."

"Have you ever heard how Kroger here in Hyde Park and the one in University Heights are great places to meet single professional men?" Dana might meet available men and surely one of them could help her get over Pat.

She shrugged. "I have, but I'm not giving up yet on Pat."

Outside Dana's condo, I called Scott. I smiled to myself when he said, "I'm here at McFadden's, waiting for this gorgeous girl I met here in this amazing belt skirt."

Twenty minutes later, I entered the restaurant and the hostess showed me where Scott was seated. When he saw me, he stood, wearing tan pants, a blue-striped shirt and a navy blue sports jacket. He kissed me smack on the lips. And he looked so hot I was afraid I'd hyperventilate right in McFadden's. I wondered if that had ever happened. I could just see the headlines, "Girl passes out in popular pub at sight of an incredibly hot guy." And of course, the guy would revive the girl. How could I have forgotten how good-looking Scott was?

He eyed my jean skirt before pulling out my chair for me. "You look great, but I'm disappointed you decided to go conservative on me."

I grinned. "This isn't conservative."

"For me, it is. You'll have to wear the belt skirt for me again before I leave town."

"I'll see what I can do."

"I guess we should decide what we want to do tonight. I'd thought about taking you to Mitchell's Fish Market in Newport and then going to a movie there. What would you like to do?"

When Jake and I were at the Pavilion, he'd talked about us going to Newport on the Levee. Funny how they both mentioned movies at Newport because it's not like we didn't have a movie theatre in Park City. Well, I knew why Jake did. Newport on the Levee could be seen from the Pavilion so that was why he'd brought it up. If Scott didn't get home much, he might not be aware that a Showcase Cinema opened six months ago.

"How often do you come home?"

He gave me a puzzled look. "I'm not sure what that has to do with Mitchell's, but usually my parents and brothers come to Florida over Christmas, and I get home about twice a year." He grinned. "But I might be making the trip to Park City more often in the future."

"I hope you do." I fingered my sweater sleeve. "I was just wondering if you knew Park City has a new movie theatre."

He nodded. "We can go there sometime. Or tonight if you want."

"I do love Mitchell's, but if we eat here maybe we'll have time to walk on the Purple People Bridge before the movie at Newport." I pictured us having a romantic night walking on the bridge and holding hands. It'd be a good opportunity to get to know him better, and I definitely wanted to before he returned to Florida.

He raised his nicely shaped eyebrows. "I bet you want to write an article about the bridge."

"I did already. I wrote how it's America's only pedestrian bridge linking two states." I gave a dramatic sigh. "If you don't want to walk with me, I'll find someone else."

He laughed. "I do. And if there's anything else you want to do, we'll do it. The developer of the Levee was smart to add so many restaurants, games, movies…"

"And shopping."

"What about the Newport Aquarium? Have you gone there?"

I nodded. "I went with my godchild, Conner, and his parents. He was fascinated with the sharks. He called them the big fish."

Fortunately, we'd looked over the menu for a few minutes before the waiter came to our table and asked if we were ready to order. I ordered a salad and their chicken melt on a roll and Scott's cheese steak also came on a hero roll. He went with a bowl of chili and got an order of cheese sticks for us to share. He told the waiter what kind of red wine he wanted, but looked up from the menu. "Is wine okay with you?"

I nodded.

After the waiter left with our order, Scott said, "Where did you park your car?"

"I left it at the parking garage down the street."

"I used the valet parking here so when we go to Newport, I'll drive and you can leave your car. It's not far and it won't take much time to drive you back to get your car."

I smiled. "Good. I can drink more wine then."

"By the way, I read your article. I'm impressed with your writing."

"Thank you. So do you think I'm a better writer than Jake?"

"You're definitely better-looking than Jake."

"Were you trying to avoid the question by making a sexist remark?" I wasn't upset, but I thought I'd tease him a little. I mean, really, if a guy had asked him that question, he wouldn't have answered about one writer being better-looking than the other one.

He shook his head. "You have different journalistic styles since you and Jake don't cover the same sections of the paper. Jake's a great sports writer and you're the best investigative reporter I know." Scott hesitated, then asked, "Did you talk to Jake today?"

I nodded. "He called this morning and—"

The waiter brought our bottle of wine and poured each of us a glass so I didn't finish. I took a sip. "I'm glad you ordered this. It's very good."

"So how's my little brother?"

"He's anxious to get back to Park City."

"Did you tell him about us?"

I frowned at Scott mentioning us like we were a couple. "About going out tonight...no, it never came up. When was the last time you talked to him?"

"Before he left for the World Series."

Setting my glass down on the white tablecloth, I said, "I never mentioned meeting you here on Saturday."

He gave me a relieved look. "That's probably just as well. He doesn't like to share with his big brother."

I watched the waiter set our cheese sticks and marinara sauce on the table. After he left, I said, "Why did you two have to be brothers? You're complicating my life."

Scott grinned. "We're complicating your life. I thought you're the type of woman who likes excitement and variety."

I dipped a stick into the sauce. "Well, your life's about to get complicated. A couple has been eyeballing you for the last five minutes. Are they mad at you for something? Did you lose a case for them?"

"Where are they?"

"To your left."

He turned his head and his eyes widened. "That's Mike and his wife Kim." He lifted his hand in greeting. "Excuse me for a minute. I'll go and say hello. We were in high school together."

While Scott chatted with his friends, I called Maggie. I told her why I was calling. "Guess what, on Thursday nights here at McFadden's, they have Ladies' Night. And they have massages for only a dollar. We should come some Thursday and get pampered."

Maggie said, "That sounds like fun. We'll have to go."

Once the food came and Scott returned, I ended the call with us planning on getting together soon.

"Mike looks a lot older than you."

"We had our fifteenth class reunion a few months ago."

I grinned. "So you're old."

"I don't think thirty-three is old."

I took a big drink of wine, wishing Kim would stop giving me dirty looks. What was her problem? She must be jealous I was with Scott. "I think Kim has the hots for you."

"Why do you say that?"

"She keeps staring at me. It's very annoying."

He shrugged. "She must think you're too young for me. We can switch seats so your back will be to her."

I shook my head. "I don't want to move. I can take a few nasty looks."

A few minutes later, Mike and Kim left McFadden's. I forgot about the incident and enjoyed the rest of our dinner.

After Scott parked his car at Newport on the Levee

parking garage, we had a little time to walk before the ten o'clock movie.

After we walked halfway across the bridge, Scott drew me close to him and his lips were hard and searching.

His moist, firm mouth demanded a response and I kissed him back, wondering what he was thinking.

He gently pushed my hair away from my face and kissed me again for a long moment. "I don't think this is going to be enough for me."

Oh no, was he going to bring up sex already? He was quiet so after a couple of teenagers walked by us, I got brave and asked, "What do you mean?"

"I'm not going to get to spend enough time with you. I fly out on Sunday."

"We still have the rest of the week."

He shook his head. "I'm afraid we don't. Before I met you, I made plans to see some friends for a few days. They're expecting me tomorrow and they live in Cleveland."

I was disappointed. I'd counted on having a week with Scott before Jake came home. Maybe it was just as well. I'd started having second thoughts about dating two brothers and could see it might not be the best situation. "I can understand you wanting to see them while you're in Ohio."

"You'll have to come see me in Florida."

"You've never told me where you live in Florida. Is it close to a beach?"

"I live in Jacksonville. I take it you like beaches."

I gave an enthusiastic nod. "I love the ocean. Mom and Dad took me and my brother on lots of vacations going to different beaches."

"Have you ever gone to Amelia Island?"

"No. Are you close to it?"

"It takes about forty minutes to get to Fernandina Beach and it's located on Amelia Island. If you come to visit me, I'll take you there."

"That's tempting."

He grinned. "Me or the beach?"

"Both, of course." I glanced at my watch. "We better head back so we don't miss the movie."

While brushing my teeth at two o'clock a.m., I thought again how bizarre it was that Kim gave me hostile glances at McFadden's. I didn't think Scott was right about the age thing. Why would she care that I was younger than Scott? It had to be something else. I rinsed my toothbrush and placed it in my pink holder.

Standing next to my bed, I threw the comforter back, wondering if she recognized me from my column and didn't like something I wrote. But if that was it, why didn't Scott just tell me? I like to know what readers think, even the angry and offended ones.

I crawled into bed and punched my pillow, trying to get comfortable. When Scott comes back, I'll just have to tell him I want to know what was bothering Kim about me. I had a feeling he knew.

I sighed. It couldn't be too terrible, could it?

Chapter Fourteen

On Tuesday afternoon, I was happy the food editor, Monica, was away. I liked her, but she was at times a distraction when I wanted to get a lot done. She'd interrupted me in the morning when I did background checking on Dana and Fred. I had to wait to make calls because she was in one of her "wish I was single again" modes. I had listened patiently to her telling me how lucky I was not to have to get children off to school in the morning before coming to work. She said I shouldn't rush into marriage and motherhood. If I did, she warned me I'd end up like her and be stressed out 24/7.

I'd thought about telling her there was no chance of that happening for a long time. I did enjoy my date with Scott, but at the same time, I was anxious to see Jake. Maybe it was the age thing. I had a feeling at Scott's age, he might want to get married soon, and that's not in my immediate future. One of my goals is to live in New York City for a year or longer and be a reporter. Scott had already called me this morning to tell me again how much he wanted me to visit him in Florida. Considering we just had officially one date, I thought this was premature. Although he was probably the best-looking guy I'd ever dated, I didn't see me rushing this relationship to a permanent one.

I clicked on my Max file and while waiting for it to open, I took a sip of coffee. I wish I had more than circumstantial evidence. Sure, it looked suspicious Max died right before he was going to make changes in his life. He was finally going to tell Tracy the truth after graduation, he planned on marrying the woman he loved, and he was buying a hardware store. Just because he died before he got to accomplish any of these things didn't mean he was murdered. Maybe he'd been thinking so much about his new life that he became careless with the boiler room equipment.

Something else bothered me as I skimmed the file.

None of the persons on my list of suspects seemed capable of murder. I sipped my coffee while I went down the names to come up with a strong motive or motives for each one.

1. Miss Evelyn Kent

—Definitely didn't like Max. Didn't want the yearbook dedicated to him.

—Tried to blackmail Karen Connelly.

2. Mr. Hudson

—Jansen witness Hudson's anger at Max about something.

—What was his secret he didn't want Max to expose?

I typed new material again in the file.

New information about Mr. Hudson:

—Hudson seemed to know a lot about boiler operations and maybe he had tampered with the gas valve.

3. Mayor Pat Connelly

—Probably wanted Max out of his wife's and daughter's

lives—but would he kill Max?

Update after mayor's interview:

—Pat seemed sincere about not wanting Max dead. However, if Dana told me the truth, Pat definitely didn't want to lose Karen to Max.

—Would he have his own daughter's biological father killed?

—One other fact—IMPORTANT ONE—As mayor, Pat had the power to hire and fire department heads. Had he used this power to tell the fire chief what to put in the report?

4. Fred

—Not likely that five years ago, the mayor's political career caused him to kill Max—but find out where Fred worked five years ago.

Since I liked Fred and he'd always been kind whenever I called him, I was happy to add the following to his column:

—Learned that five years ago Fred worked in Madison, Wisconsin. The police said nothing on Fred, no crimes, no parking tickets, he was in the clear. But then, I wasn't surprised. He wouldn't have gotten the position of campaign manager to the mayor if he had a criminal record.

Fred—not a suspect.

I opened the top drawer, looking for something to nibble on. Nothing. What happened to that granola bar I never ate? I closed the drawer. Food had to wait...needed to get back to figuring out what person had the most to gain by Max's death. It occurred to me there was a suspect I needed to add to my list, but first Dana's possible new motive needed to be included.

5. Dana

—Appears she's jealous of Tracy's life and felt she lost

Max as a father figure because of his love for his real daughter.

—In her situation, Max alive would have been the best scenario so Karen C. would divorce the mayor so he'd be free to marry Dana.

—Maybe she was bitter & wanted revenge for being dumped by the mayor and hoped he would be blamed.

Update since talked to Dana:

—Money Motive—She benefited greatly by Max's death by getting $200,000 from his life insurance.

—Was the money more important to her than Max?

—Dana might have realized the beneficiary amount would change if she had to share with Tracy.

—Dana probably knew something about boilers since she had visited Max frequently.

Suddenly I recalled something Tracy had said after she'd returned from Columbus and talked to her Aunt Gwen. She said Dana referred to Max as Dad. I'd never heard her call him Dad and wondered what was up with that. Why hadn't she used Dad even once while talking with me last night?

When had Max stopped being "Dad"?

From checking on her, I'd learned she hadn't made any large purchases or investments until she bought her condo two years ago. It didn't appear she needed the money five years ago enough to murder Max.

Now for my added suspect to the list.

6. Miss Pierce

—She felt like a scorned woman. Thought Max and she could be together until she learned he loved Karen.

—But why kill Max? If she wanted to kill someone, why not Karen? Or perhaps, Miss Pierce realized she didn't have a chance with Max and didn't want him to be happy with Karen.

Mom might have some insight into Miss Pierce's mental state from when she taught at Park City High School.

Was I missing anyone?

I thought for a few minutes and remembered how Max was going to buy Nolan's Hardware Store. Mom had been surprised since Nolan's son had been managing the store. She thought they wanted to keep the hardware business in the family. Had there been a son unhappy with his father's desire to sell the store to an outsider?

7. Nolan's son

—Possible motive—Getting rid of Max so he could keep family business.

8. The high school boys Max had arrested for drugs

—motive revenge

I couldn't think of anyone else to add to my list.

But I did know I needed a light bulb in my kitchen and what better place to purchase one than a hardware store?

Twenty minutes later, I stood on the sidewalk and stared at the Nolan's store sign. With the orange background and the big white letters, it looked great. If Max had bought it, would he have changed the name? So sad that none of Max's dreams had materialized.

I entered Nolan's store. Memories rushed through my mind as the wood planks creaked where I walked. Nolan had the same old floors that were here when Adam and I came to the store with our dad years ago. We were two small, excited children when he took us to get nails and other building supplies for our tree house. I glanced to my left at the large room which still had washers and dryers.

"Hi. Is there something I can help you with?"

I turned and saw a thin Mitch Nolan with gray hair. He looked older, but not too different from when he'd bought a yearbook ad from me. I guessed him to be in his early fifties. "Hi. I need light bulbs."

He smiled. "This is your lucky day. We happen to have light bulbs."

I smiled back. "I like your store. My dad brought me here when he built our tree house. And my mother, Leslie Steel, bought her paint here when she remodeled her coffeehouse."

He nodded. "I remember your mother coming in and she not only bought paint but got her lighting fixtures here too. I appreciated her being loyal to us because that's when Home Depot opened. We lost so many customers to them."

So that was it. Home Depot caused the Nolan family to lose business. Mitch's father probably wanted to sell to Max before they lost too much money.

"That's a shame. I hope some of them came back."

By this time we were in the aisle with all kinds of bulbs. "They did. We're doing okay now, but it's still a struggle. I do some house inspection work for realtors to make extra income. I wish every day Home Depot wasn't in our city." He frowned. "They even have the same color sign. Can you believe it?"

"But yours is brighter and better." I picked up a package of hundred watt bulbs. "I'm glad you didn't give up on the hardware business. I hate it when a big franchise tries to move into a community and take over."

"My dad wanted to sell our business and he almost did." He sighed. "Fortunately, I got my dad to retire and I'm the only owner now. When my son graduates from college, he's going to join me in the business."

"Cool. Three generations of Nolans—"

He interrupted with, "Actually four. My great-grandfather opened the first store."

A customer called for assistance in another aisle and Mitch yelled, "I'll be right there." He gave me a quick glance. "Did you need help with anything else?"

I needed more information. "I'm thinking of buying a condo and I'd like someone to do an inspection for me. Would you have time?"

"Sure. I'll give you my business card before you leave."

Several minutes later, I sat in my car in the store's parking lot. I felt light-headed and realized I hadn't had lunch yet. I must have low blood sugar or something because I get dizzy if I go too long without eating. I pulled out of the lot to go to a McDonald's down the street. When it was my turn in the drive-through, I ordered a double cheeseburger, a yogurt parfait and a Diet Coke. While I waited in line to pay for my food, I got my phone out of my bag and called my mom.

I quickly filled her in on my visit to the hardware store before questioning her about Miss Pierce. "Mom, I've been going over my list of suspects and I've been wondering if Miss Pierce had a motive. Do you think she wanted Max dead since she couldn't have him?"

"I don't think so. I went with her and some other

teachers to Columbus for the funeral. She cried a lot there and also at the memorial held at the high school."

I sighed. "I just don't have enough yet to prove he was murdered."

"I can't believe I didn't realize Karen and Max were having an affair. When Tracy and Adam were juniors, Karen helped their class with orders for fundraisers for the prom. When the orders came in and needed to be sorted, she stored them in Max's room in the basement. I see now why she did."

"I wonder if Miss Pierce ever saw Karen and Max together. It probably broke her heart since she thought Max had strong feelings for her." I dug out my wallet and said, "Hold on, Mom, I need to pay for my food."

I handed a five dollar bill to the young man at the register. While he gave me the change, Mom said, "Don't forget I'm driving to Findlay tomorrow to get my mother."

"I can't wait to see Grandma Nelson."

At eighty-five, my grandmother was still active and lived on her farm by herself. As a child, I had so much fun spending time with Grandpa and Grandma on their farm. Grandma loved coming to Park City to visit us. If she didn't have a daughter, grandsons and friends living in Findlay, I think she'd move to Park City to be closer to us. Since she couldn't drive, we took turns getting her. Whenever Mom's older sister could get away from her family, she brought Grandma Nelson.

"We'll be home in the afternoon, so I hope you can come to dinner."

I was at the second window to get my order and realized how tired I was of fast food. When you were single, you looked forward to a home-cooked dinner. "What are you having?"

"I'm putting a roast and vegetables in the crock pot before I leave."

"That sounds good." I put my Coke in the drink holder and my bag of food on the passenger seat. "Could you look up a phone number for me?"

"Sure, honey."

"I need the fire department's number."

After I parked in the McDonald's lot, I took a big bite of cheeseburger while she looked for the number. I knew she had it with other important numbers on a board in the kitchen area. I heard her oven timer dinging while she gave me the number. She got off the phone in a hurry to get a pan of muffins out of the oven.

I called the fire chief's number. I sipped my drink while the secretary connected me to the chief, Mr. Jeffries, and I thought how maybe it would be cool to buy a condo. I guess seeing Dana's condo inspired me. Instead of paying rent and having absolutely nothing to show for it, I could be a property owner. If I move to New York City, I can sell it and make a profit. Maybe I'll really need Mitch Nolan's inspection.

When I heard the chief's hello, I said, "Mr. Jeffries, this is Catherine Steel, from *The Messenger*. I'm doing an article about school safety and wondered if you have a few minutes to spare to talk to me this afternoon."

He was quiet for a moment. "I do have an appointment at four, but if you're able to come within the hour, I'll be happy to answer your questions."

I finished my burger as I drove and decided to eat my yogurt back in the newsroom. The receptionist told me the chief was expecting me and to go on in. As I walked through the doorway to the chair by his desk, Mr. Jeffries stood and shook my hand. He was huge with extremely broad shoulders and he towered over me.

"Thank you for seeing me so quickly."

Mr. Jeffries waved his hand at the chair and said, "Please sit down. Now what can I do for you?"

"When I talked to the principal, Mr. Hudson, at Park City High School about school safety, we ended up talking about the boiler room accident that took the custodian's life five years ago." I watched him closely. "I saw your report and—"

"It wasn't my report." He raised his eyebrows. "I wasn't the fire chief then."

"I thought your name was on the report."

He frowned. "I wasn't even in Park City then." He pushed his intercom. "Melissa, find the folder about the boiler explosion at Park City High School. It happened five years ago. Thanks." He looked up at me. "Wait a minute. I took over for Alan Jenkins. With my name being Adam Jeffries, you might have thought it was me."

I grinned. "Maybe that's why you got the job. You had the same initials...A.J. The city could save money."

Mr. Jeffries smiled back at me. "I bet that's it."

"Do you know where Mr. Jenkins is now?"

"He died five years ago. It was a couple of months after the school explosion."

"What did he die from?"

"Poor guy. He was killed in a hit and run accident. The police never found out who did it."

Was it an accident or had someone deliberately hit him? He might have decided to change Max's accident to a possible murder. If the killer realized Jenkins had a change of heart, he had to stop him.

Melissa brought in the folder and handed it to Mr. Jeffries. He glanced at the report before giving it to me. After I read it, I said, “The one Mr. Hudson gave me didn’t mention Mr. Jenkins’s opinion.” I read out loud from the report, “I was surprised that Max Hartman missed a faulty valve. I knew him personally and he was diligent in his responsibilities and nothing in the past got by him.” The rest of the report was the same as Mr. Hudson’s.

I was right to be investigating Max’s death. Fire Chief Jenkins had had doubts about what’d happened.

I was determined to learn the truth. I just hoped I didn’t end up like Jenkins.

Chapter Fifteen

After talking to Dana and Mr. Jeffries. I wanted to touch base with Pat and see what kind of response I'd get from him about what I had learned. I gave him a call Tuesday afternoon. He was out campaigning when I wanted to talk to him about scheduling a meeting.

Fortunately he got back to me in the evening and said, "I need to take a breather from campaigning and get some paperwork done. I'll be in my office tomorrow. I should be caught up by late afternoon. Stop in around three-thirty."

An hour after I spoke to Mayor Connelly, I heated a jar of cheese dip in the microwave and took it to the kitchen table. While I nibbled on taco chips and the hot Mexican cheese dip, I realized how lonely I felt. Alone time was nice, but right now I wanted to hear another human's voice and not anyone associated with Max. The last forty-eight hours, I'd talked to probably nine or ten people about his death. I thought about calling Jake. After glancing at the kitchen clock and seeing it was eight p.m., I knew he'd be at the baseball game. Not a good time to call him.

What about Scott? I could call and see if he got to Cleveland okay. And then ask him again about Kim's rudeness at McFadden's. I was sure it wasn't what he'd said—an age thing.

After a couple of rings, he answered. “Hi, Catherine. I was just thinking about you.”

“That’s good. I’m bored and thought I’d check to see if you made it to Cleveland.”

“I did, but I got a little tired. I forgot what a long drive it is.”

“I’m sure your friends are glad you made the trip.” I paused. “Did you ever figure out why your friend Kim gave me angry glances last night?”

“No.”

“Did you tell her I was a reporter when you talked to them?”

“No, it never came up.”

“I thought maybe Kim learned I’m a reporter and she didn’t like what I wrote.”

“She asked how I knew you,” Scott said, “and I said how we’d just met Saturday night.”

“What did you do, mention my belt skirt?”

He laughed. “No. But I bet that’s it. Kim’s jealous of your beautiful legs.”

“Will Kim and Mike be at your parents’ Halloween party? I’ll come right out and ask her.”

“No. They can’t make it. Just forget about Kim. She’s not worth it. I have another call. I need to answer it because it’s from my secretary. I’ll call you back later.”

Was he hiding something from me? His voice sounded weird.

While waiting for Pat the following day, I walked around in the mayor’s spacious office, looking at framed photos of him, starting with the recent family ones. I moved to a group taken of a young Pat Connelly with his dad. I stared at one particular photo of both Connelly men with President Reagan. And then I saw one of even greater interest to me. Pat was posing with a beloved celebrity, John Ritter.

"He died too soon."

I turned to look at Pat and said, "I was heartbroken when he died. It was so unfair."

"We shared a common goal."

If he said comedy, I wouldn't believe him. "What was that?"

"We both wanted to improve the lives of people with cerebral palsy. I met him at a fundraiser and we talked about our brothers suffering from cerebral palsy."

"I didn't realize you had that in common."

Pat nodded, pointing to a photo. "This is my brother, Michael. He's been dead for ten years and I still miss him."

"I'm so sorry for your loss. I can't imagine losing my brother."

"I appreciate how well you wrote the article about Max being Tracy's biological father." His eyes bored into mine. "I have a feeling that's why you want to see me. It's about Max, right?"

"I'm afraid so. I saw the former fire chief's report about the accident. Mr. Jenkins wrote on his that he was surprised about the accident. He said how diligent Max always was."

He sat down behind his desk. "Go ahead and take a seat. Would you like coffee or anything?"

I shook my head as I sat in a brown leather chair opposite his desk.

He sighed. "I admit Alan told me his feelings about Max

not being careless, and he questioned whether someone had tampered with the valve. But for Karen's sake, I didn't want an investigation. She was in bad shape after Max's death. And I felt justified in convincing Alan to list it as an accidental explosion. I didn't think anyone attempted to kill Max. I still don't."

"I'm wondering if someone learned Alan Jenkins thought differently and hit him on purpose with the intent to kill."

"I wish we could find the bastard who did it," he said, his lips tightening. "Alan and I were good friends. I miss him. I don't suppose we'll ever find the person who hit him and just left him to die. I think it must have been an accident because of the circumstances."

"I didn't see the police report, but I read the newspaper story about how he was in an alley."

"His wife said she'd just talked to him, and he was late for lunch. He was meeting his brother at Darcy's Restaurant and he probably ran across the alley to save time. I don't think he usually used the alley."

"That's so sad." I thought maybe it was just a terrible accident and wasn't tied to Max's death. "I talked to Dana recently. She isn't convinced of your innocence in Max's death."

He shrugged. "She probably wants revenge. I never should have had an affair with her. It was the biggest mistake I've ever made. Since I wouldn't leave Karen for her, she's going to try and make sure I don't get elected."

"Wouldn't she do that by leaking to the press about your affair before the election?"

He raised his eyebrows. "Unfortunately, you don't know

her like I do. She would never want to be known as the other woman who was jilted."

I cleared my throat. "I suppose that could be a possibility. Even though Max visited her frequently, he still left her to be close to Tracy. She might feel rejected enough by Max leaving Columbus that she doesn't want it known you rejected her."

"Did she say anything else about me?"

"Just that you wanted Max gone and you'd rather die than see Karen married to him."

"I didn't kill Max." He paused for a moment. "And I didn't hire anyone to tamper with the valve. Like I said to you before, he was Tracy's father. That mattered to me a lot."

"Maybe you should come out now about your affair with Dana. I'm surprised your opponent hasn't learned about it and leaked it."

Pat shook his head. "You just got your exclusive story about Max being Tracy's father. I think that's enough for now."

"If you ever change your mind, give me a call. I'm amazed Max and Karen kept their affair a secret."

"If I'd been faithful, nothing would have happened between them."

"I'm not so sure about that. She might not have slept with him, but she couldn't stay away with her strong feelings for Max. He was her first love." Leaning slightly forward in my chair, I asked, "Did you ever have a first love like that?"

He gave me an amused look. "You're just full of questions today."

"Did you?"

"Yes, I did. It wasn't another woman, though." He turned

and pointed to a picture on the wall back of him.

What I saw surprised me and I suddenly realized he must be bisexual. It was a picture of a popular Cincinnati Reds baseball player from the eighties. "I don't know what to say."

"You seem disappointed that my first love was baseball."

At his words I gulped, relieved I hadn't blurted out my mistake about his sexual preferences.

He continued, "My childhood dream was to become a major league baseball player."

"I guess your dad didn't approve of baseball for you."

"That wasn't it. I played in high school, but I wasn't good enough to continue." He glanced at the wall clock, then gave me a charming smile. "I've enjoyed our chat, but I need to get back to work."

"Thank you for your time. I know you're busy." I stood. "Are you going to miss being mayor?"

"It sounds like you think I'm going to win the House seat."

I nodded. "You're ahead in the polls by quite a bit."

"Are you going to vote for me? Before you say no, I should tell you Adam came to see us last night and he asked for our permission to marry Tracy."

"He mentioned he wanted to propose. I thought he'd wait a little longer."

Pat stood. "I think they're planning on having a long engagement."

Good, maybe it would be long enough for me to get married first. *Oh, stop it, you don't have to be the first one to get married in the family.* "It'll be great having Tracy for a sister."

Hopefully, we wouldn't be adding a murderer to the Steel family tree. Although the Steel ancestors were rather boring. When I was younger, I thought if only we had a Yankee woman spy in our family tree during the Civil War. Now that might have been thrilling to talk about in history class.

After I left the mayor's office, I headed home to see Grandma Nelson. I found her sitting on Mom's new claret sofa in the great room. There were several family picture arrangements on the walls. With yellow walls in this room, the space was open and bright, but at the same time, it was cozy. I felt comfortable here in this large room since I hate cramped places. I did need to buy a condo and get out of my small apartment.

"Hi, Grandma. I'm happy to see you." I bent down and kissed her cheek. Her short white hair was in a tight curl, looking like she recently got a perm.

"Hello, honey. It's good to see you too." She patted a spot next to her. "Sit down beside me."

"Did you have a good trip here?"

Grandma nodded. "Your mom's a good driver. I hear you're investigating a possible murder."

"I am. I just got done talking to someone who could be a suspect in this case."

Mom walked in, wiping her hands on a kitchen towel. "Who did you talk to?"

I glanced at Mom. "Pat Connelly."

Grandma gave us a puzzled look. "But that's Tracy's daddy. I hope you don't think he killed the janitor."

Before I could comment, the front door opened and Adam walked in. While he gave Grandma a hug, I said, "I don't really think Pat had anything to do with Max's death, but I can't rule him out completely. He had a lot at stake."

"Hey, that's my future father-in-law." Adam plopped in a chair. "I'm sure he's innocent of any wrongdoing."

"By the way, I heard you already asked Pat and Karen for their blessing to marry Tracy. You said you were going to give her more time with everything that's happened lately."

He grinned. "What's wrong? Are you upset you didn't get to put the engagement news in your article?"

I shook my head. "No, that's not it. I was just surprised."

"It's good he's engaged," Grandma said. "He's loved Tracy for a long time and I'd like to be around for the wedding." She smiled at me. "Have you been a good girl?"

I wanted to moan out loud. I knew what was coming, the sex talk again, but I didn't get a chance to comment with Adam's big chuckle. He asked me, "Should I tell her or do you want to?"

"Tell what?" I said.

He gave Grandma a grin. "Catherine's been engaged a lot since she's kissed lots of guys."

Grandma shrugged. "Oh, kissing is okay. I guess I wasn't being realistic when I said you should only kiss the person you're engaged to. That's what my mother told me."

We heard the garage door opening and Mom said, "Good, your dad's home. I'll go get the food on the table."

Adam jumped up. "I want him to take a quick look at my car. It's been making a funny noise."

"Mom, do you need some help?" I asked.

In the doorway, she shook her head. "I'm fine. You visit with Grandma."

Grandma Nelson patted my arm. "I want to see you

happy before I die. Are you in love with anyone?"

"I'm still playing the field. Are you feeling okay?"

"Pretty good for being eighty-five years old." She sighed. "I know you're a savvy granddaughter when it comes to dating and you help many single women with the dating tips you share in your articles, but don't be too quick to dismiss a potential husband based on one negative experience."

This sounded like something I heard before from Angie. A settling theory from Grandma. I raised my eyebrows. "Are you saying I'm too picky and I should settle for someone even if I'm not in love with him?"

"No, that's not it. You don't have to settle in order to get married. This is about something else. Leslie told me how Jake Michaels has moved back to Park City and he's working where you do. He made an impression on me when he used to come over with Brian and Angie. He was such a nice young man. I think you should give him a second chance."

"I am. Last Friday he took me to the Pavilion, a place in Mt. Adams, and we're going out when he gets back. He's in Kansas City, Missouri, right now covering the World Series."

"That's wonderful." She smiled at me. "You're my only granddaughter and my namesake. And I have something special in mind for you when you get married. If you stay pure until your wedding night, I have a surprise for you."

Wow, I wondered what Grandma had in mind. A set of valuable old romance books maybe. We were kindred spirits when it came to reading romances and especially ones set in England. And as an adult, I told her about Helen Fielding's book, *Bridget Jones's Diary*. She said it was a bit racy for her, but reading about Bridget was great fun.

Maybe I should tell Grandma my romantic fantasy. She

might be the only person to fully understand why it was important to me. Mom was more practical and might try to discourage me, but Grandma and I shared a certain romantic passion. She'd fully understand and want it to happen for me.

I gave her a hug. "I love you, Grandma and I'm going to tell you something no one else in the whole world knows."

Chapter Sixteen

My honeymoon fantasy thrilled Grandma, but she was definitely worried about one aspect.

After dinner we went off by ourselves into the study while the rest watched TV. I carried glasses of red wine and set them on a low table in front of a small gray sofa with two purple pillows. I'd influenced the color choice of the pillows when I'd shopped with Mom. I glanced at the overflowing bookshelves and wondered if Mom was back into buying lots of books. I'd bought her a Kindle a couple of years ago and she did like it, but I realized she must have bought several of the authors' books she displayed in the coffeehouse.

After I closed the door, I sat next to Grandma, kicked off my red loafers and pulled my legs under me. "Now this is relaxing."

While sipping our wine, I thought how cool it was that I shared my big dream with Grandma and she loved it. Some grandmas would have said I was being ridiculous, but not mine.

Grandma gave me a broad smile. "I love your whole dream of going to London for your honeymoon. Every grandmother should have a fun granddaughter like you."

"I was just thinking the same thing except in reverse."

"I'm afraid of a major problem." She lifted a pillow and placed it back of her head. "Unless you're planning on marrying royalty, I don't think you'll be able to book the place you need for your incredible fantasy."

"I'm hoping the groom will deliver."

Grandma laughed. "If he can, I'll marry him."

"I better cut your wine off."

"No way. Red wine is good for an old gal like me."

"Oh, so that's your secret to living a long life. I better stock up on wine in my apartment."

"And a sense of humor helps. Your grandpa and I laughed together a lot."

I nodded. "Humor's good when you start dating a new person too." Jake and I have had some humorous conversations ever since he returned to Park City. Although I had fun with Scott too. Hopefully, Jake would think my meeting and dating his brother was amusing. For some reason, that didn't seem likely.

"Your mother said you're going to a costume Halloween party this Friday. You always loved to dress up when you were little. I remember one Halloween you wore three different costumes to your parties."

"I didn't want to wear the same one to all of them. Sometimes I designed my own costumes and that was a blast." I paused for a moment. "Did you ever date two brothers at the same time?"

She appeared to be deep in thought and after a couple of minutes, she said, "That's a hard question since I haven't dated for a long time. But before I married your grandpa, I do remember I went out with two brothers. Not at the same time, though."

"Did they know you dated both of them?"

"They did. I went to a movie with Oren and I liked him a lot." She got a faraway look in her blue eyes. "I thought I loved him and he was the one I wanted to marry."

"What happened?"

"He fell in love with one of my girlfriends and they avoided telling me at first. I was heartbroken for a long time. Later, his brother Reno asked me to a church picnic," she paused to smile at the memory, "and it was there that I met your grandfather."

"I'm glad you told me about Oren."

"Some people think there's only one true love for each person, but I don't buy that for a minute. As much as I loved Oren, I knew there was someone else for me to love."

"I miss Grandpa."

Grandma held my hand. "Me too." She moved the pillow to her lap and sat up straighter. "Now, what was that question about two brothers all about? Are you dating brothers?"

"I'm afraid so."

My wise grandmother might have a suggestion or two on how to handle the two men at the Halloween Party, so I told her about meeting Scott. I explained how I was attracted to him before I knew he was Jake's oldest brother. I left out the part about my belt skirt.

I didn't need to tell Grandma everything.

"Jake invited you first to the party, so I'd spend the most time with him. And you need to tell Jake before the party that you've gone out with Scott." She grinned. "I'd leave the part out about Scott being the hottest guy you've ever dated."

I nodded. "I'll tell Jake when he gets back in town."

The temperature dropped a lot during the night, so on Thursday morning I teased Grandma, "What did you do, bring the cold northern air with you?"

She laughed. "I know you guys are always telling me it's ten and sometimes twenty degrees warmer in Park City, but it's cold here today. And that's not going to stop me from going out tonight with Tracy and Adam."

"Are you still going to the coffeehouse for lunch?"

"Yes, your dad's going to drop me off when he goes to work. Leslie went in too early for me."

"I'll eat lunch with you and Mom. I better go and get to work. Love you and see you soon, Grandma."

After I hung up, I finished dressing in a long, dark green skirt with a beige top. I wore tan boots and put a green scarf around my neck. I looked in the mirror, rubbing my lower lip. Something else was needed here. I know. A belt. I walked in my closet and pulled a tan belt off a hook. I buckled the belt over my top and low on my waist.

I slid my arms into a jacket and sighed, looking at my tiny apartment. It was downright depressing living here after seeing Dana's roomy condo. At dinner last night, I'd asked Dad to check out condo listings for me. He was always looking at the real estate ads and wanted to invest in some land for a retreat spot. I'd heard Park City had some reasonably-priced condos, and I was going to cut down on my expenses so I could swing the monthly payments.

I'd hit an impasse on my investigation with Max and when I couldn't fall asleep last night, I realized a change of pace was what I needed.

In the past, I'd received substantial checks for my magazine articles on dating and relationships. Now I wanted to get extra money for a down payment on a condo, so this morning while still in my pajamas, I'd emailed a women's magazine editor about a possible article on the most productive way to meet men. She'd accepted several of my previous submissions, so knew I had a good shot on this particular idea. In my pitch to her, I mentioned interviewing several single women to see what had worked for them. Where had they met the desirable men? Was it speed dating, church, art museums, concerts, supermarkets, fitness centers, coffee shops where you can sit and talk, restaurants, night spots, or sporting events?

Oh no, Jake was at the World Series. He might meet someone. There could be a girl hitting on him at the games. Why did Jane's hubby George decide not to be a silent partner any longer and suggest Jake attend the World Series games? Girls would turn out big time, knowing lots of available guys would be at the games. He could have written his pieces by staying here and watched all of it on TV. And The Associated Press offers page-ready scores for professional baseball and other sports. But no, the AP wasn't enough for *The Messenger*. George was really into baseball and wanted complete coverage by Jake, the star sports editor.

Of course, for my article I'd interview Maggie. I'll quote her about the experience she had hooking up with a lawyer at a pub. They'd gone out once with a second date planned so things were looking good. And there was the 8 Minute Dating popular in Cincinnati tonight for singles. I'd heard about it on the Cincinnati radio station, Q102. I'd go to observe and interview a few people participating in tonight's speed dating at Mama Rosa's Italian Restaurant and leave. I didn't want to stick around the whole time with a chance of seeing Jake.

After he interviewed the winners of the World Series, he'd be flying home soon.

Thursday went fast enough. I had lunch with Grandma and Mom. In the afternoon with it getting close to the election, I wrote an article about the money spent on the campaigns by both Mayor Connelly and his opponent, Mr. Marshall. It was amazing how much wealth they'd acquired in their lives. Basically, the voters had to decide which rich candidate to vote for (okay, a few political differences existed between the two) and it was looking like it would be Pat Connelly. Unless something happened in the next ten days to change the voters' minds. Although Pat didn't think Dana would want people to know he ended their affair, I felt she was a loose cannon, waiting to cause havoc right before the election.

At six-thirty, the parking lot was filled behind Rosa's so I went to a garage down the street next to Skyline Chili. As I walked by the restaurant, a customer opened the door and I smelled the combination of onions and chili sauce cooking in the restaurant. After I left Rosa's, I'd pick up an order of three-way chili to eat back at my apartment. Outside of the restaurant's door, my phone rang and I saw it was Scott calling.

"Hey," I said. "How's Cleveland?"

"I'm back in Park City."

"Oh, you left early. That's nice you're back now." I opened the door and entered the pub. "You can help your parents with the party stuff."

"That's not the response I was hoping for."

"What were you hoping for?"

"Something about us getting together tonight."

I saw lots of young professionals probably from ages twenty-five to thirty-five getting ready to start meeting other singles. "I'm in a room full of people looking for love. Or maybe just friendship."

"What bar are you at? I'll join you before you get into trouble."

I laughed, remembering Scott saying I was trouble the first time he met me. "I'm not getting into any trouble. There's a function here at Rosa's called 8 Minute Dating. I'm going to talk to a few people about it and include it as one way to meet people in an article on dating."

"I don't think we have that in Florida. How does it work?"

"You move from table to table and go on eight one-on-one dates that last eight minutes each. Each participant has a scorecard and keeps track of hits and misses."

"Do you have to write the article tonight?"

"No." I knew he called so we could do something tonight, and I decided to be available. Jake hadn't called, and I was a little hurt since he'd made a big deal out of wanting the World Series to end, so he could get back home and take me out on a date. He'd even asked me to fly to San Francisco so we could spend time together seeing the city. Since the Giants had won last night, and he'd probably flown home today, I'd expected to hear from him by now. I wondered if Scott had seen Jake.

"I'd really like to see you tonight. How about I get Chinese take-out and meet you at your apartment?"

"Were you planning on getting egg rolls?" I decided not to mention I didn't like Chinese food. I could munch on egg rolls. And oh yeah, fortune cookies.

"I guess that's a yes if I get egg rolls."

"It's a date if you also get fortune cookies."

"You got it. Call me when you leave Mama Rosa's."

Weird, I'd known Scott for less than a week and had already been in Cincinnati twice with him. Thinking about our dinner at McFadden's reminded me of his nasty friend Kim. I'd have to be sure to ask him again tonight why Kim had been so rude to me.

I spotted the event organizer since Lily wore exactly what she said she would. I knew she saw me, too, because she waved and walked toward me. "Scott, I have to go. I'll talk to you soon. Bye."

"Good," Lily said. "You do look just like your newspaper photo."

I dropped my phone in my purse. "Thanks for taking time to talk to me."

"This is a professional way to get to know a lot of people in an open setting. It's pretty cool. You should do it this evening."

"I have a date tonight, but I might register the next time when it's at The Old Spaghetti Factory." I'd heard on the radio that another speed dating would be held there in a couple of weeks.

"Good. Where else can you wear one cute outfit and have eight dates in one night?"

"I like that. Let me get that down." I wrote her comment on my pad.

"And even if you don't meet Mr. Right, you meet guys who are here to meet somebody, so you'll start some new relationships."

"Sounds like fun. Do you use a cheat list with questions

or topics to talk about in case the conversation lags?"

Lily nodded. "The back of the dating scorecard has a few conversation starters, and I jotted down a few of my own possible things to say if I get a guy who's shy. If that happens, you have to keep thinking how to get him to open up and relax."

"Do you learn a lot about the person in such a short time?"

"No, but enough to know if you want to se him again."

"Sounds like a prescreening and a big time-saver for busy professional people." I smiled at Lily and thanked her. "I should talk to a few other people."

Lily glanced around the room and pointed in the direction of a young woman. "You might talk to Samantha. She's in her first year of residency at University Hospital."

"Perfect. She's definitely a person with little time who needs to meet people quickly."

Lily introduced us and left to get something to drink.

"What made you decide to do 8 Minute Dating?"

"With my workload, it's been difficult for me to meet people in Cincinnati." Samantha pushed a lock of black hair behind her ear. "I work eighty-hour weeks so I don't have much time to go to bars and socialize. This is a great way to quickly meet guys."

"What if you see a guy you'd like to meet and he's not on your list?"

"There's an intermission when you can mingle with any singles you haven't been hooked up with yet. I had some amusing chats during the break when I did this before."

We didn't talk long. Samantha had to leave since the event was to start in a couple of minutes. After getting good quotes for my article from a few others and watching the whole process for half an hour, I decided to leave at seven-fifteen.

Within ten minutes, I was in my parked car and I called Scott first to tell him I was on my way home. He arrived ahead of me at my apartment. I hopped out of my car and realized his presence thrilled me. He brushed a kiss on my forehead.

Once inside, Scott set the bag of food on the table. “First, I want to show you how much I missed you.” He drew me into his arms, and his kiss was slow with his tongue sending tremors through my body. It was incredible. I felt like I was kissing Henry Cavill. Superman, himself.

After I recovered from our passionate embrace, I looked up at him. “I missed you too.”

We went ahead and filled our plates, or rather Scott did. I took a few egg rolls and scooped out some of the shrimp fried rice.

“When I got the take-out, I noticed a Kroger store and thought we could go there to look at the movie selection. I know they have Redbox. Would you like to get a movie?”

I nodded. “We can save the fortune cookies for later and eat them while we watch the movie.”

“I’m not sure cookies will suffice for my appetite. I might need a bigger dessert.”

I gulped. The smoldering flame I saw in his eyes startled me. Great, was he referring to having me for dessert? Or maybe he was serious about wanting an actual edible dessert. “I have ice cream in the freezer. Or if you don’t want that, we can get something else when we get the movie.”

“You’re so sweet. You can be my dessert.”

Between the dessert comments and the hot kisses, I felt giddy and couldn't wait to snuggle with Scott and watch a movie. I completely forgot to ask him about Kim.

Even though I mentioned having several movies, we decided to go out anyhow to find something to watch. We'd look at the movies in the Redbox kiosk. Scott said we needed popcorn to eat while we watched the movie.

Inside the Kroger store, we looked at the movie selections listed on the Redbox kiosk. Finally, Scott and I decided on *Guardians of the Galaxy*, an action adventure movie with a superhero who survives all kinds of implausible escapades.

While Scott put his information on the screen, he said, "I love this type of movies. I get so involved in the main character's unbelievable exploits that it helps me escape my own boring life."

"I hope I'm not boring you."

He smiled at me. "I haven't been bored since I met you."

After we had the movie, we went inside the store and grabbed a bag of white cheddar popcorn. I couldn't resist also getting a bag of caramel corn. The cashier had an irresistible dimple. He was cute but irritating the way he stared at me. I'd been to this store several times but didn't remember seeing him, so it couldn't be he recognized me as a customer. On his shirt I saw his name plate and read Bruce. When we were next, I insisted on paying for the popcorn and a few other items I decided to get. I had trouble when I slid my debit card to pay.

Bruce asked to see my card. After I handed him my debit card, he said, "Catherine Steel. I don't recognize your name."

What a jerk. He was hitting on me while I was obviously

standing next to my boyfriend. "I didn't know that was a requirement to have to recognize the cardholder's name."

"Sorry. I thought your name was something else." He looked disappointed. "You don't remember me, do you?"

I shook my head. "Should I?"

"You were at a bar wearing this incredible belt skirt and dancing on the bar counter and..."

"When was this?" Scott asked.

Bruce shrugged. "Maybe a month ago."

Scott turned to me, laughing. "I'm glad it was before I met you. I didn't realize you liked dancing on bar counters. I'll pay for Catherine's stuff."

Bruce shook his head. "It went through now."

After signing my name, Scott and I grabbed the bags on the way out. He opened the door of his black Mercedes Sport Sedan for me. Once he was behind the steering wheel, he said, "I was right. I said you were trouble when I met you. You better not wear that skirt any more."

"Would it make a difference if I promise not to dance on any bar counters when I wear it?" What I'd do for a hot guy.

He didn't answer since his cell phone rang. "Great, it's Chad. I better take it."

I read the synopsis on the back of the DVD while Scott talked to his brother. I knew something was terribly wrong when I heard him say, "I'm coming, but I wish Jake was home to bail you out. I'll have to find out how to get there too."

When he closed his phone, I asked, "What's wrong with Chad?"

He frowned. "He got pulled over for running a red light then got arrested for being under the influence of alcohol while driving. At least he didn't have an accident."

"I'm glad no one was hurt. Did he try calling your parents?"

Scott started his car. "He doesn't want to upset them before the party, he says. I think he's worried Dad will stop paying his tuition at college."

"He's lucky you're in town."

"Yeah, except I came back early to spend time with you. By the time I get Chad, it's going to be late. I'm sorry. Maybe we can watch the movie Saturday night."

"Or even after the Halloween party." Now why did I say that? I might want to see Jake after the party. It might be good Scott's returning to Florida on Sunday. Too much stress with seeing two brothers.

Chapter Seventeen

After Scott dropped me off, I changed into a pair of flannel pants with a monkey pattern and a pink T-shirt. I broke open a fortune cookie and from the slip of paper read, *Don't play with fire if you can't stand the heat cuz you will get burnt.* Interesting fortune since I was investigating a gas explosion.

As I chewed the cookie, my phone rang. My heart raced when I saw it was Jake calling. I hoped my voice sounded calm as I said, "Hey. Where are you?" I hoped he wasn't still in Missouri.

"Would you believe I'm right outside your apartment? I came straight here from the airport. I know it's short notice, but I'd like to see you."

"I'd like to see you too." Thank God, Scott had left half an hour ago.

I shoved my feet into a pair of green flip-flops and ran down the stairs so fast I lost my balance on one step, but I reached out for the railing, stopping the fall. Jake stood there grinning at me before I opened the glass door, and I knew he saw how I almost fell. I grinned back and opened the door. As soon as Jake stepped inside, he grabbed me and I felt his warm lips on mine.

His hands moved to my butt and he squeezed both cheeks hard. "I like what you have on. It's soft, like your butt."

"Are you saying I have a flabby butt?"

He shook his head. "It's firm but soft."

I held his hand and pulled him up the stairs to my apartment. "How was your flight?"

"It was awful. I didn't call you earlier because it was delayed. Some kind of an engine problem."

"That's okay. I'm glad you're here now."

"I'm starving. Would you like to get something to eat?"

"I'm not dressed to go out."

"That's okay. I'll get a pizza and bring it back here."

While he waited for someone to answer at the pizza place, he said to me, "There's a Redbox close to Papa John's. Why don't you go with me? We can get a movie."

"Did you see *Guardians of the Galaxy*? I rented it tonight and haven't watched it yet."

"I saw it. I liked it, but I don't want to see it again."

"Well, you can pick a movie. I'll stay here." With my luck, Bruce would see me with Jake at the Redbox kiosk. He'd probably mention how I was just there with another guy.

With the phone next to his ear, he said, "I forgot to ask you what you want on the pizza."

"Anything except peppers and anchovies."

"How does mushrooms, pepperoni, and bacon sound to you?"

I rolled my eyes. "It's everything I like, but it'll probably make my butt flabbier."

"Your butt's fine." He grinned. "If you go with me, you'll get a little exercise walking to Kroger to get the movie."

I could help pick the movie and hope that Bruce didn't

see me. If he should see me with Jake, he'd probably mention how I was just there with another guy. His register and checkout spot just had to be across from the movies, but hopefully, Bruce would be too busy ringing up orders to notice me. "You win. I'll go."

After Jake ordered the pizza, I gave him a quick kiss and grabbed a jean jacket to throw over my T-shirt. Although I'd mentioned not going out before because of how I was dressed, I wasn't worried about going in my flannel bottoms to the pizza place late at night. Lots of girls wear them in public, even to school.

So strange, riding now with Jake after being with Scott a short time ago. A bit confusing too. I started thinking something must be wrong with me for going from kissing one brother to kissing another brother in the same night.

Jake looked good in his dark jeans and blue ribbed sweater.

Inside his car, I told him about Grandma's visit.

"You're lucky to still have a grandparent. None of mine are alive."

"That's too bad. I don't want to think about losing Grandma Nelson. She's so cool." I laughed. "She has a thing for One Direction. Here's she's eighty-five and loves popular music by a boy band."

"If they come to Cincinnati for a concert, you'll have to get her tickets."

"She'd love that."

"Your grandma sounds like she believes in staying young."

"She says I keep her young by telling her about all the exciting stuff that happens to me."

He raised his eyebrows. “Did something exciting happen while I was gone?”

Yeah, I’ve been having fun making out with your brother. But I failed to use his opening to mention Scott. I didn’t want to blurt it out. The timing had to be right. Maybe while we’re curled up on the sofa watching the movie would be the most opportune moment to tell him.

While we were in front of new releases, I saw Bruce eyeballing me. Of course, he didn’t have a customer in line so was free to stare at me. A chubby female employee with red hair stood next to him. I pretended to be looking at the movies, but out of the corner of my eye, I watched them chatting. She was probably asking him if I hadn’t been there an hour ago with a different guy. He might be telling her I was an immoral person doing two men in one night.

She laughed. I bet Bruce said the first guy dumped me because of my flabby butt. I pulled up my pants.

Jake glanced at his watch. “It’s almost time for the pizza to be done. Do you see anything?”

I pointed to one with Chris Pine. “I heard *Jack Ryan: Shadow Recruit* is good.”

He turned away from the screen and raised his eyebrows. “It’s a thriller. I thought you’d want a romantic comedy.”

I shook my head. “I love thrillers and action films.”

When Jake got a call on his cell, he said, “I better take this. It’s George.”

While Jake spoke with George, I felt relief and selected the movie. After the transaction was finished, I took the DVD out of the slot. Whew. I’ll make it out of here without Bruce coming over to us and making a comment in front of Jake.

"Hi, Catherine," Bruce said, suddenly standing next to me. "Back so soon and with another guy. I'll have to say you were dressed better for the first one."

"I was still in my work clothes earlier."

Leaning against the kiosk, he said, "Yeah, I figured that since your skirt was longer. Maybe the next time you get a movie, you can wear your belt skirt."

"Bruce, you better get back to work."

He gave me a broad smile with his dimple appearing. "It's getting a little late to see this movie, but I guess you'll be ready for bed?"

How dare the creep act like I was ready to hop into bed with Jake?

I leaned very close to Bruce. "I think you better watch how personal you're getting with me. One more remark and I'm going to the manager."

He narrowed his eyes but said nothing, then went back to his register.

In the kitchen, Jake poured glasses of wine while I put pizza on plates. I never ate much of the Chinese food Scott had bought so I was hungry. But I only put one piece on my plate because I didn't want to look like a pig in front of Jake. Well, that was only part of it—the Halloween party had something to do with it. I didn't want to be known as the chubby Poison Ivy.

"Hey, take more than one," he said, leaning over and taking another piece out of the box to put on my plate. "You'll have to come over to my condo this weekend and I'll cook you dinner."

I smiled at Jake. "I'd love to. After seeing Dana's condo,

I'm thinking of buying one if I can handle the payments."

"I'm sure condos in Park City are cheaper than Dana's in Hyde Park. Did you find out how she could afford it?"

I stuck the movie in the DVD player before carrying my wine and plate to a glass table. Sitting down next to Jake on my sofa, I told him about Dana being the beneficiary of Max's life insurance policy. I mentioned the old fire chief being surprised about what happened to Max. Then how he died in a car accident just a few months after Max. While movie reviews played, I continued filling him in about murder suspects and mentioned Nolan not wanting to sell the hardware store to Max.

Jake swallowed a mouthful of pizza. "You've covered a lot of ground here."

"Oh yeah, I went to the high school and talked to Ralph, the janitor, Mr. Hudson and Miss Pierce."

"Are you getting closer to finding out what really happened to Max?"

I shook my head. "No. The people I interviewed seem suspicious to me, but it's hard to imagine any of them killing Max. And I can't prove he was murdered. Everything's pure speculation at this point."

"You might never find out."

Something just occurred to me. "I wonder what Max did with the down payment money he saved for the hardware store?"

"Maybe he left it to his sister." Jake stood. "I'll get us some more wine and pizza, and we better start the movie or we won't be able to get up tomorrow to go to work."

"We can play hooky."

"We could."

I glanced at the clock and saw it was eleven o'clock already. "But you're right," I grabbed the remote and pushed play, "we better get the movie started."

Jake wasn't kidding when he said he was starving. He polished off the pizza quickly. He kissed me a few times before pulling me against his body, and he kept his arm around me.

When the movie ended, I said, "What a great movie. I'm glad I picked it."

"Here, I thought you'd want a romantic movie instead where the girl gives a guy a hard time at first, but then he wins her over. So do you want to be swept off your feet?"

I laughed. "Definitely."

He grinned. "I think I might have done that already. You practically fell down the stairs when you saw me."

"You're so conceited. I had flip-flops on and took the stairs a little too fast."

"But why'd you take them like that then? I think it was because you couldn't wait to get your hands on my body."

I gave a dramatic sigh. "That's it. I wanted your body." I paused for a moment. "But I bet I'll be the one doing the sweeping off the feet when you see me in my costume tonight."

"I can't wait."

On Friday evening, I stared at myself in the full-length mirror, dressed in my Poison Ivy costume. I only needed to do one more thing before I went to show Grandma, Mom and Dad my costume. It wasn't complete without the red wig. I walked to the bed where I'd left the wig, remembering the night I bought it. I'd seen Jake in the store buying his pirate costume. He'll make a great pirate. While I adjusted the wig over my head and pushed my own hair out of sight under it, I realized how I'd changed since that night. Originally, I'd told Angie how my outfit just had to be sexy so Jake wouldn't be able to take his eyes off me. Back then, I wanted revenge for him dumping me to go out with his cousin and for not showing up on prom night. I wanted to drive him wild before I agreed to go out with him.

I didn't regret giving in sooner than I'd planned. The few times we'd been together had definitely been fun.

But I did regret one thing—not telling Jake about Scott. Tonight I'd tell Jake as soon as I got to the party. If he asked why I hadn't mentioned it earlier, I'd explain how I would have, but he'd been gone and I didn't feel it was necessary to tell him when he'd called. Really it wasn't a big deal. It wasn't like I'd slept with Scott.

It might be a good thing I'd kept quiet. If I'd told him while he'd been in San Francisco or Missouri, he might've thought I was using Scott to make him jealous. Jake would realize he couldn't take me for granted in the future. It just seemed whenever I was always available for a guy, stopped dating others, and went out of my way to be thoughtful, I wasn't treated as well. The guy started being too comfortable in the relationship, and I was no longer a high priority in his life.

In the beginning, I didn't get serious and that seemed to make the guy more interested in me and even to profess love for me too quickly. I didn't like it when that happened. If I acted like I cared too much, then the guy wasn't as fascinated. Very confusing.

I glanced at my watch and saw I better hurry if I wanted

to stop at Mom and Dad's before picking up Miranda and Kevin.

Fifteen minutes later, I stood in the foyer of my parents' Cape Cod house. I never get claustrophobia here with the cathedral ceiling in the foyer and the huge family room. While Mom held a magazine in her hand, Grandma sipped tea next to her on the sofa. As usual, Dad was in his tan recliner, looking very comfortable watching a rerun of *The Middle*.

I noticed a pile of toys on the floor, but no Connor. He'd been discharged from the hospital on Wednesday, but Angie and Brian didn't want to take him to the party. With the music, costumes and being outside, they decided it'd be a bit much for young Connor. Mom had volunteered to babysit. "Where's Connor?"

"They're running a little late." Mom pushed up the sleeves on her aqua shirt. "I got some of your old toys and Adam's out for Connor to play with."

I leaned over and kissed Grandma on the forehead. She set her cup carefully on the oak end table and grasped my hand. "You're going to be the hit of the party. You're so beautiful."

Mom gave me a look of approval. "Angie and you did an awesome job."

Dad took his gaze off the television to look at my costume. "Do you think those leaves will stay on?"

I pulled on my green cape. "If I lose the leaves, the cape is my backup."

With a puzzled expression, he said, "I don't see how the cape will cover you enough."

"Dad, I was kidding. Don't worry, I won't lose any leaves. And even if they come off, they're attached to a steel-boned corset. I'm sure it won't fall off."

"That's good. So who are you suppose to be?"

Mom rolled her eyes at Dad. "Harrison, she's Poison Ivy." At his blank expression, she said, "You know, from Batman."

When the doorbell rang, I said, "I'll get it."

It was Angie, Brian and Connor. Angie spun around in her red flapper dress, showing it off, and dangled the ends of her black feather boa across her arms. Brian tugged on his black gangster hat, then pulled an authentic-looking reproduction of a tommy gun out of his black pants.

"I know what I want to be next Halloween," I said, eyeing Angie's dress.

"It was an easy dress pattern and I just had to sew rows of fringe and sequin trim on it. With Connor being in the hospital, I forgot to tell you the Park City Playhouse wants me to make costumes for a roaring twenties play. That's where I got the idea for the flapper and gangster costumes."

Brian grinned. "I refused to be Robin Hood or wear any costume with tights."

"Look at you, Connor. You make a great lion," Mom said.

"He wanted to dress up too," Angie said. "If he falls asleep in it, that's fine. You might just want to take the headpiece off when he's sleeping."

"Hey, buddy," Brian said to Connor. "Do your lion roar."

Connor let out a very convincing roar and we all laughed. He waddled over to me and rubbed his hands over my tights where Angie had hot glued a line of leaves on the outside of both legs.

Angie said, "He's so fascinated with the leaves on your costume."

I leaned over and gently removed Connor's small hands from my legs. "Sorry, Connor. I better go. I need to pick up Miranda and Kevin."

"Catie, me go."

I shook my head. "Not this time, but I'll take you soon to the mall to ride on their train." Connor loved the kids' train in the center of our mall.

Angie and Brian decided to stay for a few minutes so we didn't all leave Connor at the same time. Grandma stood and walked with me to the door. "Did you get to tell Jake about dating Scott?"

I shook my head. "His flight was late getting in. We ordered a pizza and Jake wanted to rent a movie. There wasn't a good time to bring it up. I'm going to tell him as soon as I get to the party."

"Good luck with that. You lead an interesting life. And a tiring one. I'm glad I can put my flannel nightgown on and go to bed early."

I laughed. "You won't go to sleep early. I bet you have a romance you're dying to read."

Grandma grinned. "You just know all my secrets. If I finish my novel, I'll give it to you before I go back home. You get going. You have some partying to do."

Chapter Eighteen

Miranda and Kevin were waiting on the porch for me, so I didn't get out of the car. Mrs. Carter waved from the doorway. I thought it was cute when Miranda didn't get in the front seat with me, but got in the back seat with Kevin.

I turned around and smiled at the young couple. "You two look great. I love your costumes." Miranda, dressed in a bodysuit with an attached light green skirt and wings, made an adorable pixie Tinkerbell. Kevin looked good as Peter Pan, wearing a jagged tunic with a rope tie, matching tights, and a hat with a red feather.

"Thank you, but I wanted to be Wendy instead of Tinkerbell. Mom couldn't find a Wendy costume."

I put the car in reverse and backed out of the driveway. "Sorry you couldn't be Wendy. I'm surprised Tinkerbell wasn't your first choice. I do like you as a little fairy."

"But Wendy gets the guy."

I nodded. "You have a point."

Twenty minutes later, we were at the Michaels' house. After I put a small mask on my face, we got out of the Civic. "The band is outside and there's going to be dancing on the patio. If you get too cold outside, you can go in." Fortunately, it'd been a warmer day than yesterday.

"The graveyard is cool," Kevin said.

Miranda and I agreed while we stared at several tombstones in the front yard. A blue flood light illuminated the graveyard. Fog slowly drifted over the ground around the tombstones.

We walked around to the back where a good size crowd was already dancing. An orange flood light shone over a table loaded with food, punch and other drinks. Several strings of decorative lights hung from the tree branches and on the fence surrounding the yard. Skeletons dangled from tree branches, swaying in the wind. When I saw the outdoor patio heaters in different spots, I realized Mr. and Mrs. Michaels and their sons had thought of everything to have a successful party.

While Kevin and Miranda went to dance, I searched the group of costumed people, trying to see Scott or Jake. I picked out a pirate with his back turned talking to Hilary, a Bengal cheerleader, and Keith, a Bengal football player. Both were dressed in the team's orange and black colors. Hilary's auburn hair was pulled back into a ponytail. Before I could go talk to Pirate Jake and tell him about Scott, I saw Batman in full costume moving toward me. It had to be Scott. Although I thought it a shame for him to have half of his handsome face covered with a black mask, there was something so sexy and thrilling about a man disguised as a superhero.

I took a deep breath when he stopped next to me and said, "Well, Poison Ivy, I've been watching for you."

"I'm glad you're Batman. How did you know I'd be Poison Ivy?" I'd never told Scott I was going as Poison Ivy so it was a surprise he knew.

"I have my sources." He groaned. "Seeing you in that costume is making me want to kiss every inch of you. I think we better dance."

"Okay, Batman."

He drew me into his arms and I put my arms around his neck. Thank God, it was a slow dance. I loved being pressed against him, feeling his manly strength.

"Everything looks great," I said, "but I especially like the fog around the graveyard."

"Chad built the fog maker."

"Was he trying to redeem himself after his accident?"

He ignored my comment and squeezed my butt. "Of course, I don't know for sure, but this costume has to be better than your belt skirt."

Now both brothers have squeezed my butt, and I was reminded of Jake. "I'm going to tell Jake tonight about meeting you at McFadden's and going out together."

He stopped dancing. "Who do you think I am?"

I swallowed hard. "You aren't Scott, are you?"

"You've been dating my brother?"

My body stiffened in shock and my heart pounded. I tried to absorb the fact that Batman was Jake and not Scott. "I thought you were the pirate."

"Scott told me to pick up a costume for him. We need to talk." He pulled me a few feet away from the crowd.

My heart raced as he pushed me against a tree. In a gruff voice, he said, "I'm disappointed you would even date Scott."

Was he disappointed because I dated his brother or because he didn't want me to date anyone else? "He approached me at McFadden's on Saturday night when I took Maggie there. When he first kissed me, I didn't know he was your brother."

His jaw tightened. "I bet you were wearing that damn skirt I keep hearing about."

"Yes. But I don't see the big deal. Scott and I only saw each other a couple of times."

"I bet Valerie would think it's a big deal."

"Who's Valerie?"

"Scott's wife."

I grabbed Jake's shoulders. "I didn't know he was married. He didn't wear a ring."

"I can't believe no one told you he was married."

"I hadn't made an announcement I was dating him yet."

"Did you sleep with him?"

"It's none of your business, but no I didn't. I should've Googled him. The one time I don't, look what happens."

Footsteps startled both of us. We turned our heads and saw Scott. I raised my hand to smack Scott for being such a louse and dating me while he was married all the time. I've never dated married men and hated him for lying to me. But Jake punched Scott in the face before I made contact.

Scott's head reeled back and his body smacked against a tree. The skeletons dangled in an angry motion around him. When Scott regained his balance, he said, "So Catherine told you we've met. I should hit you back, but one of us has to be civilized. There's a party going on, remember?"

"You're married, remember," Jake said in a sarcastic tone.

"Not for long. We're separated."

Jake said, "Valerie doesn't want a divorce."

Suddenly it hit me why Kim had given me dirty looks while we were at the pub. And Scott knew why, but since he didn't want to tell me he was married, he couldn't say anything. "That's why your friend Kim gave me nasty looks at McFadden's. She probably thought I was the other woman and blamed me for your broken marriage."

Unfortunately, Hilary and Keith joined us. With hands on her hips, Hilary asked, "Catherine, what did you do to get two brothers fighting?"

Keith grinned. "Yeah, nice punch, Jake."

Great, the drama queen was present. "If you must know, Scott failed to tell me that he's married."

Hilary's eyebrows went up. "Oh, is Jake defending your honor?"

I sighed. "Hilary, why don't you go bob for apples or something?"

"I hope you didn't go all the way with Scott. Adultery would be a problem," Hilary said. "His wife might use that in the divorce settlement."

What a jerk! Sometimes Hilary made me want to strangle her. And this was one of those times.

Jake grabbed my hand. "Excuse us. We need to have a private conversation. Scott, you need to come."

After we left the tree area, Hilary said, "Maybe you can use this experience in one of your magazine articles and tell how to pick up a married man." She snapped her fingers. "I know. Your title can be 'How to Tempt a Married Man'."

I started to turn to go back because I wanted to slap her face. I'd put up with enough of her comments for years, and it was going to stop right now. But Jake must have sensed there could only be trouble if I went back and talked to Hilary because he kept a tight grip on my hand.

When we were a few feet from Hilary and Keith, Jake

said, “We’ll go inside to talk.”

Scott said, “I need something to drink.”

I was in the middle with a brother on each side when Miranda came out of the house. “Hi, I had to go to the bathroom.” She glanced at Jake and then Scott. “None of you looks happy and it’s a party. Catherine, maybe you should just have one boyfriend. I don’t think they like to share you.”

I nodded. “Thanks, Miranda. That’s good advice.”

Once inside, Jake took off his mask and I removed mine too. Scott opened the door of a stainless steel refrigerator and got a beer. He held up his bottle and asked me, “You want a beer or a glass of wine?”

I shook my head.

Scott put his hand on my shoulder. “Catherine, I’m sorry.”

“Let’s go into the study,” Jake said.

As I slowly followed them, I kept thinking how I’d let my guard down by not thoroughly checking Scott out. No, that wasn’t right. I hadn’t done anything. Not even asked him if he was married. I’d assumed because he wasn’t wearing a wedding ring and came from a good family that he wasn’t the type to cheat on a wife.

After I sat in a deep red chair, I glared at Scott. “You asked me to come see you in Florida. When were you planning on telling me you had a wife?”

He cleared his throat. “I was going to tell you as soon as the divorce is final. I know I didn’t behave right, but when I saw you that night at McFadden’s, I couldn’t help myself. You looked sexy in that skirt yet had a young cute look about you.”

My stupid freckles probably made me appear wholesome. “I’m getting rid of that skirt. It never occurred to me you were married. If I'd known it, I wouldn't have gone out with you."

"I don't feel married. Our marriage has been over for a long time and—"

Jake leaned forward in his chair. "Damn it, Scott. Stop making excuses. You're married and you had no business keeping it from Catherine."

Scott ignored Jake and his gaze met mine. "After I'm divorced, the invitation to visit me in Florida is still open."

I shook my head. "I don't think so. I'm Catholic and I'd never consider dating a divorced man."

Scott took a few sips of beer. "All I can say is again how sorry I am for everything." He glanced at Jake. "I'm going back out to the party."

After he left, I clutched my cape and felt awful. "Was he telling the truth about being separated from Valerie?"

Jake nodded. "He moved out of their house, but Valerie wanted to come this week with him to try and fix things between them."

"I wish she'd been here."

"Mom said she called. Scott and Valerie have been married for five years, so it's hard on my parents too. They love Valerie. She's like a daughter to them."

"I hope they can work it out, but Scott was good at acting like a single male." I gave Jake a straight face and asked, "Do you have a wife stashed away?"

"No wife. And Angie would've told you if I did."

"I guess she told you I was going as Poison Ivy."

He nodded. "If Scott wasn't married, would you choose me over him?"

I grinned. "We'll never know."

"I know one thing. I'll never lie to you."

"I'll have to admit, I do prefer Batman over an old pirate any day." I stood. "I better go check on Miranda and Kevin."

"They can wait a minute." He shut the door, then walked to me and tilted my chin. "Do you really think I can just let you leave here without kissing you?"

I looked up into his very sensual eyes. "I probably shouldn't tell you this, but the day you slammed me against the wall and kissed me was a big turn-on."

He chuckled. "You got to me in your short skirts. I couldn't resist you any longer. Just like now."

Jake drew my body against his and kissed me. Then his lips left mine and he planted tiny kisses all over my neck. "Did Scott ever kiss your neck?"

I murmured, "No."

Gently, he lifted the cups of my bodysuit away from my breasts. His warm lips caressed each breast. I didn't stop him. I couldn't. I tingled all over from his touch.

He paused for a moment, staring at my face. "What about here? Did he kiss your beautiful breasts?"

I pushed him away and covered myself up. "I'll tell you what happened exactly so we can put this whole situation behind us. Scott started talking to me when Maggie and I were at McFadden's."

"Out of all the people there, he happens to talk to you."

"I suppose he went there to meet someone while he was in town, and what can I say, I looked good. And I was attracted to him. The Michaels brothers are hotties."

"Oh, great. Now I have to worry about you and Chad."

"You don't have to worry. Chad's just a kid." I sighed. "Oh yeah, when Scott got back from Cleveland last night, we were going to watch a movie when Chad called from jail."

Understanding crossed Jake's face. "That's why you said what you did about Chad trying to get in good by building the fog maker."

I put my hand on the doorknob. "I'm going to wrap this up so I can get something to eat. When I learned that Scott was your brother, I told him how I planned on dating you. And if you hadn't been away, I'd have told you right away about Scott. We went out on Monday night to dinner and a movie. And we kissed on the Purple People Bridge. And no boob kisses. Just lips."

"I'm glad I wasn't gone any longer."

I turned the knob at his annoying questions. Jake had no business asking where his brother kissed me. "And you should put your mask back on. You look stupid as Batman without your mask."

On Saturday morning at eight-thirty, I was curled up in a blue flowered chair Grandma Nelson had given me. Since I'd woken up early and couldn't go back to sleep, I'd taken a shower. After I dressed in jeans and a pink blouse with white polka dots, I opened my laptop to work on the article about the most creative ways for women to meet men. The editor had accepted the proposal on the basis of my query letter.

Not much happened at the party after the crisis of learning Scott was married. I danced a few times with Jake, talked to Brian and Angie a little, ate and was relieved I could use taking Miranda and Kevin home as an excuse to leave early.

It was just too much for me to absorb how Scott had been dishonest and cheated on his wife. I know people do it a lot of the time, but not to me. I believe no messing around while you're married or separated. And I was extremely hurt he'd never mentioned his marriage. I regretted I hadn't told Jake about meeting Scott when he'd called me from Kansas City. At least that way I'd only have kissed Scott the first night at McFadden's and that would have been it.

My cell phone rang.

"Good morning. I hope I didn't wake you."

I closed my eyes at the sound of Jake's voice. His voice wasn't angry but normal. I needed that. "I was up. I'm surprised you're calling so early."

"I figured if you were asleep, you wouldn't answer it. How are you?"

"I'm okay. I've been working on an article. How did the cleanup go after the party?"

"Not bad. Some of Chad's college friends pitched in and helped. Are you hungry? I'd like to take you to breakfast at IHOP."

"Thanks, but I just need some alone time." I could just see Hilary being there with IHOP just opening recently. I didn't feel like hearing another comment from her about me dating a married man. "I wouldn't be good company this morning."

"Angie, Brian and your favorite godchild are going too."

I was hungry and IHOP has terrific food. Oh, forget Hilary. She probably wouldn't be up yet and if she was at IHOP, I'd pour coffee on her. I laughed. "Why didn't you say that in the first place? I'll go since Connor's going."

"I should be hurt that you prefer Connor over me, but he is cute."

At nine o'clock, Jake and I were in a booth with Angie

and Brian across from us. Connor sat in a high chair and gave me a sad face and said, “Leaves gone.”

Everyone laughed and Jake said, “I’m with you, Connor. I miss the Poison Ivy costume.”

I smiled at Connor. “I’m glad you’re feeling better.” I looked at Angie. “When does he have to go back to see the doctor?”

“We have an appointment on Wednesday.”

The waitress came. Angie and I ordered a combination plate with scrambled eggs, bacon, hash browns and stuffed French toast. Brian and Jake each ordered a ham and three cheese omelette served with three pancakes. Connor wanted juice and pancakes. After the waitress poured coffee for us and brought Connor his juice, Angie asked, “I’m glad you came. This is fun, all of us eating breakfast together.”

Jake grinned. “I had to use Connor to get her to come.”

“I was happy to hear from Jake this morning, but I didn’t know whether I felt like going out to breakfast,” I said.

Angie gave me a puzzled look. “What’s wrong?”

I glanced at Jake. “I woke up early this morning after I had a dream of Hilary chasing and yelling at me for breaking up Scott’s marriage. And look at this place, half the residents in Park City are here. I didn’t want to see Hilary or anyone this morning to remind me some more of what an idiot I was.”

“You didn’t know the creep was married and,” Angie stopped, giving an apologetic glance at Jake, “sorry, Jake. I didn’t know Scott was married. Catherine, how would you know? We were never in school with him since he’s so much older than us. I just knew Jake had an older brother.”

“That makes me feel a little better. I kept thinking I

should've mentioned him to you when Connor was in the hospital."

Brian grinned at Jake. "So how did it feel to have competition from Scott for Catherine?"

I said quickly, "I doubt I would have seen Scott again anyhow. I don't think we had much in common. I was mainly attracted to him because he looks so much like Henry Cavill."

"Oh, so it was a celebrity look-alike thing," Jake said.

Angie put down her coffee cup. "He is dreamy. I can see why you went out with him."

Jake squeezed my knee. "Apparently, I'm dreamy too. She thought I was Scott in my Batman costume."

"With that mask," I said, "you looked just like Scott."

Brian chuckled. "I heard Cavill's going to be Batman in a movie."

"I told Jake how you like Batman movies," Angie said.

I raised my eyebrows at Angie. "And that I was going to be Poison Ivy."

"Hey, that's what friends are for."

When Connor banged his highchair tray with a spoon, I said, "And just look at your cute son. He's going to be a heartthrob someday."

Angie groaned. "Don't say that."

The waitress served our food. Angie cut up the pancakes in small pieces for Connor, and Brian gave him one of his sausage links. I saw Jake eyeing my toast, so I asked him, "Would you like to try a bite?"

He nodded.

I jabbed a piece of toast and raised my fork to Jake's mouth and smiled at him as he enjoyed the sweet food. I took the next bite of the stuffed toast. After I swallowed it, I said, "I love the cream cheese filling. It's delicious."

Jake said, "I should have gotten what you did."

The waitress came back and refilled our coffee cups. Looking at me, she said, "There's a gentleman wanting to talk to you when you're done eating."

"Where is he?" I asked. I followed her hand pointing to a table a few feet from our booth. When I saw it was Ralph, I waved to him. "That's Ralph Tindall, the janitor from Park City High School."

"I wonder if he has something to tell you about Max's death," said Jake.

I shrugged. "He's pretty interested in getting his name in the paper, so he might just want to ask when I'm going to finish the article about school safety."

When I finished everything except one remaining toast, I scooted out of the booth. "Jake, you can have the last stuffed toast. I'm going to talk to Ralph."

Ralph introduced his wife Martha to me. She smiled. "It's so nice to meet you."

"It's nice to meet you, too. Ralph has been helpful telling me about boiler safety and other things."

"I'm glad you're here this morning," Ralph said. "You saved us a trip. We were going to call and see if we could come to your apartment after we ate."

His wife opened her purse and handed me a paper. "I found this yesterday."

"Remember that old brown couch of Max's?" Ralph asked.

I nodded, opening the folded paper.

"Well, Martha stopped in to see me. After I talked to her about the possible murder, she suggested looking for clues."

"I stuck my hand pretty deep in the couch, and this paper was in there," Martha said.

I read out loud, "You can't have Max. He's mine. You have a husband. If you don't start acting like a wife, then I'll have to tell everyone what kind of a person you really are."

Obviously, it was meant for Karen Connelly, but I didn't want to tell Ralph and Martha that. Someone had cut out letters for the words and pasted them on the paper. And I wondered if the threat was from Miss Pierce. It seemed like a logical conclusion, but maybe there was someone else in love with Max. Maybe one of the cooks or a school volunteer.

"It sounds like Max had a couple of girlfriends," Ralph said.

"Ralph, thank you for showing this to me. I'd like to keep it and see what I can find out."

And I knew exactly the first person I would visit.

Chapter Nineteen

From my seat in Jake's Mustang, I leaned over and kissed him on the cheek. "Thank you, for taking me to breakfast. And I have to tell you, I'm pleased with what Ralph's wife found."

"So are you going to talk to Mrs. Connelly?"

I nodded, fingering my scarf. "I'm going to call Tracy and tell her about the note and talk to Mrs. Connelly. She must have given the note to Max. She never mentioned it to me."

Jake put his key in the ignition and started the car. "Maybe it was from Miss Kent, and that's why she didn't say anything to you."

"I don't think it's another note from Miss Kent, but I'll definitely ask Karen and Miss Kent. Maybe it's from Miss Pierce, but then I can't see her cutting out letters and pasting them on a paper. I'll see her at school on Monday. Do you suppose one of the cooks was in love with Max?"

He pulled out of IHOP's parking lot. "That's possible."

"I'll have to find out if any cook hung around Max a lot." I bit on my lower lip. "But I doubt if a cafeteria worker would know how to mess with a gas valve to cause an explosion."

"Maybe she got someone else to do it."

"And why kill Max? Why not kill Karen Connelly

instead?"

"Maybe he wasn't supposed to die. You said earlier Mrs. Connelly sorted the orders in the basement for the class fundraisers, and it could have blown before she was around."

My mind raced as Jake drove. "Maybe the note has nothing to do with Max's death. The person just threatened to tell the media. Not to kill anyone."

"I think I'll stick to being a sports editor. It's easier." He took his gaze off the street for a second, glancing at me. "How about I cook you dinner tonight?"

"I do like to eat."

"I'm working the rest of the morning and this afternoon." He grinned. "Well, if you can call it work writing about sports and watching college football." He braked the car when the traffic light turned yellow and gave me a questioning look. "How about if you come over at seven?"

"Perfect. That'll give me time to call Tracy, see my grandma and finish an article." And take a long soak in a bubble bath for our date and add shaving my legs to my list of stuff to do. I was glad Jake invited me for dinner this evening. I had always loved Saturday night dates. Plus a breakfast date already. Who needed old, married Scott anyhow—I could live without that kind of problem.

"What article is that?"

"A magazine editor accepted my pitch about writing how women meet guys. Did you ever hear of 8 Minute Dating where you pay a small fee and get to meet young professionals at some place like a restaurant?"

He shook his head. "Single men, I hope."

"Yes, single or divorced."

He put his foot on the accelerator when the light

changed. “Did you participate in this dating thing?”

“No, I just observed.”

“I feel like a boring writer. I just cover sports and you write about so many different things.”

“Yeah, you’re a little boring.” I stared at his brown eyes. His lashes aren’t as thick as Scott’s but almost. “You just covered the World Series and you’ll go to the Super Bowl while I stick it out in Park City, trying to find something a little interesting to write about.”

“I don’t know. Excitement seems to follow you. Recently you’ve interrupted a drug deal, caused a married man to fall for you, now don’t get mad,” Jake turned and rolled his eyes at me, “I’m not mentioning his name, and...”

“And the best is yet to come, going to a big sports editor’s condo on a Saturday night. I can bring something, a vegetable dish, dessert, or whatever you like.”

“If it’s not too much trouble, I love your mom’s cheesecake. I’ve had it a couple of times at the coffeehouse and it’s the best. I’ll give you some money for it.”

“No, you don’t need to pay for it. She’ll be thrilled I’m seeing you. In fact, she’ll probably even throw in a coffeecake.”

“I’m glad she approves of me. What did she think about Scott? I guess she didn’t know he was married.”

I frowned, irritated. “I didn’t mention Scott to her. I know I talk a lot, but I don’t blab everything about my dates to my mom. And Scott and I only went on one official date.”

He winced. “Sorry, it slipped out about you and Scott. I guess I have a little sibling jealously.”

I was quiet for a moment. “I never thought of something until now.”

"What's that?"

"Scott and I are both the firstborn in our families. It never would have lasted. We'd have been at each other's throats. But dating a middle child might work," I teased.

"Whew. That's a relief."

"So what are we eating tonight besides cheesecake?"

"What do you like the best? Chicken, beef, fish?"

"I like everything except Chinese food."

After Jake dropped me off at my apartment, I called Tracy. She answered on the first ring.

"Hi, Tracy."

"I'm glad you called," Tracy said in a rush. "I want you to see my engagement ring. I just keep staring at it."

"Congratulations. I knew Adam talked to your parents, but I wasn't sure if he'd popped the question to you yet. I'm happy you'll be my sister-in-law."

"It'll be cool to be part of your family."

"I want to see your ring soon." I opened up the note and laid it on the table. "I have something I want to read to you. It's a note the janitor's wife found in Max's old couch. Is your mom around?"

"Wait, I'll get her and I'll put you on speakerphone."

While Tracy was gone, I thought how nice it'd be to throw an engagement party. Although traditionally the bride's parents might host an engagement party, I could have a fun, spontaneous one. In their position, I was sure Mr. and Mrs. Connelly would do something more formal.

Tracy interrupted my party thoughts. "I'm back and Mom's here to listen to the note."

"Hi, Mrs. Connelly."

"Hi, Catherine. You can call me Karen," she said warmly.

"Thanks, I like that. Just this morning Ralph showed me a note his wife found in Max's couch. Ralph's the janitor at school. I'm hoping you know something about it to help me in my investigation. I'll go ahead and read it to you." I smoothed the paper and read, "You can't have Max. He's mine. You have a husband. If you don't start acting like a wife, then I'll have to tell everyone what kind of a person you really are."

Karen said, "You must think me a real dunce. I guess with the campaign, and Tracy learning Max was her father, and everything, I forgot about the note. After I got it, I gave it to Max."

"That's okay. You remember it now. Did you or Max know who sent it?"

"No, we didn't know." Karen paused, then said in a funny voice, "This is going to sound weird, but I thought of Dale at the time."

"Mom, why would you ever think that it was from Mr. Jansen? Is he gay?"

"I don't think so, but I thought he probably wanted us to think a woman sent it and never wanted us to suspect he sent it. He acted jealous whenever Max canceled on him to see me. See, Dale and Max watched sports together, played on the same basketball team, and Max seemed to fill a void in Dale's life. He didn't have many friends and his parents died a long time ago."

"I guess we can't rule him out," I said, "except he pushed for more investigation of Max's death. He acted pretty upset when more wasn't done."

"Oh, I don't think he killed Max." Karen cleared her throat. "I'm wondering if Dale thought Pat had something to do with it."

I considered asking her if she thought Pat had anything to do with the accident, but realized I already knew the answer. Karen wouldn't still be his wife if she felt he had anything to do with Max's death. "Oh yeah, how was the note delivered and when?"

"It was in my school mailbox right before Christmas break," Karen said. "I did so much volunteer work at the high school that Miss Kent gave me my own box."

"Mom, do you think Miss Kent gave you a second note?"

"No."

I asked, "Is there anyone else you remember that you or Max might have suspected?"

"I mentioned Miss Pierce to him. Max said she was a lonely woman and had acted like she had a crush on him, but he didn't think she'd carry it that far."

On Monday morning, I was definitely going to the high school to see Miss Pierce and Mr. Jansen. It'll be interesting to see their reactions when I told them about the newly found note.

As I soaked in a peach-scented bubble bath for my date night, I thought how one positive thing came out of Scott being married. It definitely was a deciding factor in breaking up with him. Well, maybe there hadn't been anything to break up—we knew each other briefly, but it did make it easier to stop seeing him.

I had to face the facts. Even though I enjoyed my time with Scott, I saw him mainly because of how he looked. He was a major hottie, looking like movie star, Henry Cavill. Our relationship would've fizzled out eventually. There just wasn't any chemistry like I had with Jake. It'd always been there.

Sparks flew between us. His kisses made me want more of him. That's why he'd hurt me so much when he went away to college—he forgot about me. But I hadn't been very gracious when he'd apologized to me about missing the prom, and the broken dinner date had angered me.

I climbed out of the tub, grabbing a big lavender towel. While drying off, I realized I better be up front with Jake and tell him something I'd decided on a long time ago. It was something he needed to know before our relationship developed any further. I hoped he would be okay with it and understand.

With the towel wrapped around my body, I stood in front of my closet, trying to figure out what to wear. I decided to wear jeans, but would wear my black heels with them. I wanted to be casual but yet a bit dressy. I also put an aqua silky tee and a gray single-button jacket on the bed. While I was putting on my underwear, Jake called and asked, "Do you want me to pick you up tonight?"

I had my cell phone lodged between my ear and shoulder and I answered, "Thanks, but I'll just drive."

"I don't know. Do you think it's safe? Stuff seems to happen to you."

Was he really concerned or just being funny? "I'll risk it."

"You can come before seven."

I laughed. "Is that so I'll cook our dinner?"

"Of course not. I like company while I cook."

Glancing at my clock radio, I saw it was five. I still needed to stop and pick up the cheesecake. If Mom didn't chat too long, I could get there early. "I'm not ready yet, but getting there. I'll be there around six-thirty."

"Wow, you look fantastic," Jake said to me as I walked into his condo, carrying my mom's cheesecake. He kissed me before taking the box out of my hands. "And you smell as good as you look."

"Thanks." He wore jeans and a dark green knit shirt with long sleeves. I squeezed his shoulder. "You look pretty good yourself."

"It's almost ready. Did you get your story done?"

I nodded. "I did and I emailed it to the editor."

While he went to put the cheesecake in the refrigerator, I smelled bacon and saw a dirty frying pan on the stovetop. I grabbed the skillet. "I'll wash this for you."

"Watch out. It's still hot. I just used it to cook the chicken breasts."

I wrinkled my nose. "I smell bacon."

He nodded. "I cooked bacon and poured the grease out of the skillet, but didn't wash it. I put olive oil in the same pan and cooked the breasts. Then the chicken goes in a baking dish. Oh yeah, I fried the onion and garlic in the skillet, too, and mixed it with the crumbled up bacon and all of that is dumped over the chicken. And I sprinkled the whole mess with cheese."

"I'm impressed. I thought you'd throw steaks on a grill for us." While I ran hot water in the sink and squirted some detergent in it, I saw the table was already set with vibrant blue dishes, matching salt and pepper shakers and wine glasses. I wondered if he cooked often for women. He seemed pretty adept and relaxed about entertaining me.

"You don't need to wash the pan now. It can soak." He lit two white candles on the table. "Would you like wine?"

"Yes, I'd love to have some."

"White or red?" he asked.

"White, please."

The timer went off and Jake opened the oven door. "The cheese is melted." He removed the pan and set it on a potholder in the middle of the small table. "I heard you like potatoes, so I hope you like how I fixed them."

I laughed, wondering what else Angie had told Jake I like. "I'm surprised you haven't been snatched up by a woman yet."

"Me too." He put a dish of asparagus next to the chicken. He slid the small, nicely browned potatoes in a bowl and after I took a seat, he poured my wine.

"How about a toast?" I said as he sat down. "My family's big on toasts."

He nodded.

I held the glass up and said, "To a wonderful cook and a lovely evening."

Jake clinked his glass to mine and smiled. "I hope you still think I'm a good cook after you eat."

"I like your dishes," I said as I stabbed a potato.

"When Mom got new plates, she gave me her old ones."

A comfortable silence existed between us while we ate. After a few minutes, I said, "The seasoning's good on the potatoes. Everything's delicious. If you ever decide to quit writing for the sports section, you can get a job cooking."

Jake grinned. "I guess we both have backup jobs then. Remember how I teased you about bagging at the Halloween store and said you could do that in your spare time?"

"Oh yeah, when I bagged stuff for Maggie after upsetting her about Halloween."

"I couldn't believe that. She really lost it for a few

minutes. Is Maggie worried about vandalism this Halloween?"

"A policeman's going to drive by her house several times on Halloween night, and she's going to give out lots of candy plus she used her employee discount and decorated her porch for Halloween." I didn't add that it was all my idea, to discourage kids from being mean to Maggie again.

"That's good. So after we eat, would you like to go to a movie?"

I took a sip of wine. "Maybe. Sometime I'd like to walk around your neighborhood. Aren't you close to Hennessey's Bar?"

"I've walked there before, but I'm surprised you mentioned it."

I raised my brows. "Why's that? I went there with Angie and Brian and liked it."

"Angie and Brian told me how you like dancing on the bar counter. I heard they frown on girls dancing on their counter. We could walk there and ask if they'd allow you to, since you're an experienced bar counter dancer."

I sighed. "I'm never going to live that down. I had too much to drink on a couple of occasions. And I wasn't the only one dancing on the counter. Hilary went first and I followed."

We finished eating and decided to wait on the cheesecake and go for a walk. We held hands and hadn't gone far when I noticed a basketball court. "We have to play sometime. Maybe we can get Brian and Angie to play with us."

"That's right," Jake said. "I remember you played basketball in high school."

"I love basketball," I said. "I'm hoping the weather will

be nice enough for us to play on Thanksgiving day. We try to do something physical so we burn some calories. Even Mom and Dad play."

While we stood in front of the court, Jake covered my mouth with his before I could tell him more about our holiday celebrations. When he deepened the kiss, I wound my arms around his neck.

We stopped kissing and I said, "I'm glad the World Series is over."

He chuckled. "Okay, I kiss you and the World Series pops out of your mouth. I better work on my technique."

I ran my finger lightly over his lips. "I have a rating system with ten being the highest. Your kissing is a number nine."

"I'm disappointed you don't think it's a ten."

"Few are perfect, but I'm sure with practice, you'll be a ten soon." I grinned. "Hey, Scott was a seven."

"I'm not surprised." He pushed a lock of my hair away from my face. "Do you want to get a drink at Hennessey's?"

We were only a block from the bar but I shook my head. "Not really. We can go to a movie if you like."

"I'd like that."

We went back to his condo. Before sitting down, he grabbed his smartphone off the coffee table. "You can pick the movie since I did last night."

I sat next to Jake on the brown leather sofa. I noticed his great room was tastefully done in a mixture of browns, dark green, and blue. "You did a good job decorating."

"I can't take credit for it. Mom's an interior decorator and she helped me a lot." He got the movies up on the phone's screen. "Here are the times of the movies."

I peered over his shoulder, skimming the movie titles. "There are three good movies on at nine-thirty. Or at least, I heard good reviews about them."

He looked at me. "Nine-thirty sounds good. We can eat cheesecake before we leave."

I grinned. "I wondered when you were going to mention eating the cheesecake."

While Jake made coffee, I cut our pieces and slid them on plates. After the coffee was done, we carried everything to the great room and put the cups on the coffee table. I noticed Jake had put photos under the glass and leaned closer to see if he had any of Brian and Angie. He did, but it wasn't just our friends in the picture. Jake had his arm around a pretty blonde.

"Who's the girl?"

"Kelly. We dated for three years in college and I planned on marrying her."

Since he just said I instead of we, I wondered if she was the one to break it off. "What happened?"

"We were engaged for a few months when she met someone else." He frowned. "And it was over, just like that."

"I'm sorry. I didn't know." Hopefully, he still didn't have feelings for Kelly. I wondered if Kelly married the guy she met while engaged to Jake.

"Angie probably didn't mention Kelly because she only saw her once. I didn't tell Brian a whole lot about the breakup. I was pretty depressed, but he and Angie were happy and busy with their lives, so I just kept quiet about it."

Was this the time to tell Jake my personal philosophy about sex? Probably shouldn't put it off and get it out in the open. I put my fork down and took a deep breath. With dating a lot and being twenty-five, I've had a lot of practice with the sex topic. Even so, my pulse raced. Maybe because I cared what Jake thought of me.

I looked him straight in the eye. "I need to talk to you about something."

With concern on his face, he said, "Geez, this sounds serious."

"It depends on how you look at it. A few years ago, I decided to remain a virgin until marriage."

"You know, Steel, you have guts. I bet it wasn't the easiest thing to tell me you're a virgin. And it takes a lot of backbone to decide on a certain moral principle and stick to it."

Relief slowed my heartbeat. "So you're okay with this?"

"Hell, no." He ran his fingers through his black hair. "I mean, yes, of course. Everything's cool." He muttered, "I'll just take a lot of cold showers."

After my virgin announcement, I was delighted to hear from Jake on Sunday while he was tailgating at Paul Brown's stadium before the Bengals game. He said, "I'm sorry I don't have an extra ticket for you. I should have a ticket for you next month for one of the games."

"That's okay. I want to see Grandma before Mom drives her home, and I'll watch some of the game with Dad."

"After I get my article done for the paper, would you like to do something tonight?"

"Sorry, I can't. I invited Angie and Maggie over to watch *Downtown Abbey*."

Jake groaned. "Yipee. A girls' night."

He sounded disappointed. I wanted to see him, too, but

couldn't cancel. "I'm surprised you aren't tired of me by now. We've seen each other a lot the last couple of days."

"If the girls don't hang around after *Downtown Abbey*, how about I come then to see you?"

I laughed. "I don't know. I guess I can boot them out of the door right after it's over."

At eleven-fifteen p.m. the girls left and Jake came. I poured glasses of white wine for both of us and had cheese, crackers and pepperoni slices on a glass plate. It was from a set of party dishes I used at a bridal shower for Angie. I remembered then that Jake hadn't brought a date to the wedding reception. At the time, I was dating a philosophy instructor from UC.

I put a piece of cheese and a pepperoni on a whole wheat cracker and fed it to Jake. "You didn't bring a date to Brian and Angie's wedding. Were you serious about anyone after Kelly?"

He shook his head. "Not really. I've been a free spirit until you. If you hadn't been with that geeky guy, I'd have talked to you more at the reception."

"He wasn't geeky. I missed you at the rehearsal, but we all understood why."

"It sure worked out Brian's best man was his brother instead of me since my grandpa died the day of the rehearsal. To be honest, I don't remember much of their wedding or reception."

"You didn't stay long at the reception."

He grinned. "So you noticed I left while you were with the geek."

I set down my glass of wine. "Enough talk." I covered his mouth with mine.

His kissing became so intense that my lips felt bruised. Finally, I buried my face against his shoulder.

Jake asked, “So am I a ten now?”

“You’re more than a ten.”

Chapter Twenty

Miss Pierce did not look happy to see me. As soon as the last student left her classroom, I walked in. I'd seen Mr. Hudson in the hallway and he hadn't been happy to see me either. He asked, "When's this article going to be in the paper?"

I answered, "Soon."

"Catherine, I don't have very much time, so what do you want?" Miss Pierce tossed me an impatient scowl from behind her desk.

"It won't take long. I just need your help in figuring out a note found in Max's couch." I pulled the paper out of my bag. After I put it on the desk, I watched to see her reaction.

Her face showed nothing. She lifted her eyes to mine after reading the note. "I can't help you. I never saw this before."

"Someone gave it to Mrs. Connelly and she gave it to Max."

"Did she accuse me? I know she was jealous that Max brought me coffee. He stopped because of her."

I shook my head quickly. "No, she didn't accuse you. Just one more question. Do you think someone wanted Max dead?"

"But Max wasn't killed. It was an accident."

I shrugged. "I'm not so sure. I think there's a good possibility someone tampered with the gas valve."

"I disagree. Everyone loved Max."

I wanted to say someone loved Max too much and couldn't bear the thought of not having him, but knew that would definitely be going too far. "You're probably right, Miss Pierce."

Miss Pierce straightened the papers on her desk and folded her hands. "I can tell you aren't convinced. But the note doesn't prove he was murdered. It was obviously meant to scare Mrs. Connelly so she'd stop her affair with Max. There's no story here."

"That's a shame. I was hoping for a good scoop and to right a possible wrong."

She removed her reading glasses and stood. "I need to make copies of an exam. I'm sure it would be a glamorous story for you if Max had been killed because he was in love with the mayor's wife, but boiler room fires happen frequently and they're accidents. Sorry you'll have to look elsewhere for a scoop."

On my way out, I glanced at Mr. Jansen's classroom. He stood reading something out of a textbook to his students. I didn't want to disturb him.

Before I left the school, I went back to the main office and Miss Kent was now available. I told her about Ralph's find. She motioned for me to follow her into the principal's empty office. She glanced at the paper and a flicker of remorse crossed her face. "Poor Karen. She tried so hard to keep her affair a secret."

"Since it was in her school mailbox, do you think it could

have been a school employee?"

"I always suspected Miss Pierce."

"Max told Karen he didn't think it was Miss Pierce."

"What do men know? He wouldn't blame her. He liked Miss Pierce because her classroom was always so orderly and clean."

I nodded. "He probably appreciated her saving him time in cleaning. Wasn't Max quite a bit younger than Miss Pierce?"

"Ten years difference and that might have been a little bit of the attraction." She paused for a moment, then continued, "but I think the main thing was Max could melt the hardest heart."

But not yours. Not in the beginning anyhow. While I was in high school, she'd complained about my class dedicating the yearbook to Max. "Did he melt your heart, Miss Kent?"

She frowned. "Not at first. I thought he was a devious man and using Karen to get money. But I was wrong. He truly loved Karen and wanted to have a life with her and Tracy."

Miss Kent seemed fond of Karen. Strange, since she'd originally blackmailed Karen for money. "I know Karen gave you money. Did you two become friends?"

She lifted her chin. "She loaned it to me. I paid her back, but yes, I think a lot of her. She's a good person. She never told me Max was Tracy's father, but just that she needed my help in keeping her affair a secret. She told me in confidence about the mayor's affair, but I'm sure you already know about that."

Had Karen been totally into Max just to make her husband jealous and to get back at him for his affair with Dana? Maybe she had changed her mind about marrying

Max.

The school phone rang so Miss Kent answered it. I waved to her as she started writing down a message for Mr. Hudson. I left Park City High School. While driving to Mom's coffeehouse, I thought hard about everything I'd learned about Max and Karen's affair, Pat Connelly, Miss Pierce and others involved in Max's life.

I was missing something. My gut told me it hadn't been an accident in the boiler room. Max was killed. Before he died, there'd been too many disturbing occurrences. Mentally I listed them.

—Karen and Max were going to start a new life together and tell Tracy the truth. I'm still going to assume she really wanted to marry Max and hadn't changed her mind.

—Max planned on buying the Nolan's Hardware Store and quitting as janitor.

—Mr. Jenkins, the fire chief, was killed in a hit and run accident.

—Dana was the beneficiary of a big life insurance policy when Max died.

—Miss Pierce wanted Max and was jealous of Karen.

—Mr. Hudson had words with Max before he died.

—Teenage boys mad at Max for telling on them to the police.

When I entered the coffeehouse, I looked for Mom. She stood by the cash register, ringing up a customer's to-go order. "I hope you enjoy your lunch and come back to see us," she said.

I went and got myself a latte while she finished ringing up customers.

After a few minutes, she joined me. "You don't look happy. What's wrong, honey?"

I told her first about my visit to the school. Then I said, "I've been going over everything in my mind, and I still feel Max was killed. But I can't figure out who wanted him dead the most."

"Who had the most to lose if he lived?"

I sighed. "I keep asking myself that question. Pat Connelly, probably. He'd have lost Karen if Max had lived. But I just don't feel he could've done it. He wouldn't kill Tracy's real father, and I can't imagine him doing it since he's a man who cares enough to raise money for cerebral palsy."

Mom touched the green gemstone in her necklace and was quiet for a moment. "The person had to know a lot about boiler room equipment."

"As an administrator, Mr. Hudson learned a lot about maintenance. He said how he wanted everything to be safe."

"Personally I never liked Mr. Hudson, but I doubt he'd tampered with anything."

I sipped my latte. "Tracy's depending on me to find out the truth about Max."

"You just started investigating." Mom put an arm around my shoulders and grinned. "You've always had patience in short supply. Just give it time."

"Thanks, Mom." I checked my watch. "I better get to work. Do you want my help tonight passing out treats?"

She nodded. "And what you have on is perfect for Halloween. I like the pumpkin-colored blouse with your black jacket and skirt."

"I took your advice about the designer suit sale at Dillard's." With the top, I wore a three button jacket and a

"Shelly" skirt. At the last minute, I'd decided to wear boots.

Back at the office, I stared at my consumer report about digital cameras. With Christmas less than two months away, I knew readers might be interested in purchasing a new camera. They would need information about the different features on the cameras with so many on the market.

"I guess writing about cameras is serious stuff."

I looked away from my monitor and saw Jake. "Oh, sorry, I didn't notice you. Have you been standing there long?"

He shook his head. "Did you get to talk to Miss Pierce?"

I moved my swivel chair around. "I did. She didn't show any reaction to the note, but Miss Kent thinks it was Miss Pierce."

"It seems like she's been teaching forever. I wonder when she's going to retire."

"I'm surprised she's taught this long. The kids always made fun of her."

"Would you like come over and watch Monday Night Football with me?"

"I'm going to pass out treats for Mom tonight, but it's only from six to eight."

"At home or the coffeehouse?"

"Coffeehouse." I laughed. "Why, are you going to dress up and go out?"

He smiled. "Only if you do in that sexy Poison Ivy costume."

I ignored his comment and said, "If I'm not too tired, I'll be over to watch a little football. I'll call either way to let you know."

On Monday evening, I enjoyed seeing all the cute costumes. Mom always had good treats and this year was no different. I passed out at least a couple hundred pieces of Reese cups, Snicker bars and other chocolate candy. At eight o'clock, my legs ached from standing so long.

"Mom, I'm leaving after I call Jake."

"Okay. Drive carefully and thanks for taking care of the treats."

My purse was stashed behind the check-out counter. As I walked around to the back of the register, I bent to pull my cell phone out of the bag. I sighed, feeling a little depressed and realizing it was that time of the month. And I get such bad cramps while on my period.

"Hey," I said to Jake after he answered. "I'm done treating all the children of Park City."

"Oh no, you probably don't have any candy left for me."

"How about a kiss instead?"

"I was hoping for more than one."

"You got it." I hesitated, wondering if he was serious about me watching football with him. "Are you sure you want me to come over? Wouldn't you rather watch it with Brian or some guys at a sports bar?"

"No. I need to concentrate and write about the game. And you might distract me some, but at the same time, you'll be an asset."

I laughed. "So you want another reporter on hand. I'm on my way." I'd considered going to my apartment to change into jeans, but decided just to drive to Jake's.

Before I left, Miranda and Kevin came in dressed in their Halloween costumes. With a straight face I said, "You two are late. We're out of candy."

"That's okay," Miranda said. "I want to show your mom our costumes."

"She has candy left. I was just teasing." I opened the door. "I'm leaving to go to Jake's. Enjoy the rest of Halloween night."

When I'd arrived, the closest spaces were full, so I parked at the far end of the lot. An uneasy feeling swept my body as I pulled my set of keys out of my purse. I walked quickly to my car and pushed the button to automatically unlock it. Before I could get in, someone whacked me on the head with a heavy object. Pain shot through my skull. I stumbled against the car. I regained my footing and screamed, hoping to scare the mugger away. I threw back my fist to punch him in the gut. Thoughts of being raped or murdered crossed my mind. Before I could turn around to fight off my attacker, he hit me again.

I must've blacked out. I woke up in a trunk of a moving car. How long had I been unconscious? I pushed the little side button on my watch to light it. It was nine o'clock. I'd been out for approximately thirty minutes. My assailant must have been desperate to take a chance of abducting me right in my mother's parking lot. I tried to open the trunk, but there wasn't any release latch inside. I'd have to be stuffed in an old vehicle. Did the kidnapper plan on raping me? I'd fight and kick him in the balls before he'd dare touch me. What if he killed me? I didn't want to die. Tears ran down my face. What if I never saw my parents and Adam again? Or Jake? Angie, Brian and Connor? Or Grandma Nelson? At her age, my death would break her heart.

If only I'd seen my attacker and knew what he planned

on doing with me. My pulse pounded in my ears. My lungs ached for fresh air. Every bump in the road jolted through my tense muscles. But I knew I had to fight every second to keep calm. I couldn't lose it and had to be ready for whatever was going to happen when the trunk opened.

I needed to make it known I was a prisoner. Kicking out the tail lights and sticking my arm out one of the holes and waving should alert someone. My boot smacked against something hard, so I explored with my hand. I found that both lights were protected by a metal covering and kicking with my boot didn't knock out either light. A woman might know that's one of the life saving tips if she's abducted and put in a trunk. Could my attacker be a woman or have an accomplice?

I felt around, but couldn't locate my bag and hadn't expected to—only a stupid person would throw my bag with my cell phone into the trunk with me. The only thing I felt as I searched was a big hardcover book. As I flipped it open, my head throbbed. I could throw the book when he came for me. Would it stun him enough to give me time to escape?

My breathing became shallow. I couldn't wait and needed to do something now. Maybe if I tore out a page, I could get it through a crack. I could keep shoving out pages.

The car must have been hit sometime in the back because one side of the trunk had a wider gap. I pushed a page through the crack. I must have already torn fifty pages out and got each one to the outside when the car stopped. Oh no, the driver saw what I did or maybe it was time to get rid of me. I decided to kick the person with my boot as soon as he opened the trunk.

I heard the car door slam shut. Then footsteps coming

closer to the back. At least I only heard one set. I might only have to protect myself from one person.

"Catherine, I have a gun pointed at the trunk. Don't try anything when I open it."

Oh my God, it was Miss Pierce.

"Would you like me to knock you out before I throw you over the hill to the highway? There are some nice big semi-trucks traveling this time of night."

"Miss Pierce, why do you want to kill me?"

She laughed. "Come on, Catherine, don't play innocent with me. You didn't come again to question me for no reason. You know I tampered with the gas valve and if you didn't, it was only a matter of time. I plan on this being my last year teaching before I retire. And then I'm leaving Park City. You aren't going to ruin everything for me."

"I thought you loved Max."

"When he told me he was quitting soon as janitor, I begged him not to. I told him how much I loved him and he looked at me with pity in his eyes. I thought he'd realize I was the right woman for him when I confessed my love, but he wanted Karen. It was always Karen. I knew once he left the high school, he'd be in her clutches forever."

"So since you couldn't have him, you didn't want her to either."

"Yeah, that's it. Guys always want the pretty ones. And I decided pretty Karen was going to know what it felt like to lose a handsome guy like Max."

"You don't have to kill me."

She opened the trunk. In a gruff voice, she said, "Get out."

I looked up and was surprised to see Miss Pierce wearing

a blonde wig. I decided to run in a zigzag pattern for my life once I got out of the trunk. Hopefully, Miss Pierce was a bad shot. Or maybe I should try to fight her and get the gun.

I climbed out with her gun pointed at me.

Several police cars suddenly surrounded us, and one cop hopped out of his police cruiser. "Miss Pierce, put the gun down."

Another officer grabbed me before Miss Pierce could respond. After a slight hesitation, she dropped the gun. Once the officer handcuffed Miss Pierce and read her the rights, she turned to me. "It wouldn't have been hard to kill you. I always hated you."

I couldn't think of any reply to her cruel remarks. I stared back at her until I heard another car and saw it was Jake's Mustang. His car screeched as he came to a quick stop. Within seconds, I was in his arms, and only a little behind were my parents. They'd ridden with Jake.

"Oh baby," he said as he held me tightly. "I was so afraid when your mom called to see if I'd picked you up. She saw your car in the parking lot."

I rested my head against his chest. "You feel so good right now." When my parents were beside me, I reached out my hand and Mom grasped it. "Boy, am I glad to see all of you."

Mom's eyes filled with tears. "I'm going to give Miranda a raise. She spotted your vacant car. You forgot your laptop. She ran out to see if you had left. And she saw a woman with blonde hair driving away and told us it was a silver car."

"Did she recognize Miss Pierce?" I asked.

Mom shook her head. "I thought of Dana, but I found out she was with Fred."

"That was so smart of you to toss papers out of the trunk." Dad squeezed my shoulder. "A young couple in a car behind you saw them and called the police."

A policeman examining the trunk took out the book and held it up for us to see. He gave us a small smile. "And my daughter says her calculus won't be of any help to her."

His flashlight shined on the cover of the old calculus text. Thank goodness I had Jake's body to lean against. Chills went through me, and Jake said, "You're shivering. I'll give you my jacket." He removed his jacket and put it around my shoulders.

What if that book hadn't been in the trunk? Or no one saw the pages fluttering out the crack? And thank God for Miranda noticing my car and Mom not assuming I'd gone in Jake's car.

Being alive wasn't something I'd ever take for granted again.

Chapter Twenty-One

Two weeks later, I was still a celebrity in Park City. It wasn't everyday a local girl was on the *Good Morning America* show. When I was interviewed on live TV, it was very exciting. You wouldn't think throwing torn math pages out of a trunk would be big news, but apparently people were fascinated by my story and what had really happened to Max in the boiler room. Pat Connelly being elected to the United States House of Representatives helped boost my story into national news too. He promised to give me scoops from Washington D.C. whenever possible because I'd uncovered the truth about Miss Pierce killing Max.

And things were going well with Jake. To make a boyfriend attentive, just get abducted.

Maybe dating Scott had started the process, but realizing Miss Pierce could've tossed me down the hill to meet my death had a sobering effect on Jake. He told me he loved me, and I said the same thing back to him. The night he expressed his love for me, I called Angie and said, "You were so on target telling me to date Jake. I think he's Mr. Right for me.

Yes, I was definitely falling ardently in love with him. With butterflies in my stomach and my heartbeat accelerating around him, I was where I wanted to be in my life at this time.

We spent two or three evenings a week at his place. My kitchen was just too tiny for us to cook together. Tonight I prepared vegetables to steam, and he fried the steaks.

"What time does your family eat Thanksgiving dinner?" he asked, throwing mushrooms into the skillet.

I stopped cutting broccoli to look at him. "I can't believe Thanksgiving is coming so quickly. We eat around one-thirty. What about yours?"

He groaned. "The same time."

"Grandma Nelson is coming this year to our house. She wants to see you again."

"We can go to my parents' house later."

"Thank you."

We were eating when I remembered to tell him about my interview. "Guess who I'm interviewing tomorrow?"

He grinned. "Miss Pierce. And you're going to ask her how prison food is."

I laughed. "No way am I going to see her. I'm meeting with the interim mayor, Sam Philips." The city council had appointed Sam as mayor until the election was held in a few months.

"I'm sure you'll find out if there's any special news about him to share with the citizens in Park City."

I chewed a piece of steak, thinking how I did wonder about this new mayor. He hadn't been on city council very long, but Pat Connelly had encouraged the members to appoint Sam as a replacement. "I know little about him, so it'll be interesting to see who he really is."

"How's Tracy these days?"

I sighed. "She's a strong woman, but all this has been hard on her. And she hates it that her parents and Max didn't tell her he was her father. Karen regrets very much not being honest and telling Tracy the truth years ago. She wonders if things would have worked out differently had Miss Pierce known Max had a daughter."

"I guess we'll never know."

After we ate, Jake cleaned the skillet and I rinsed the plates before putting them in the dishwasher. As I finished wiping the table, Jake's cell phone sounded. His face showed surprise at the caller. And when I heard him say "Kelly", I knew why. From what he'd told me, they hadn't talked to each other for a long time.

After ten minutes of conversation, the call ended. He stared at me for a moment before speaking. "Sorry, I'm trying to absorb what I just heard. Remember I told you about Kelly?"

I nodded.

"She called to ask me to come to Seattle to be with her. She's in the hospital with leukemia."

"Oh no, I'm sorry she has leukemia. What about her husband?"

"She's divorced and her ex has remarried. Her father's dead and she needs me there."

I didn't want him to fly to go see his old girlfriend. "What about her mother?"

"They've never been close. I don't think she even told her mom yet."

"I can help you order flowers or a planter for her."

He shook his head. "I'm going to get online and book a flight. I'll get flowers there."

I stiffened. Flowers and traveling to the other side of the country for a woman who broke his heart. "Why? You two broke up years ago. You can call her and send cards and flowers. Washington is so far away. I'm sure she doesn't really expect you to come."

He kissed me and searched my eyes. "If Ricardo called you, I bet you'd fly to Costa Rica to be with him when he needed a friend."

I shrugged. "My breaking up with Ricardo is more recent and I don't know what I'd do."

"She sounded so alone and afraid. She doesn't have any siblings. I told her I'd be there soon. I'll talk to Jane about Austin covering more local sports while I'm away."

What could I say to stop him? He clearly had feelings for Kelly after all this time if he planned on spending money and time to fly to Washington to be with her. I didn't want him to go and hoped that after he thought about it longer, he'd decide to stay.

Thirty-six hours later, we stood in Dayton International Airport's terminal. Jake looked so hot and I didn't want him to leave. Wasn't there a time limit on how long to expect an old boyfriend to come to your beck and call? Obviously not in Jake's mind when the woman was Kelly. I thought about begging him not to go, but realized I didn't want to appear a loser. So big deal, right, he was traveling to see an old beautiful girlfriend. And what could be the worst thing to happen? That would be Kelly wanting to resume their boyfriend-girlfriend relationship. But Jake wouldn't. He loved me.

He'd come back soon and we'd have Thanksgiving together and that'd be it.

So why did I feel like it was so wrong for me to be saying

goodbye?

Jake leaned down and his kiss was gentle. I deepened the kiss, not wanting to stop. But soon he raised his mouth from mine. He gazed into my eyes. "I love you. I better board."

"I love you too." I put my hand on his arm. "Did you tell Kelly about us?"

"She knows. Actually she knew before I told her. She saw the picture of us in the newspaper and it made her think of calling me."

Oh yeah, the picture of us standing next to Miss Pierce's car with Jake's arms wrapped around me. Drew had followed the police and taken a few shots. That photo had been picked up by the presses across the country. Since Kelly saw the photo, she must have read underneath that Jake Michaels was my boyfriend.

I exhaled a deep breath. Being a celebrity wasn't so great if it caused my hot guy to travel miles away to reconnect with a previous lover.

As Jake walked away, I had an urge to call all my old boyfriends and ask them if I had a terrible disease would they care enough to drop everything and visit me.

Apparently it worked for Kelly.

While I drove back to Park City, I said a prayer for Kelly to have a complete recovery from her leukemia. Then I added, "Thank you for my boyfriend, Jake."

Hey, giving God a reminder of Jake being mine shouldn't hurt.

Epilogue

Several months later

So did I get my sexual fantasy? Was Jake the guy I lost my virginity to?

Before answering these two big questions, I need to mention Jake's old girlfriend. Kelly was quickly out of the picture. Oh no, not that. She didn't die. She went into remission. Jake only stayed three days in Washington. Once her mother arrived, he was out of there. I was happy to hear that Kelly's mother showed up at the hospital. Actually, Jake planned on returning back to Park City that soon to be with me regardless when her mom came.

When Thanksgiving, Christmas and Valentine's Day came and went without a proposal from Jake, I wasn't surprised. We hadn't been in a relationship very long.

On St. Patrick's Day, Jake brought me a bouquet of deep pink tulips with a light pink ribbon tied around the stems and surprised me with an Irish cottage music box playing, of course, what else, an Irish song. How sweet of Jake, but I didn't realize people gave gifts on St. Patrick's Day. I admired the detailed shamrocks, thatched roof and pink roses on the cottage. “Thank you so much. I love it.” I lifted my eyes to look at Jake, feeling embarrassed. “I’m sorry I didn’t get you anything.”

“There’s something else for you in the chimney.”

As I leaned over and peeked inside, my eyes widened at the sight of a diamond ring. It was such a shock that I was speechless.

Jake picked up the ring. “I love you, Catherine. Will you marry me?”

I hesitated for a brief moment. Was it too soon for us to become engaged? *You dummy. You love him. Answer him before he changes his mind.*

A glint of amusement was in his brown eyes. “Who is this reserved woman? I expected you to throw your arms around me and scream yes.”

In a breathless voice, I said, “I wasn’t expecting this. Yes, I’ll marry you. I love you so much.”

He slipped the ring on my finger and gave me a long, passionate kiss. Shortly after, we went to my parents’ house to tell them about our engagement. From there, I called Grandma Nelson, Maggie, and Miranda, but not Angie. We were meeting Angie and Brian at McFadden’s Irish Pub to celebrate St. Patrick’s Day and now our engagement.

In the months before the big day, Jake and I had a hard time waiting to make love. One particular time, I wasn’t the one stopping us from going too far. Jake was. “I’ve taken more cold showers than I ever thought possible.” He groaned. “I just can’t break an old woman’s heart and her trust in us.”

I nodded, remembering what Grandma had told Jake when she met him. “I know you have the hots for Catherine, but if wait, you won’t regret it.” She straightened her glasses and said, “I’ve decided to pay for your honeymoon to London.”

Six months after St. Patrick’s Day, we were married in St. Christopher’s Church in September, my birthday month. Angie was my matron of honor and Brian was the best man.

I didn’t get my exact sexual fantasy of making love on our honeymoon in a famous London landmark. By the way, poor Grandma and Jake tried to find a relative in the royal family or a friend of the queen so we could consummate our marriage in Buckingham Palace. None was found.

It didn’t matter since we checked into a very romantic French chateau-style hotel just a few blocks from the Houses of Parliament, a mile from Buckingham Palace and Oxford Street shopping. From the lobby we stopped to look across the Thames River at the London Eye Ferris wheel.

I stared at the tourist attraction and squeezed Jake’s hand. “I’m excited about going on it with you. It’s going to be so cool.” Mom and Dad paid for a flight called Cupid’s Capsule on the London Eye as a wedding gift to us. We would be in our own private capsule, complete with a bottle of champagne. We could lounge in the seating area of our own “pod”, or stand by the glass enclosure and view the tall buildings in London.

Jake nodded. “Chad was jealous when I told him about it.”

“I don’t know, it might be too tame for Chad since he likes wild rides. The wheel rotates only a few inches every second.”

Later, in our hotel suite, Jake took my face tenderly between his fingers and kissed my lips. “I’m going to warm you up first."

I winked. "I'm not a shy bride." I unbuttoned his khaki pants and pushed down his zipper.

"I love a woman who knows what she wants." He stepped out of his pants.

The room phone rang and I raised my eyebrows. "Who would be calling us?"

"Ignore it." He kissed the pulsing hollow at the base of my throat.

"I'll hurry and answer it." With the receiver next to my ear, I heard a male British voice telling me hello. Then he said, "I am Detective Cornwell. I'd like to speak to Catherine Michaels."

"I'm Catherine Michaels."

"We could use your help in solving a mystery here in London. We heard you like to investigate and thought you might like to try your hand at a case while visiting our city."

I heard a giggle in the background and it sounded like Tracy's laugh. "Okay, Adam, the gig's up. I can't believe you're calling me on my honeymoon."

"Sorry. I didn't get to tell you goodbye. You and Jake left so fast after the reception."

"I love you, Adam. Thanks for being a great groomsman and give Tracy a hug for me." I sighed. "Now be a good brother and let me get back to my husband."

"You got it. This is costing too much anyhow. Love ya, sis. Bye."

I laughed as I replaced the receiver. "Can you believe it? Adam pretended to be a British detective and asked me to investigate a case." I pulled Jake to me, squeezing his butt. "The only thing I want to investigate is you."

We went back to removing clothes. Jake unzipped my skirt and slid it down over my hips. I unbuttoned his blue shirt and ran my fingers over his chest. Once we got my white cami off, he leaned down to kiss the tops of my breasts. With one hand he managed to unhook my bra. After he fondled and kissed my breasts, I throbbed all over. Every inch of my body exploded from a deep consciousness of my husband. The intense physical caressing built to a climax and I clutched him. "Oh, Jake, I need you inside me."

He pulled me into bed and kissed me all over my body. "I've wanted you so long."

I murmured, "I love you."

We made love slowly and passionately for a long time. A very long time. We decided the sights of London could wait.

So here we are—happily married.

Was it worth waiting for? You bet. Even if we hadn't gone to London for our honeymoon, I'd still give the same answer.

I'll just say that Jake is definitely my Mr. Right in every way possible.

About the Author

As the youngest in the family, growing up on a farm in Findlay, Ohio, Diane often acted out characters from her own stories in the backyard. In high school she was the student sitting in class with a novel hidden in front of her propped up textbook. Her passion for reading novels had to be put on hold during her college years at Ohio State University due to working part-time on campus and being a full-time student.

Before starting on her writing career, Diane was a school teacher and play director. She enjoys her life with her husband, six children, daughter-in-law, son-in-law and three grandchildren in southwestern Ohio. Her husband of thirty-nine years is very supportive, as well as her awesome children.

She writes Amish fiction, contemporary romance, Christian romance, historical fiction, women's fiction and chick-lit mystery. *A Fiery Secret, When Love Happens Again* (previous title was *No Greater Loss*) and *Never The Same* were published with Samhain Publishing, but Diane asked for her rights back last year. All three Samhain books were revised and given new covers when Diane self-published them recently.

Learn more about Diane Craver and her books at

www.dianecraver.com.

Join Diane's blog at www.dianecraver.com/blog. She also has an author Facebook page at: https://www.facebook.com/pages/Diane-Craver/153906208887?ref=bookmarks. When you visit her here, please give Diane a like. Reviews by readers are always appreciated.

www.ingramcontent.com/pod-product-compliance
Lightning Source LLC
Chambersburg PA
CBHW022155170626
46807CB00005B/2222

* 9 7 8 0 6 9 2 4 3 0 4 1 5 *